CAUGHT IN THE ACT

Coburn's strong arm caught her, grappling her roughly against his chest. It might have been a gallant gesture had he used two hands, but he had already used one to snare Volume I. Releasing Maggie quickly, he proceeded to examine the binding, while she in turn backed against the bookshelves to steady herself.

"Do you have any idea how rare this is?" he growled as he tested the book's spine. "Did it not occur to you that it was placed out of reach for a reason?"

Maggie wanted to answer—in fact, she wanted to berate him for daring to suggest that the mishap had been *her* fault!—but the only sound she could make was a raspy one as she struggled to calm her pounding heart and to return her breathing to normal.

For the first time, Coburn turned his full attention to her. After a moment's study, he grinned and assured her, "You'll live. You just had the wind knocked out of you."

"By *you,*" she managed to retort.

He seemed about to argue, then shrugged instead. "Didn't we have this conversation last night? Yet here you are, roaming the library half-naked."

"Be quiet!" she warned between gritted teeth. "You almost killed me."

"You were quite a sight. Unfortunately, I'm not looking for a damsel in distress." Setting the book down, he stepped to within inches of her, then lowered his face toward hers and murmured, "What are *you* looking for, Maggie-Margaret?"

Dear Readers,

In July of 1999, we launched the Ballad line with four new series, and each month we present both new and continuing stories set everywhere from medieval England to the American West—the kind of passionate, romantic stories you love best, written by the most gifted authors. At the back of each book, we tell you when you can find subsequent books in the series that have captured your heart.

First up this month is **With His Ring,** the second book in the fabulous new *Brides of Bath* series by Cheryl Bolen. What happens when a dedicated bachelor who marries for money discovers that his impetuous young wife has married for love—his? Next, Kelly McClymer returns with **The Next Best Bride.** A jilted groom marrying his errant fiancée's twin sister is hardly romantic, unless it happens in the charming *Once Upon a Wedding* series.

Reader favorite Kate Donovan is back with another installment of the *Happily Ever After Co.* This time in **Night After Night** a young woman looking for a teaching job instead of a husband finds the key to her past—and a man with the key to her heart. Finally, ever-talented Cindy Harris concludes the *Dublin Dreams* series with **Lover's Knot,** in which secrets are revealed, friendships are renewed . . . and passion turns to lasting love.

Why not start spring off right and read them all? Enjoy!

Kate Duffy
Editorial Director

Happily Ever After Co.

NIGHT
AFTER
NIGHT

Kate Donovan

ZEBRA BOOKS
Kensington Publishing Corp.
http://www.kensingtonbooks.com

ZEBRA BOOKS are published by

Kensington Publishing Corp.
850 Third Avenue
New York, NY 10022

All Kensington titles, imprints, and distributed lines are
available at special quantity discounts for bulk purchases for
sales promotion, premiums, fund-raising, educational or in-
stitutional use.

Special book excerpts or customized printings can also be
created to fit specific needs. For details, write or phone the
office of the Kensington Special Sales Manager: Kensington
Publishing Corp., 850 Third Avenue, New York, NY 10022.
Attn. Special Sales Department. Phone: 1-800-221-2647.

First Printing: April 2002
10 9 8 7 6 5 4 3 2 1

Printed in the United States of America

Prologue

Dear Mr. Braddock,

I've heard so many wonderful stories about your mail-order bride business. I'm hoping perhaps you are aware of other opportunities for young women such as myself, who are as lonely as any of your brides, but who do not wish to marry. Instead, I would like to find a position as a schoolteacher, as far away from Chicago as possible. I assure you I am well qualified, as you can see from the references I have enclosed.

Before you suggest I consider a husband as well as a position, let me assure you my reasons for not marrying are good ones. I trust you will hold them in confidence. Suffice it to say, I am the sister of Brian and Ian Gleason. You were still living in Chicago when the scandal dominated the newspapers, and so I am certain you know that Brian is dead, murdered by Ian, who was thereafter sentenced to life in prison. But perhaps you didn't hear about Ian's death, in a cold, lonely cell. My only remaining relative was my father, and we buried him today, although in truth, we lost him five years ago, when the shot that killed Brian rang out.

My family is in ruins, and I have no desire to

*start another. I do adore children, however, and
if you can assist me in securing a suitable position, I will be forever in your debt. I am prepared
to pay the fee you usually charge to your prospective grooms. Don't worry—I have no need of the
modest legacy my father left me, and would be
more than happy to exchange it for the peaceful
life I hope to find. Thank you ever so much.*

*Yours truly,
Maggie Gleason
Chicago, Illinois
January 1868*

Russell Braddock watched as his daughter read and
reread the letter. Finally he asked, "Do you see why
I was so distressed?"

Noelle sighed. "It's heartbreaking. And odd, too.
She refers to both boys as her brothers, when we know
only one of them was."

The matchmaker nodded. "She was still so young
when it all happened. And she had no one to explain
it to her. I've heard her father was a bitter man even
before the murder, because his wife died giving birth
to Maggie and her brother, leaving him with all the
responsibility of raising the children alone. And to be
fair, he may well have missed his wife to distraction,
which would account for his bitterness also."

"I didn't realize Maggie and her brother were twins.
It's more bizarre by the minute! I can almost understand why she doesn't want to open her heart to another family. We're so fortunate, aren't we, Father?"

Braddock smiled and patted Noelle's trim waist,
thinking of how it would soon swell as his first grandchild continued to grow within her. "We are indeed.
And we mustn't take any of it for granted. I want you
to be especially careful these next few months."

Noelle's gray eyes twinkled. "I've promised my husband I won't jump out of carriages or onto the backs of wild stallions anymore. Or at least, not until the baby is safely tucked into his or her cradle." Sobering slightly, she added, "If only Maggie Gleason's mother had lived to see her grow up. She needed her so desperately."

"That's true. Motherhood is a daunting responsibility."

"But not more daunting than *your* responsibility to the brides. And now, to Maggie. You have to find a way to help her open her heart to a new family. And to true love."

"Do I? Or should I respect her wishes and simply find her a comfortable teaching position?"

"You'll find a way to do both." A knowing smile flitted over Noelle's features. "After all, it's not just a responsibility. It's a challenge to your matchmaking prowess."

Braddock chuckled. "First things first—the teaching position. With any luck, when Maggie's heart is ready for true love, I'll be able to help with that, too."

One

Maggie Gleason stood on the front steps of her new home—Mrs. Eleanor Blake's boarding house—and inhaled deeply. Crisp, cold, mountain air—as clean and pure as anything she had experienced in her nineteen years of life—filled her lungs, reminding her that this was a fresh start in every conceivable sense. No one here knew about her tragic past, and so when they looked at her, it would be with light hearts and confident expectations. After all, they had brought her to their lovely hamlet for a single, glorious purpose—to entrust her with the minds of their precious children. It was an honor and a refuge, and Maggie vowed there, on that step, never to let them down, nor to wish for more than this comfortable second chance Russell Braddock had arranged for her.

A voice from a second-story window burst into Maggie's reverie. "Mercy sakes alive! Don't tell me you're the new teacher? Wait right there, and don't move another inch until I get my wrap!"

The landlady, Maggie told herself, her heart pounding at the prospect of actually meeting one of her new neighbors. Until now, she'd been surrounded by fellow travelers, first in the ship that had brought her to San Francisco; next, in the stagecoach that had brought her deep into northern California; and finally, in a rickety buckboard with two brothers who made a living delivering provisions to various shopkeepers in the area. They had been curious about Maggie, but she had managed to stay comfortably anonymous, explaining only that she had accepted a position as schoolteacher in the town of Shasta Falls.

Everyone along the way had given her the same cheery response: "A pretty girl like you? Won't last a month, before some lucky man makes you his bride and takes you away from all that. You'll have your pick of husbands, just you see." Several had added that if they were only ten years younger, or some variation on that theme, they'd marry her themselves, while one had actually proposed! Maggie had assured one and all that she had no desire to find a husband. She was a dedicated teacher, and would be for the rest of her years, thank you kindly.

At least you had a chance to practice your new surname, she reminded herself. *I wonder if it would have pleased Mother to know you adopted her maiden name for your new life. Maggie O'Connor. It sounds fine, and at least no one will ever again refer to you as "the poor little Gleason girl."*

"Mercy me! Just look at you!"

Startled, Maggie steeled herself for the embrace that was aimed in her direction, but still almost toppled from her step as a pair of hefty arms grabbed her with unbridled enthusiasm. Gasping for air, she managed to ask, "Mrs. Blake?"

"Who else would I be? And you're our little Maggie! We heard you were young and pretty, but that doesn't do you justice!" Frowning slightly, she demanded, "Where's Sheriff Riordain? I can't believe he had the nerve to leave you standing all alone on this dusty street."

"I know he planned on greeting me, but I arrived much earlier than expected. The driver offered to fetch someone to assist me, but I had already seen your sign—not to mention your beautiful garden—and I just couldn't resist heading right over."

"Well, I'm glad you did. Come on inside. It's too chilly out here for a skinny girl like you. You're not even wearing a wrap!"

Maggie wanted to assure her that the sturdy brown jacket of her traveling outfit was as warm as toast, but she was already being whisked into an entry hall flanked by a narrow staircase on one side and a flower-filled parlor on the other. "What a lovely room!"

"I'm glad you like it. You'll be spending many an hour in there with us."

"Us?"

"The other boarders, and all my friends. We gather here every night, to sing and play the piano. You'll be courted in this parlor by every unmarried man in town, I predict."

"Mrs. Blake?" Maggie took the woman by the hand and explained softly, "I hope this doesn't sound presumptuous or ungrateful, but you should know I'm not interested in being courted, much less married. I came here to teach. It's my dream, and I'm grateful to you and Sheriff Riordain for your roles in making it come true."

Eleanor Blake laughed fondly. "Dreams can change, Maggie. When you find out what nice fellows we have in this town, you won't be so quick to reject them. In the meantime, come and see my kitchen. I have a roast in the oven, just for you. I hope you like spicy food."

"I'm sure I'll love it," she said, trying to sound agreeable, although her nose had detected an odor that wasn't altogether mouthwatering. *That can't be the roast,* she assured herself as she hurried after her landlady. *It smells more like burnt hair . . .*

"We'll have you fattened up in no time," Mrs. Blake was promising her. "Sit down and have a cup of tea and some cookies, and tell me all about yourself."

Maggie started dutifully toward an enormous pine dining table, but her attention was captured by another room, visible through a wide doorway at the far end of the kitchen. "What's in there? It looks like a library!"

"That's because it is. My husband—rest his soul—had two vices, Maggie. Gambling and reading. Between the two of them, it's a wonder we managed to hold on to this house at all."

"I never heard reading referred to as a vice before," Maggie said with a smile. Edging toward the mysterious room, she guessed, "Are you saying he bought too many—oh! Oh, my goodness . . ."

Her breath had actually caught in her throat at the sight of the books—hundreds upon hundreds of them! She had never seen anything like it, outside a public library.

"Do you see what I mean?" Mrs. Blake demanded. "Take a lesson from it, Maggie dear. *Anything* can be a vice if it's done past the bounds of common sense."

"But this . . ." She stared in rapt delight as her eyes began to pick out individual titles on the spines of the imposing, leather-bound collection. "It's as though every book ever written is here! He must have been an amazing man."

"He was an odd sort, but I loved him. Come along now, dear. You haven't even seen your bedroom yet!

When the fire's not burning, this room is so dreadfully cold."

"I don't think I could ever be cold in here," Maggie murmured. "But if I were, this fireplace is magnificent."

"Built from stone hauled four hundred miles, down from Oregon. Our children could stand straight up inside there till they were nearly full-grown."

"I can imagine." Maggie studied the room hungrily, noting that even the furnishings were perfect—an overstuffed sofa that could serve as a bed for the largest man, and two black leather armchairs pulled up to the inviting hearth. But it was the books—row after row of them—that truly made her pulse race.

"First there were the mountains, all covered with snow. And the air, so crisp. And everyone being so friendly. But this—" To Maggie's dismay, tears were actually welling in her eyes, and she brushed them away hastily. "It's like I'm in heaven."

"If it's heaven you want, just wait until you taste my roast."

"Pardon? Oh, of course! I can't wait." Maggie chided herself for neglecting her hostess, then insisted, "You offered to show me my bedroom. I'm sure I'll love that, too. And there'll be plenty of time for me to get to know this library better, so—"

"We don't actually spend much time in here. None of us except Mr. Coburn, that is."

There had been a hint of something—a rebuke, or perhaps even a warning—in Mrs. Blake's tone, so Maggie was cautious as she asked, "Mr. Coburn?"

"One of my boarders."

"Oh."

"His room is over there." The landlady gestured toward a closed door at the far end of the library. "When Mr. Blake was alive, that was *our* room. But

when Mr. Coburn came, I moved upstairs. He's a very
private man, Maggie. We try to respect that around
here, given that he pays me so generously, and doesn't
ask for much in return."

*Not much, except the nicest room? And the library
for good measure?* Maggie silently rebuked the greedy
boarder, but forced herself to smile at Mrs. Blake. After all, the widow seemed to be at peace with the arrangement. Or more likely, at the mercy of it, if indeed
Coburn paid her well for his privileges.

The town was paying for Maggie's room and board,
and she had the feeling it wasn't nearly so generous
a sum. She could hardly complain, at least until she
learned more details. Perhaps she could eventually
find a way to subsidize the town's payment, to help
out Mrs. Blake, and to gain greater access to the remarkable library. Until then, she counseled herself, she
should remember that even without the amazing collection of books, she had found exactly what she was
looking for in Shasta Falls. It was foolish to allow
unimportant details to annoy her.

It's just like Papa always told you, she scolded herself silently. *You expect too much of people. It's a bad
habit—a habit you inherited from Papa himself!—and
you'll never find a moment's contentment if you don't
overcome it.*

A man's voice, booming from the entry hall,
brought Maggie back to reality. "Mrs. Blake? Where
in blazes are you? They're saying the schoolteacher's
here somewhere, but I'll be darned if I can find her!"

Maggie felt her chest tighten. "Oh, dear. Is that Mr.
Coburn?"

Eleanor Blake burst into laughter. "Mr. Coburn
doesn't raise his voice. He doesn't need to. And he
doesn't look for schoolteachers or anyone else. That's

Denny Riordain, so don't look so worried. He's the finest man you'll ever hope to meet."

Relieved, Maggie smoothed back a lock of hair that had come loose during the buckboard ride, anxious to make a good first impression on the man who, together with matchmaker Russell Braddock and a kindhearted priest, had made this new life possible for her. Then she followed Mrs. Blake back to the kitchen, where a brawny giant with a wide, welcoming smile was waiting.

"Well, now. Father James told me you were a pretty little thing, but I didn't expect an angel. You'd think a man of the cloth would remember to mention a detail like that."

Maggie smiled at the mention of the kindhearted pastor who had acted as a go-between for Russell Braddock. For reasons she was determined to respect, the matchmaker hadn't wanted anyone else to know that he had arranged a position other than bride for an unmarried young woman. And she had to admit, it was best for her as well. If people knew she'd used the services of a marriage broker, they might not believe her claim that her only goal was to become a schoolteacher.

"Sheriff Riordain? It's so wonderful to finally meet you. Father James told me so much about you. I hope you know how grateful—"

"None of that, now. Just stand there and let me look at you." The sheriff shook his head, his blue eyes twinkling with mischief. "I can see I have my work cut out for me."

"Oh?"

"I promised the town you'd teach for a least a year. But seeing you standing here—"

"I intend to teach in Shasta Falls for many, many years, Sheriff. Your promise to the town is quite safe."

She stepped forward and stretched out her hand. "You have my word on it."

"I'll not shake your hand on any such promise," he said with a grin. "And I'll not ask more than a year of you. You'll be having babies of your own after that, and I'll be writing to the good father again, only this time, for an ugly teacher of the *male* persuasion."

Maggie had to laugh. "We'll take it year by year then—how does that sound?" Dropping the bantering tone, she added softly, "It's everything you promised it would be. From my first glimpse of the mountains, to my first whiff of Mrs. Blake's cooking, I just knew I'd found myself a home."

"Well, then . . ." He cleared his throat, as though choked up by the tribute. "You'll eat here tonight. Tomorrow, my wife insists you'll be *our* guest. And I never argue with my June, so that's how it'll have to be."

"I can't wait."

Mrs. Blake rested a hand on the sheriff's arm, as though warning him against further monopolization of her new boarder. "I was about to show Maggie her bedroom."

"Well, I don't want to interfere with that." Riordain grimaced slightly as he added, "It's a small room, but a cozy one. If we could have afforded more—"

"Don't be silly. Why would I need a large room?"

"That's right," Mrs. Blake said. "It's not as though she'll be spending any time in it. That's what the parlor is for, and it's a fine room."

"That's a fact." The sheriff grinned. "Mrs. Blake's parlor is famous for miles around, Maggie. The friendliest room in town, aside from the ones over the saloon."

"Dennis Riordain!" The landlady blushed to a deep

crimson. "What will Maggie think? And if I told June—"

"Don't go threatening me, now." He feigned distress, then leaned over and kissed Mrs. Blake's red cheek. "I'll just be going before I scare little Maggie away." He took Maggie's hand in his own. "Welcome to Shasta Falls, missy."

"Thank you."

"I saw your bags in the hall, and took the liberty of bringing them up to your room already. If you need anything else—"

"If she needs anything else, I'll see to it," Eleanor Blake reminded him with a sniff. "Go on now to your precious saloon."

Denny grinned. "Is Amos over there?"

"He'd better not be. He's supposed to be fixing the Widow Clausen's fence."

"And His Lordship? Is *he* back yet?"

"No. Still off on one of his adventures."

"That's for the best." The sheriff's eyes twinkled. "He's not exactly a man who likes surprises."

Eleanor Blake shrugged. "He knows about this, so where's the harm? Run along, now. And give Junie a kiss for me."

"I'll do that. Maggie?" He touched her cheek. "I'll be by for you in the morning, to show you our new schoolhouse."

"That sounds wonderful. I'll be ready."

"Come early and I'll feed you with the others," Mrs. Blake told the sheriff briskly. "We'll have something special, to celebrate Maggie's first day."

"I'll be looking forward to it." He grinned broadly and backed toward the hall. "Take care, missy."

Maggie waved, and then, when the sheriff was out of sight, turned to Mrs. Blake to ask, "Amos? Is that one of the boarders?"

"That's right. Amos Gentry—a lovely widower who helps out in exchange for room and board. He was a gun salesman in his prime, but that was years ago."

"I see. And I assume 'His Lordship,' who doesn't like surprises, is the famous Mr. Coburn?"

"Yes. Fortunately, he's away on one of his adventures at the moment. That man *loves* to travel."

Maggie cocked her head to the side and studied her new landlady. "You'd think this was his house, rather than yours."

"It's only because of him that it *is* my house. I would have had to sell it long ago if he hadn't been willing to pay me so well. He's a saint, in his own way," Mrs. Blake added solemnly. "Just try not to annoy him, and stay out of his path, and everything will be fine. Like the sheriff said, he doesn't like surprises. Or change. Or too many questions. But if you stay away from him, everything will be fine."

Some saint, Maggie grumbled to herself. *But he loves books, and traveling, and he helped Mrs. Blake keep this house, so how bad can he honestly be?*

Putting the mysterious Mr. Coburn out of her mind completely, she hurried down the hall and caught up with her guide on the second-floor landing. Four doorways beckoned, but to Maggie's surprise, Mrs. Blake kept right on going, up another flight of stairs—which had narrowed ominously—and into the attic. "Here it is. Small but cozy, just like the sheriff said. How do you like it?"

Maggie stared at the tiny quarters, trying not to allow her expression to betray her disappointment. It wasn't simply the floor space that was lacking. She could barely stand up in the "room"! And there was no door! Did they truly expect her to sleep soundly under such circumstances, much less to change her clothes or groom herself?

Eleanor Blake seemed to be reading her mind. "Look here, Maggie. Mr. Gentry installed a curtain, just for you." She pulled a length of white muslin across the doorway. "There, do you see? Better than a door really, because the night breezes can sneak right past it."

Maggie laughed despite herself, hoping that the night breezes were the only things that sneaked past the ineffectual barrier. "Please thank him for me."

"Thank him yourself. You'll meet him at supper. Which reminds me, I'd better go check on that roast. We wouldn't want your first meal here to be ruined, would we?"

Maggie shook her head, although she suspected it was too late for the ill-fated roast. "I'll just unpack my things, then. And I'll join you in the kitchen at . . . ?"

"Six sharp, every night. Rain or shine, summer or winter."

"I like that." On impulse, Maggie gave the woman a quick hug. "I think I'm going to love it here, Mrs. Blake. How can I ever thank you for welcoming me into your home?"

"Thank me by being happy," the landlady suggested. "It's something I insist on, you know."

Surprised by the perception behind the sentiment, Maggie summoned a grateful smile and promised, "I'll try."

It's been so long, she added as her hostess disappeared through the muslin curtain. *But I really am going to try. To be happy. Or, at least, useful. After all, that's more than I ever dared wish for, once they came and took Ian away . . .*

* * *

It was long past midnight when Maggie tiptoed down the two flights of stairs, oil lamp in hand, and stepped back into the library, if only to convince herself that she hadn't imagined the magnificent fireplace or the endless rows of books. She had longed to curl up in one of the leather armchairs after dinner, but Mrs. Blake had made it clear she was expected to spend the entire evening socializing with the other boarders in the parlor. She hadn't wanted to be rude, even though she was exhausted from three days' traveling, and overwhelmed by all the new faces and personalities.

They were all asleep now, and so with a shiver of anticipation, she pulled a slender volume of sonnets from its shelf, set her lamp on a side table, and eyed the chairs mischievously. Was one the domain of the reclusive Mr. Coburn? If so, she had no desire to touch it, much less snuggle into it.

The sofa looks much cozier, she decided. Nestling into the rich, black-tweed upholstery, she pulled her thick dressing gown securely about herself to keep out the cold air that seemed to have come all the way from the snowcap of Mount Shasta itself. *You must remember to bring a shawl tomorrow night. Or perhaps Mrs. Blake will allow you to keep one down here. Perhaps the quilt . . .*

Maggie winced. What would Mrs. Blake and the others think if they knew that their schoolteacher slept every night under a blue-and-yellow quilt that had obviously been intended for a baby's use, not that of a full-grown woman? Of course, once they heard it was all Maggie had to remind her of the mother she had never known, they'd understand.

And it was pretty—threadbare but pretty—with its fourteen blocks, each one lovingly stitched with a letter of the alphabet, from M to Z. Her twin brother's quilt had been identical, except for the fact that his letters were A through L. They had buried *that* quilt with Brian, and, of course, that had been appropriate, but still . . .

As always, a chill ran through her as she imagined another boy's final days, and how cold those must have been. Ian, alone in his prison cell, cut off from the world because of his transgression, and cut off from Maggie by choice. It was difficult to guess which was colder—that cell, or his grave on the edge of the prison churchyard. If only Maggie had heard about his death in time to attend the funeral, she would gladly have contributed her own little quilt to keep him warm. A loving remembrance of the sister who would never, ever forget him . . .

You promised yourself you wouldn't dwell on such thoughts in this new place, she reminded herself firmly. *Think about the new people in your life! Mrs. Blake, for one—isn't she loveable? She can't cook, and she's more of a matchmaker than Mr. Braddock, but such a big heart! And the others are wonderful, too, in their own ways.*

Her thoughts turned easily to Amos Gentry, a sweet, shy man who for some unfathomable reason had chosen to become a salesman—of guns, no less! And there was a strident, opinionated widow named Gladys Chesterton, who lived next door to the boardinghouse. She had done more than her share of complaining and gossiping, but had also played the piano beautifully, which Maggie suspected was the reason Mrs. Blake had nurtured a friendship with her. Two other women—spinster sisters of advanced years—completed the group. They had been quiet—almost disoriented—during the evening's conversation, and Maggie had been touched to see how Eleanor Blake catered to them.

And last but not least, there's Mr. Alex Coburn—the bookworm, she reminded herself. *He sounds like an actual hermit, and a rather rude one, from all accounts. But he loves books, and values his privacy. In other words, you have more in common with him than you care to admit. Wouldn't it be odd if you and he grew to be friends one day? Perhaps his reclusiveness is actually born of shyness, which he chooses to mask, inartfully but effectively, with obnoxious behavior.*

Her imagination began to dance with images of the absent boarder. He'd be pale, of course, from hiding indoors in a windowless library. And because he had never taken the time to hone his social skills, he'd be awkward, especially with women. Or perhaps, he hid indoors *because* of women! Perhaps they had been cruel to him as a child.

Her thoughts turned to Ian again. The other children—boys and girls alike—had taunted *him* mercilessly, and he had responded just as Coburn had, by retreating from the world, determined to shut it out.

In an instant, her heart warmed for her mysterious fellow boarder, whom she now pictured in Ian's likeness, from the frail body, to the thin face, to the anxious wheezing that insinuated itself into his voice whenever he was tormented or belittled. No one but Maggie had ever seen the real person—a thoughtful boy with so much love to give. So loyal. So innocent. So kind and gentle and hopeless.

If Alex Coburn's moody retreat from society was rooted in an unhappy childhood—from bullying and taunting, just because he was slight, or clumsy, or somehow deformed—Maggie would find a way to befriend him, slowly, over the next few years. She might even help him see that shutting himself away with his books wasn't any way to live out his life.

The hypocrisy of that particular thought wasn't lost

on Maggie. *"You* intend to teach him that? You, who would gladly follow the same course if circumstances didn't require you to earn your own keep?"

She forced herself to reshelve her book. In less than six hours, the sheriff would be coming to escort her to the schoolhouse, which she would prepare for its opening, less than four days away. There would be opportunity enough, in the coming weeks and years, to explore the plight of Alex Coburn. And to read every book in this library. For now, it was definitely time to go to bed.

Two

If Sheriff Denny Riordain hadn't been married, Maggie imagined she might have become ever so slightly infatuated with him, despite her vow to lead a celibate life. There was his smile—so broad and infectious; his cheerful, booming voice; his twinkling blue eyes; and a physique so powerful, the gun hanging at his side would have seemed completely unnecessary even if Shasta Falls were a den of iniquity rather than a quiet town.

And he was a kind man—kind enough to wolf down a generous serving of Mrs. Blake's egg-and-onion pie, an unforgivably salty dish that the landlady claimed had been handed down through her family for generations. She cautioned Maggie not to ask for the recipe: "If it were up to me, I'd share it in an instant, but I was sworn to secrecy by my dear, departed grandmother." Maggie solemnly agreed not to press the issue, all too aware that the sheriff was grinning from ear to ear at the absurdity of her plight.

Not that Maggie could have eaten more than a few bites, even if the dish had been fit for a princess. She was too anxious to see the new schoolhouse, and to meet a few of her students. After all, news traveled fast in a small town, did it not? And so the children would hear that the new teacher was on the premises, and they'd want to catch a glimpse of her. She intended to coax them inside, one by one, so that she could get to know as many of them as possible on an individual basis before the official first day arrived.

How would they react to her? she wondered. Her stomach knotted slightly, despite the fact that she was confident in her teaching abilities. After all, she'd had years of practice, assisting Headmaster Robert Grimes in Chicago from the time she'd turned thirteen. At the beginning, her only compensation had been free tutoring sessions—a priceless gift, given the depth and breadth of Robert's education—but for the last year or so, she had actually earned a modest sum along with the lessons.

But the children always behaved because of the respect they had for Robert, she remembered nervously. *What if you aren't able to earn that sort of respect on your own? What if they run about the room creating havoc, or simply walk out the door?*

"Maggie?"

"Pardon? Oh, dear—were you speaking to me? Forgive me, I was lost in thought."

"I was saying it was time we started over to the school. Are you ready?"

"Yes, absolutely. I'm ever so slightly nervous, for some reason." She grimaced as she asked, "Is it evident?"

Denny grinned. "I'm guessing one or two of the little ones are feeling the same. Worried that they won't measure up to your big-city standards."

"My big-city standards?" Maggie studied his expression anxiously, and was relieved to see that he was teasing her. "It's silly, isn't it? There's nothing for *any*one to worry about. I'm sure everything will be fine." She pushed back her chair and gave the other boarders a hopeful smile. "Excuse us, won't you? I'll see you all this evening. Mrs. Blake, thank you so much for the wonderful meal."

"And don't forget," the sheriff interrupted. "Maggie will be dining at the Riordain home this evening, so you'll all just have to find some way to amuse yourselves without her."

Gentry, the gun salesman, stood up respectfully. "Best of luck, Miss O'Connor. I'm sure the children will fall in love with you at first sight."

"They'll adore you," Mamie Lowe, one of the spinster sisters, agreed easily. "That's why the town decided to hire a young woman, in spite of Mr. Coburn's advice."

"Pardon?"

Denny laughed. "His Lordship was against it. Of course, he's against most everything, so I wouldn't take it to heart. He was sure we'd go to the trouble of bringing you here, only to see you run off with a jack in less than a week."

"A Jack? Oh, a *lumber*jack." Maggie smiled icily. "I've heard how much Mr. Coburn hates surprises, but I'm afraid he has one in store for him, because I shan't be running off—unless, of course, the children hate me."

"That's enough of that." Denny wrapped his huge arm around her shoulders and ushered her toward the door, grabbing her satchel with his free hand. "Is this all you need? Did you remember to pack a whip?"

Maggie smiled at the silly remark. "It's all books and pencils and paper, I'm afraid. It's heavy, I know—"

"Light as a breeze," he assured her. "Now let's head on out before you start losing your nerve again."

As Denny explained it, there had been quite a controversy over the location of the new schoolhouse. The owner of the logging camp had offered to supply all materials and labor if it were built west of town, so that the children of the "jacks" wouldn't have far to travel. But the townspeople didn't want *their* children passing through that end of Shasta Falls, which was dominated by two rowdy saloons that provided liquor, gambling, and all manner of female companionship for the lumberjacks.

As a compromise, the school was built to the north, against the face of the mountain—a beautiful spot more or less equidistant from both groups, although not really convenient for anyone. Denny complained that it wasn't as close to his office as he wanted it to be, given the fact that the school-teacher was a pretty young girl. He had insisted on installation of a bell, and lectured Maggie strictly on when she was to ring it.

"The slightest hint of trouble, or any suspicious persons lurking about, or one of those boys from the camp being disrespectful, or even just an uneasy feeling that you can't explain—"

"I'll be fine." Maggie gave him a teasing grin. "One would think we were living in Sodom or Gomorrah, rather than this beautiful little town."

"Just the same—"

"Just the same, I'll ring the bell at the slightest hint of trouble," she promised cheerfully.

He took her arm as they ascended the stone steps that led to the schoolyard, then he swung open the gate of the low, white-picket fence and bowed with playful gallantry. "After you."

"It's so pretty." Maggie's gaze traveled over the simple lines of the new white building. Two gangly oak trees shaded a portion of the yard, while the rest was covered by myriad wild grasses that had been stomped into a soft mat. She could see that some wildflowers were trying to re-establish themselves, but no formal planting had been done, and her first resolution was to send for seeds so that the walkway could be lined with posies. Perhaps she could even convince Mr. Gentry to build a few flower boxes for the narrow windows that flanked the wide front door.

"This spot gets too much wind," Denny complained. "You'll catch cold if you're not careful."

"If I start feeling sick, I'll ring the bell."

He chuckled. "Father James told us you were sweet and docile, but I'm learning there's another side to you. Come along now, and see the inside."

She followed him into the building and clapped her hands with absolute delight. Row after row of sturdy desks, just waiting for eager young students, confronted them. And at the head of the room, a grand oak table for Maggie, beyond which was a long, narrow chalkboard.

"It's just right!"

"There wasn't a lot of money for extras—"

"It's perfect." She smiled into his beaming face. "You've built a wonderful school here, Sheriff. The whole town should be very proud."

"That they are. They can't wait to meet you, missy. Did Eleanor tell you about the picnic we're planning for Sunday after church?"

Maggie nodded. "It will be wonderful to meet everyone. And then, on Monday morning, I'll meet the children. Which means, I'd best get busy." She patted his arm. "Thank you for escorting me, but I'll be fine alone now."

"When you're ready to go back to the boarding house—"

"I'll find my own way. Truly, sheriff, I don't want the children to see me as weak or timid. This spot is perfectly safe—you wouldn't have built a school for

your children here if it weren't—so let's have no more
nonsense."

Denny laughed. "So? I'm the first person chastised
by the new schoolteacher? I'm thinking the boys'll be
lining up to be scolded by the likes of you."

Maggie arched an eyebrow in playful rebuke.
"Aren't there any criminals you could go and chase?
I for one have work to do."

When he hesitated, she added with an exaggerated
sigh, "I'll ring the bell if I need you. You have my
solemn word."

He nodded. "I'll close up for the day at five
o'clock, and come by the boardinghouse to fetch you
for supper. You won't forget?"

"Of course not. But you don't need to come for
me. I'll be at your office promptly at five, and you
can show me the way to your house from there. I can't
wait to meet Mrs. Riordain."

"You and Junie will get along fine. Both stubborn
as mules." He turned and ambled back onto the front
steps, calling over his shoulder, "Ring the blasted bell
if you need me."

Laughing lightly, Maggie waved to him until he was
outside the yard, then returned eagerly to the schoolroom, studying every inch of it with admiring eyes.
A blank slate, waiting for her to create an exciting,
stimulating, provocative environment for the young
minds entrusted to her.

She had few illusions that she would produce clas-
sical scholars in this little room. But she could give
her students a good basic education, and could inspire
a handful of them to seek something more, either at
other institutions of learning outside Shasta Falls, or
from books. In the meantime, they would learn to read
and write; to do enough arithmetic to pursue a trade;
to locate oceans and continents on a map; and to ap-

preciate the incredible events of history, beginning with the ancient Greeks and Romans. She would read great literature to them every day, and teach them to recite poems and soliloquies, and to identify—

Wait! She stopped herself with a sheepish smile. *You'll scare them away with your enthusiasm. Remember how Robert did it? He simply allowed them a glimpse of his passion, and they practically begged him to share more.*

"Miss O'Connor?" a soft voice interrupted from behind her.

She whirled toward the speaker—a skinny girl of perhaps thirteen years of age. Two younger girls—one with long, golden hair, the other with dark brown braids—were with her. And all three had bouquets in their hands, and tentative smiles on their freshly scrubbed faces, as though they were unsure of the reception they'd receive.

Maggie beamed. "What a lovely surprise! I was hoping I'd have visitors today." Dropping to one knee, she asked gently, "Are those for me? Daffodils and daisies? They're beautiful."

"We didn't want to bother you, but we were curious," the older girl explained. "We won't stay long."

"Stay as long as you'd like. Let's sit over here, shall we? And please tell me your names."

"I'm Angela Deighton. Everyone calls me Angie. This is my sister, Mary Ellen." She paused to rumple the hair of the blond child fondly, then tugged playfully on one of the brown-haired girl's braids. "This is our neighbor, Becky Green."

"I'm delighted to meet you." Maggie perched on the edge of her table, then watched with a smile as the two little girls crowded into one seat together, directly in front of her, while Angela slipped into a seat to their right. "I want to hear everything about you."

"We're all girls," Becky explained simply.

"I can see that. Very pretty girls, in fact."

"You're pretty, too. Papa said you'd be homely as his hunting dog, but—"

"Becky!" Angie grimaced. "I'm sure Mr. Green didn't say that, Miss O'Connor. Everyone tried to guess what you'd be like, though. We've been so anxious for you to come to Shasta Falls. A real teacher at last. I've tried to teach these two a little," she added carefully. "And I've tried to teach myself from books, but it isn't easy."

"Angie's real smart," Becky explained.

"Too smart for her own good," Mary Ellen added. "That's what Father says."

Maggie laughed. "That's exactly what *my* father used to say about *me*. Believe it or not, it's their way of expressing their pride in us."

Angie nodded. "We have a brother who's smart, too."

"He doesn't want to come to school, though," Mary Ellen told Maggie. "He says girl-teachers don't know the things *he* wants to learn."

"He'll come, though," Angie interjected. "Father will see to that. But some of the other boys won't come."

"Oh?"

"Mostly the boys from the camp. And the Lawsons."

"The Lawsons are mean," Becky explained. "We don't want them here."

Maggie sighed. "I want them to come, but I certainly won't allow them to be mean while they're here." Turning back to Angie, she asked, "What's your brother's name?"

"Joshua."

"And what is it he wants to learn about?"

"Battles. And ships. And weapons. And famous men—especially famous generals."

"I see." Maggie bit back a smile. "My brothers loved all those subjects, too. You tell Joshua I'll do my best to find something of interest for everyone. Maybe even for the boys from the logging camp."

"But not the Lawsons. They don't care about anything but being mean," Mary Ellen said with staunch insistence.

Maggie grinned. "I appreciate the warning. How many Lawsons are there?"

"Three. Joey, and Patrick, and Junior. Junior's big. Really big. He's mean to Angie. Joey and Patrick aren't big yet, but they're mean, too—to us."

Maggie moistened her lips, no longer amused. "As I said, I won't allow them to be mean to you here."

"You won't be able to stop them. Even Josh can't, and he's really strong."

"It doesn't matter, Miss O'Connor," Angie assured her. "They won't want to come to school very often. And even if they wanted to, their father probably wouldn't let them. He's the meanest of them all."

"He whips them," Becky said with a shudder. "One time, Joey cried and came to our house, and Papa sent for the sheriff, and the sheriff was so mad, his face turned purple and he used curse words."

"How unfortunate."

"It was *real* unfortunate," Becky agreed. "Can we climb the trees?"

"Hmm? Do you mean, in the schoolyard? I hadn't thought about that—"

"I'll watch them," Angie offered.

"We'll both watch for a while," Maggie said, relieved that the subject had changed so easily. Over time, she had a feeling she'd become more and more involved in this sordid business of the cruel Lawson boys and their crueler father, but for now, she intended to seek a different sort of information from Angela Deighton.

By the time she and the older girl reached the play yard, Becky and Mary Ellen were already scampering up the larger of the oak trees. Settling down onto the grass, Maggie asked casually, "You said you've been teaching the girls. Did you enjoy it?"

Angie nodded. "But I didn't make much progress."

"I used to do that—teach little children, when I was your age. I was an assistant for our schoolmaster. I helped the little ones with their lessons for a few hours each day, so he could concentrate on the older students, or on the ones who were having unusual difficulty. In exchange, he tutored me after school, in advanced subjects, such as Latin." She hesitated. "Perhaps, as time goes on, you might want to try that sort of arrangement."

"I'm not very advanced, but . . ." Angie's eyes danced with excitement. "I can read and write and do arithmetic. And I'd like to learn more. I'd *love* to learn more. It sounds wonderful, Miss O'Connor."

As Angela began to detail the many, *many* areas of learning that she one day hoped to master, Maggie listened with wary delight. She hadn't dared hope she could find such an able assistant so quickly, and the possibilities for success now seemed limitless. She would pour herself into this school and its students, and over time, she would manage to keep her vow to Robert and herself, to stop dwelling on the past. To make peace with her sorrow, her guilt, and her pain, and above all, to stop thinking about the fact that she'd never had a chance to say goodbye to either of her beloved brothers, nor to convince Ian that he was well-loved, despite all the horrendous evidence to the contrary.

* * *

By the time she returned to the boardinghouse, she was weary, and would have thrown herself onto the tiny attic bed for a nap had five o'clock not loomed so near. She barely had time to scrub her face in the tiny washroom on the second floor, then scurry back up to her room, where she changed—with one eye on the "door"—into a modest green-and-white checked dress. Finally, she brushed her long, golden-brown locks into thick, shimmering waves, which she corralled into a loose braid that hung halfway down her back. *Just like Mother,* she informed herself, thinking wistfully of the woman she knew only through stories and a few worn but beloved pictures.

The aroma of burning chicken tickled at her nose, and she almost felt guilty as she hurried downstairs to bid goodbye to Mrs. Blake. Promising to "save room for pie," she slipped out onto the porch, inhaled deeply, and then made her way toward the middle of town, where the sheriff's office and jail were located.

For the first time, she wondered about June Riordain. What sort of girl had caught the eye of the handsome sheriff? Someone soft and feminine and demure?

But stubborn, she reminded herself with a smile. *That's what he called her this afternoon. And when he talks about her, his eyes sparkle, like he's still falling in love with her. I wonder if she knows how much he cares for her. I wonder how it feels to know you're loved that way.*

She caught herself, all too aware of where her thoughts were going. If she wasn't careful, she'd be having regrets about Ian again, wondering if he knew *he* was loved, there at the end, all alone in his cell.

You promised Robert you'd stop yourself whenever

you began to worry about things you could never change, she reminded herself.

She decided to think about Robert himself instead. If he were there at that moment, he'd persuade her to concentrate on her new students, and the progress she hoped to make with them. And he'd ask her to marry him again, although she had gotten the distinct impression that his last proposal had been habit, rather than true desire. She certainly hoped so, since she knew he wanted to have children of his own. Wasn't that why she had introduced him to her neighbor Marie? And they had seemed intrigued by one another, hadn't they? Perhaps by this time . . . ?

She smiled wistfully. June Riordain was a fortunate woman, but not more fortunate than Marie, if she in fact became Mrs. Robert Grimes. Maggie had turned down that honor, despite her admiration for the headmaster, because she knew she couldn't be a good wife and mother. She'd be too afraid that something would go wrong . . . that someone would die . . . or worse. . . .

She was blessedly distracted from the familiar litany by the sight of two boys scampering across the dusty street in the direction of the livery stable. They were clearly plotting some mischief, and she decided to join in their little game, whatever it was. Perhaps that would convince them that a "girl-teacher" wasn't completely useless.

By the time she reached the far side of the street, the boys had disappeared behind the stable, and Maggie hesitated. She didn't want to be late for her appointment with the Riordains, and so she couldn't follow the potential students forever. She'd simply check around the back, and if they were nowhere to be found, she'd abandon the search.

Stepping carefully through a hay-lined alleyway, she

reached the back of the building, where a huge, dark
doorway granted access to the stable. There wasn't a
soul in sight, nor a horse, although she could hear a
gentle neighing sound emanating from the darkness.

They're in there, she assured herself. *Little boys and
horses—the ultimate love match. Remember how
Brian would sneak into the stalls at Mr. Sinclair's, and
pretend the stallion was his trusty steed, ready to carry
him into battle?*

Angela Deighton's brother, Joshua, had sounded
like that sort of child, and Maggie wondered if perhaps
he was one of the boys she'd spied. It would be a
lovely coincidence, giving her an opportunity to tell
him she planned on reading adventure stories such as
Moby Dick to the class. That would improve his view
of the new teacher, would it not?

Brimming with playful confidence, she crept to the
doorway and peered into the shadowy interior of the
stable, intent on discovering the boys' game before
joining it. As her eyes adjusted to the dim light, she
realized that she was staring at the back of a full-
grown man, dressed in a long, dark coat covered with
dust. His hand rested on the rump of a powerful black
horse, precariously close to the butt of a sheathed rifle.

The man was silent and motionless, his attention
plainly riveted on something or someone other than
Maggie. Still, her every instinct told her *she* was in
danger, and she was about to turn and run when his
voice split the silence with a menacing growl of
"Who's hiding there? Come out and show yourself."

As he spoke, he drew a shiny pistol from under his
coat, and Maggie almost shrieked aloud, despite the
fact that he clearly wasn't addressing *her.* Instead, his
stare was fixed on a dark corner of a stall near the
front of the stable.

Then he cocked the pistol and repeated his instructions, and to Maggie's horror, the two little boys scurried into view, their hands above their heads.

Without thinking, Maggie lunged forward, insinuating herself between the gunman and the children. "Put that pistol away this instant! Can't you see they're just children?"

His steely gaze now fixated on her so completely, she knew the boys were safe, and so, without turning away from the man, she murmured, "Go on now, you two. Run along home. No one's going to hurt you." To the gunman, she dared add, "Tell them it's fine for them to leave."

For a long moment, he didn't react. Then he gave a curt nod, and the two youths scrambled toward the corral. She thought they weren't even going to look back: then the taller of the boys spun back for a moment to stammer, "We're s-sorry, Mr. Coburn. D-don't hurt the new schoolteacher—*please?*" before darting out of sight.

Maggie stared in confused disbelief at the tall, dark-haired figure before her. He still had a cocked pistol in his hand, although he had allowed his arm to drop down by his side. And his eyes—the color of midnight ice, and dangerously narrowed—told her he hadn't fully relaxed. Was it true? Was he . . . ?

"Mr. Coburn?"

"So? Those fools ignored my advice, I see." Holstering his weapon, he rested his hands on his hips and surveyed her with a grin. "They spent good time and money bringing an unattached female into these parts, knowing that even the homeliest girl could find a husband here in a week's time. I shouldn't have wasted my breath trying to convince them to hire a man. What's your name?"

"It's Maggie—Margaret, I mean. Margaret Gleason—Oh! I mean, Margaret O'Connor." Her voice had become a wail, and she forced herself to take a deep breath before informing him more firmly, "I'm Miss Margaret O'Connor. And you're Mr. Alexander Coburn? I've heard quite a bit about you, sir."

Her statement brought a scowl to his face. "Such as?"

"Such as, you don't like change. Or surprises. What you do like is your privacy. And so, if you'll excuse me, I'll get out of your way."

"That's a good idea."

All too aware that her cheeks were burning bright red, she bade him a haughty, "Good evening, Mr. Coburn."

"Good evening, Miss Maggie-Margaret Gleason-O'Connor," he replied with a slightly mocking bow.

His sarcasm infuriated her, and she tried to summon the strength to stay and chastise him, but her nerve failed her, and she bolted for the corral, where she leaned against a fence post and tried to steady her pounding heart.

Had he actually dared to draw a pistol on two innocent children? And to mock her name, and call her 'homely'? And had *she* actually been misguided enough to feel sympathy for him the night before? To suspect that his infamous rudeness was born of unhappiness? She had imagined him to be a pitiful victim, like poor Ian, when in fact, he was the consummate bully!

She wanted to march back into that stable and give him a tongue lashing, but what would that accomplish, other than to make her late for her appointment with the Riordains? And did she really want to engage in a full-scale feud with a fellow boarder?

Be thankful he was in fact a fellow boarder, and not some villain, she scolded herself. *What were you thinking, jumping in there to confront an armed man?*

Did you see his hands? His eyes? Did you actually think you could protect those boys from him?

But she knew the truth—that her behavior had been pure instinct. Little Maggie, jumping to Ian's defense when bullies of every size and shape came to plague him. She had done so from the age of five, or perhaps even earlier. In fact, she couldn't remember a time she *hadn't* been Ian's defender!

More than once, it had occurred to her she might have grown up to be a dainty, bashful coquette, had destiny not given her the task of protecting her sickly brother. Her mother had reputedly been a delicate beauty—too delicate, in fact. But Maggie knew in her heart her mother would have approved of her little girl's efforts to protect little Ian, even if technically—

"Teacher?"

Maggie opened her eyes and was charmed to see the face of the little boy who had entreated Coburn to spare her. When he took her hand and said, "Let's go," she followed him gratefully across the street to join his shamefaced companion.

"We're sorry we left you alone with him, miss. Did he yell at you?"

"Mr. Coburn knows better than to raise his voice to a schoolteacher," she assured them. "He'd be standing in the corner of my classroom at this very moment if he did such a thing."

The two boys laughed.

"I'm Miss O'Connor."

"We know."

"Why did you go into the livery stable?" she asked gently. "To spy on Mr. Coburn?"

They nodded. "We wanted to see him up really close. No one ever does. From far away, he always looks so big and strong and mean."

"And up close?"

"He looks worser."

Maggie laughed. "I agree."

"Did you see how shiny his pistol was?"

"It seemed quite formidable."

"He would've shot us if you hadn't've saved us."

"Don't be silly. Any man would react that way if he sensed an unknown opponent hiding in the shadows." Maggie felt her shoulders relax for the first time since the encounter with Coburn, and realized that the words she had just spoken were true. His reaction to the children, while a bit harsh, had been perfectly understandable. Arriving back in town after a long, exhausting journey, he had become aware that someone was lurking in the darkness, and had instinctively drawn his weapon before instructing them to show themselves. What could be more natural?

And if *she* hadn't rushed to their aid so inappropriately, he would have simply scowled and sent them on their way. She had complicated matters by implying he would hurt a couple of innocent children! All because of her instincts—her lifelong duty to protect little Ian Gleason.

"You're the bravest lady we ever saw," the taller boy was informing her solemnly.

Maggie started to protest, then smiled instead. "I expect to see you both in my class, bright and early Monday morning. Agreed?"

"Sure. We'll come, if our pa says we can. And when we tell him about you, he'll let us."

"Tell me your names."

"I'm Joey Lawson. This is Patrick, my brother."

Maggie bit back a gasp. The bullies? These sweet little boys? "Bright and early Monday morning," she repeated lamely, trying not to remember which boy had been beaten so severely it had caused Denny Riordain to cuss. "I'm having supper with the sheriff and his wife, so I need to run along. It was nice meeting you both."

"Don't tell the sheriff what happened with Coburn," Patrick pleaded.

"I won't."

"Coburn'll tell him anyways, idiot," Joey muttered. "They're friends, remember?" Then he flashed Maggie a weary smile. "Someday, when we're big, we'll be braver. Then if some bad man points a gun at you, we'll kill him for you."

"I appreciate the sentiment. Go on home now, boys. It's suppertime."

"Goodbye, Miz O'Connor!" They were gone in an instant, shoving playfully at one another as they ran.

"It's a day for surprises," Maggie murmured aloud as she resumed her journey to the sheriff's office. "Mr. Coburn wasn't a helpless, intimidated bookworm—he was a beast. And the Lawson boys weren't beastly—they were helpless and intimidated! I have a feeling June Riordain's going to surprise you, too, so best prepare yourself for the worst. And *hurry,* because the sheriff will be certain you've been waylaid if you're even one second late!"

Three

Unlike Eleanor Blake, June Riordain proved to be a marvelous cook, plying Maggie with mouthwatering roast chicken and buttery biscuits. Unfortunately, it was difficult to find a moment to actually eat the food, since the pretty, red-haired hostess also served her guest a dizzying assortment of questions, along with provocative observations and advice concerning the townsfolk.

June had something to say about each of the boarders except Coburn. For example, she deemed Mamie and Francine Lowe, the spinster sisters, to be "lost in the past, and enjoying themselves there immensely, so who are we to judge them?" Predictably, she adored the gun salesman, Amos Gentry. And just as predictably, didn't care much for the nosy neighbor, Gladys, whom she succinctly labeled a gossip who "never had a life of her own and resents the rest of us ours." Maggie wondered how June could call someone else a gossip, given the nonstop barrage of information she was sharing with a virtual stranger, but she had to admit, there was something endearing about June's manner that kept it all from seeming mean-spirited or wrong.

Eleanor Blake herself was apparently nothing less than a saint in June's eyes. The hostess explained to

Maggie that the landlady's daughters were sweet, but lived in Sacramento with children too young to travel well. "Eleanor goes to see them once a year, but she should go more often. Speak to her about that, won't you, Maggie?"

Fortunately, June didn't really seem to expect answers to her many questions, or reactions to her diatribes. In fact, she usually provided both question and answer, and moved from subject to subject so rapidly, her guest simply had no time to utter a meaningful response.

And as if that weren't bizarre enough, June flirted shamelessly with her husband right there at the supper table! It was sweet and amusing, but Maggie had been raised in such a different and reserved environment, she found herself mentally gasping for air, or at the very least, for a moment alone to gather her thoughts and digest the information along with the food.

But there was no time for reflection in the Riordain household, it seemed. Even when they moved to the parlor for coffee and cake, June didn't leave Maggie alone for a second. Instead, she sent her brawny husband back and forth to the kitchen to serve them, shocking Maggie even further. But Denny followed June's instructions with a smile, pausing only to kiss his bride every time he passed by her as he went about his tasks.

June chose this time to address the subject of the town's bachelors. "I've made a list of them for you," she informed Maggie cheerfully. "I may have omitted one or two names, but if I did, they're probably not worth your attention in any case. For every wonderful quality a man has, I placed a star next to his name. And for every fault, an X. Do you see?"

Maggie turned confused eyes to Denny, hoping he would rescue her from his wife's ridiculous scheme,

but he only grinned sympathetically as he settled into
a huge rocking chair. "Junie's a born matchmaker. Between herself and Eleanor, you'll be married by
autumn, so you might as well stop resisting."

Maggie cocked her head to the side, wondering if
June had planned this from the start. Two full hours
of nonstop chattering on every subject under the sun,
including the story of Denny's courtship; of the fire
that had swept through the town its first year; of the
dramatic feuds between loggers and townspeople, and
the equally dramatic love matches that had erupted
from time to time out of the same rivalries. It had
been mind numbing, yet interesting. And the only real
danger had been that Maggie herself might be perceived as having engaged in prolonged gossip. But
this?

A list of the town's single men? With June Riordain's personal assessment of each in the margin?

"You'll see that Kirk Waller has five stars and only
two X's. In other words, he's my recommended choice.
But of course, if he doesn't make your knees
buckle . . ." June shrugged her slender shoulders.
"Do you prefer a beard?"

"Mrs. Riordain—"

"June," she insisted for the hundredth time.

"Fine." Maggie exhaled sharply. "June, I appreciate
the time and effort you devoted to making this list.
But I'm begging you, *please* believe me when I say
I'm not interested in finding a husband."

"I understand completely. You think there's no man
in the world who can measure up to the ideal you've
set for a prospective spouse. I felt that way myself,
before I met Denny. But as you can see, a man can
have dozens of faults and still be a perfect husband."

The sheriff pretended to glare. "Dozens of faults?"
Jumping to his feet, he crossed to the sofa in two

strides, then pulled his wife into a rough embrace and "punished" her by nuzzling at her neck until she screamed for mercy.

Maggie pretended to examine the needlepoint on a cushion of her chair, all the while questioning the sanity of her hosts. Of course, their behavior was loving in its own way, but so embarrassing! And it seemed they honestly had no idea how inappropriate it was.

"Behave yourself, Dennis Riordain. You're making Maggie blush. Take this tray back to the sink, then go outside and have a smoke while we finish discussing the men in this town."

"That's hardly necessary," Maggie interrupted. "And it's time I started back to the boardinghouse. Mrs. Blake will wonder where I am."

"She knows you're here." June arched an eyebrow toward her husband, who dutifully grabbed the tray and disappeared into the kitchen.

"I appreciate your interest in my happiness, June—"

"Shh," she warned, craning her neck to be certain her husband was out of earshot, then she grinned mischievously. "There's really only one man I want to talk to you about, and that's Alex Coburn. But Denny made me promise not to mention his name, so I have to be careful."

Maggie stared, certain now that June was insane. "You can't possibly consider Mr. Coburn to be a romantic prospect—"

"Him?" June shrieked with laughter. "I'd strangle you with my bare hands before I'd let you become involved with that horrible man. I just wanted to be certain you'd been warned about him."

Maggie smiled warily. "Yes. I've been warned." She considered adding that she'd actually had the pleasure of meeting the "horrible man," but decided against it, just as she'd decided against telling the sheriff during the short walk from his office to the house. If she told them, they'd ask her what her impression was, and she actually wasn't sure anymore. After the initial shock of seeing a dusty, scowling stranger point a gun at innocent children, she had begun to suspect she had overreacted to the bizarre situation.

After all, he had put the gun away as soon as he knew there wasn't any danger. And he had let the boys go without a lecture about lurking in dark places. His only real offense had been calling Maggie "homely," and it seemed hypocritical on her part to be offended by that, considering her supposed lack of interest in attracting male attention.

And she did look rather plain, in this threadbare dress and shawl, with her hair in a braid. And in Coburn's defense, he had been trying to make a point, which was that even a homely girl like Maggie could find a husband in these parts, so he hadn't actually pronounced her repulsive. As a recluse, he hadn't had an opportunity to refine his social skills, because he didn't care what others thought of him.

It's a good thing he enjoys being alone, because with those manners, it is a self-fulfilling wish, she decided with a pragmatic shrug of her shoulders.

June was watching her with curious intensity. "You needn't be afraid of him, you know. Denny would never let him hurt you."

"What? Oh, dear, I'm not at all afraid. I feel wonderfully safe in Shasta Falls. And frankly, I have so many new people to meet and become friends with, I simply don't have much time to worry about Mr. Coburn one way or the other. Mrs. Blake tells me he likes to be alone, and I intend to respect that completely."

"Everyone lets him misbehave. Even Denny. It's so very, very frustrating."

Maggie smiled. "I've been told Coburn and the sheriff are friends."

"Some friendship." June sniffed in complete disgust. "Friends visit one another's homes, the way you've come here tonight. But how many times has *he* come to supper?"

"Never?"

"Once, and halfway through the meal, he stood up and left, muttering some sort of half-baked apology under his breath. After I slaved over a meal for him." Her hazel eyes narrowed. "And try making conversation with the man! He doesn't say a word. Denny and I had to do all the talking."

Maggie suddenly had an image of June and Denny flirting with one another in front of Alex Coburn. Given how much the behavior had bothered Maggie, it must have made a reserved man like Coburn even more uncomfortable. With a teasing smile, she told June, "He was probably jealous that Denny had such a wonderful wife, who could cook so well."

June grinned. "Don't defend him. He's just plain rude. Denny defends him, too—says he's like a wild stallion, and we need to be patient."

"A wild stallion?"

"How does it go?" June pursed her lips as though struggling to remember the wording. "Coburn just wants to be left alone. He stands apart by choice, because it suits his purposes. He isn't afraid of anything, so you can come near him, and it doesn't bother him as long as you ignore him. But show a bit too much interest, and all you'll see is his dust. Just like a wild stallion."

"Well, now," Denny muttered from the doorway. "I thought we had an understanding, Mrs. Riordain. Didn't I ask you not to poison Maggie against Coburn? He'll do that himself soon enough," he added philosophically. "And at least he doesn't break his promises, which is more than I can say for my own wife."

June's eyes twinkled. "I'm prepared to accept my punishment."

"Are you? Come over here then."

Maggie almost groaned aloud as she realized that what appeared to be a disagreement was actually just another excuse for the lovebirds to indulge in a mating ritual. Eyeing the door, she murmured, "It's late. And I have a thousand things to do tomorrow if I'm to be ready for school on Monday."

This time, Denny didn't protest. "We'll go, then. Junie, can I count on you to behave while I'm gone?"

"As long as you hurry back."

"That I will."

June pulled her guest into a warm embrace. "Goodbye, Maggie dear. I'll come to the school tomorrow and help you get everything ready for the children."

"I'd like that." Maggie wriggled free, then backed a safe distance toward the door before adding sincerely, "I can't remember when I've had a nicer time. Thank you for everything—the food, the hospitality, and the advice."

"And the list! You almost forgot it." June scooped up the piece of paper and handed it to her husband, instructing him, "Make certain she has this when she gets back to the boardinghouse."

"Yes, ma'am." He lowered his mouth to June's and kissed her with relish, then turned to his houseguest and announced cheerfully that it was time to go.

The temperature had dropped twenty degrees in a matter of hours, and as Maggie strolled at Denny's side, she silently thanked her hostess again, this time for insisting that she borrow a fur wrap to augment the thin wool shawl that had seemed more than sufficient just three short hours earlier. Above her head, the sky was so crowded with clear pinpoints of light, Maggie almost believed Shasta Falls had its own private constellations intermixed with the ones shared by the rest of the world. As she'd done during her first hours in town, she inhaled deeply, and while the air was now so cold it almost stung, she still welcomed it, knowing that it could cleanse her right down to her soul if she let it.

"We'll be expecting you for supper weekly from now on," Denny told her as they neared the boardinghouse. "Junie loves to entertain, and I can see she's taken a special liking to you, so it's settled. No sense in arguing."

"The food was delicious, the conversation was lively, and you and June made me feel instantly at home. What more could I ask?"

"She's stubborn, though." His smile faded. "Don't let her sour you on Coburn. He's not as bad as she makes him sound."

"I'm sure he isn't." Maggie moistened her lips before explaining. "The truth is, I'm very much the same as he is. I'm private, I tend to keep to myself and to dread change, and I love books."

The observation made Denny chuckle. "You're nothing like His Lordship, believe me. When you meet him—"

"I've met him already."

"Huh?" They had reached the walkway to the boardinghouse, and her escort rested his hand gently on her shoulder so that she wouldn't proceed further. "When was this?"

"I was on my way to your office this evening when

I encountered him. He had just returned from his 'adventure,' apparently."

"And?"

She smiled mischievously. "For a grouchy recluse who hates surprises, he was inoffensive."

Denny threw his head back and roared with laughter. "Learned your lesson, did you?"

"Yes."

The sheriff's eyes twinkled. "If he were any other man, I'd say he'll change his tune when he gets to know you better. But Coburn *won't* get to know you—not even if you keep your promise and stay in that boardinghouse for a full year."

Maggie studied him, fascinated. "But he got to know you, didn't he? I mean, you're his friend, so I assume you've done what friends do—talked, and spent time together, and learned to appreciate one another's strengths."

"And learned to forgive one another's faults?" Denny shrugged his brawny shoulders. "I doubt we would've become friends at all, if it hadn't been for a posse I had to rustle up a few months after he moved into the boardinghouse. I was short on men and shorter on time, so I took a chance and asked him, despite his unfriendly manner."

"And?"

"He was armed and saddled up in the blink of an eye, and for three days straight, we watched each other's backs. *That's* the kind of friend a sheriff needs, missy, so I look past his lesser qualities."

"I see." Maggie smiled. "How long ago was that?"

"A year, more or less."

"How did he come to live here? It's so remote. And he doesn't seem to have any real ties to the area—no employment, no family."

"If you have questions, you should ask Eleanor. Or

better yet, just let them go. Why he's here—why he's the way he is . . ." Denny shrugged again. "He's the only one who knows that for sure, and I don't advise asking him."

They had reached the boardinghouse walkway, and Maggie asked slyly if he'd like to come inside, knowing that he was eager to return to more amorous pursuits.

"Junie's waiting," he confirmed. "Give Eleanor my best."

"I will, but not right away." Maggie inclined her head toward the parlor window, from which boisterous laughter and the tinkling of piano keys were pouring. "Once they settle down, I'll join them, but I plan to get my bearings in my room first."

"Overwhelmed, are you?" He took her arm and walked her around to the rear porch. "Everyone means well—"

"I know that. It's just what I need, actually."

"But in small doses?"

She smiled. "As I said, I'm a bit like Mr. Coburn in that regard." Before Denny could protest, she squeezed his arm and insisted, "June's waiting. Go on now, and thank her again for me, won't you?"

"Good night, missy." He gave her a brisk hug, then started back for his house.

Smiling to herself, Maggie slipped through the door, remembering that just inside the service porch was a back staircase. With any luck, no one would be in the second-floor hall to see her as she made her way to the other, narrower stairs that led to the attic.

She resisted a wave of guilt at avoiding her fellow boarders, after they'd been so warm and welcoming to her. She had had enough merriment for one night, and longed only to curl up with a book for a while. She had spied a copy of *Ivanhoe* on a shelf in the library, and was tempted to borrow it—it had been one of her favorite stories for years—but she wasn't completely certain Mrs. Blake would approve of volumes leaving the dark-paneled confines of the room.

You could read downstairs for just a while, couldn't you? she asked herself, edging toward the doorway to the room. Then she realized a fire was blazing in the library's fireplace. Coburn? At this hour, after all his traveling?

Why are you surprised? she thought wistfully. *Have you ever been too tired to read for a few minutes before bedtime? And even at your most exhausted, those minutes can become hours if the book is sufficiently intriguing. It's simply more proof that you and he have something in common.*

She challenged herself on the spot to go and speak with him—to clear the air, if nothing else. And perhaps, when he learned she was a fellow book lover, he'd invite her to join him! With a fire burning, she could only imagine how cozy the wonderful library could be on so chilly a night, and that image helped her to square her shoulders and step right into the room.

"Mr. Coburn?"

He was seated to the left of the fireplace, and had repositioned his leather chair so that he could prop his feet on the raised stone hearth. His clothing—black shirt, black trousers, shiny black boots—appeared fresh and clean, so she assumed he had changed, although she couldn't guess why he would dress this way for an evening by the fire. The outfit was more appropriate for a gunfight, although his pistol wasn't anywhere in sight. He was armed only with a thin, leather-bound volume, which he half closed as he raised his gaze to hers.

No further acknowledgment, either through a greeting or, more appropriately, by his rising to his feet, was forthcoming, so Maggie took a deep breath, then smiled warmly. "I'm so pleased you're awake. We started off badly, all because of a misunderstanding. But since we're going to be neighbors of a sort, we ought to try again. Don't you agree?"

He seemed to consider the statement for a moment, then shrugged. "You won't be living here for long, Maggie-Margaret, so there's no need to engage in the usual niceties. Just pretend I don't exist, and I'll return the favor."

"My name isn't Maggie-Margaret. It's Miss O'Connor, if you don't mind."

"Miss *Gleason*-O'Connor, wasn't it?"

She bit back an angry retort, and tried again to be civil. "I'm told you have a fondness for books. It's something we have in common, sir. I was simply hoping . . . well, that we could coexist. In silence, if you wish, but companionable silence. This library is large enough to accommodate us both, wouldn't you say?"

With an exaggerated sigh, he set his book on the hearth, then stood to tower over her, his midnight blue eyes suddenly blazing with condescension. "If you're looking for male companionship, Maggie-Margaret, may I suggest you try the logging camp west of town?"

"How dare you!" Maggie stepped backward, but didn't look away from his scornful expression. "I was trying to be polite, but apparently, civilized behavior is quite lost on you."

"Quite," he agreed with a mocking grin. "But if you're interested in engaging in some *un*civilized behavior, we could adjourn to my bedroom—"

"Be quiet!" She forced herself not to run away from his leering invitation. After all, Mrs. Blake and the others were close at hand, so presumably Coburn wouldn't physically advance on her against her will. And she simply had to stand her ground, if only to ensure that he'd never make so alarming a suggestion again, so she advised him in a suitably icy voice, "Don't *ever* dare speak to me like that again. In fact, don't speak to me at all, from this moment forward."

His grin faded into an expression of cool victory. "We understand each another, then?"

"Completely."

To her chagrin, he then retrieved his book, returned to his seat, and began to read again as though nothing had transpired.

She wanted to make a graceful, even haughty, exit, but the experience had played havoc with her nerves and so she dashed for the back staircase instead. Taking the steps two at a time, she didn't pause for a breath until she flew through her little muslin "door" and threw herself onto her bed.

"Now you know the truth: that you have *nothing* in common with that beast!" she warned herself aloud through gritted teeth. "To think you compared him with Ian! He isn't simply ill-mannered or uncivilized, he's perverse and ignoble. How tragic that Mrs. Blake's need for income forces her to house such a hideous man."

For the first time since the age of fourteen, Maggie was actually tempted to go out and find herself a husband—a very wealthy one—who could give Mrs. Blake whatever she needed to live comfortably for the rest of her years. And he could punch Coburn in the nose for good measure! Which meant, of course, that he'd have to be bigger and stronger than Coburn, although Maggie wasn't sure she could ever again enjoy the sensation of feeling dwarfed by a male. It had often made her feel protected in the past, but now and

forever, it would remind her of danger. And humiliation. And Coburn.

"We missed you at supper last night. And then
when you didn't join us in the parlor—well, I was
sick with worry, until I realized you had used the back
stairs to go up to bed."

"I meant to come downstairs and wish you good
night after I put my things away and read for a little
while," Maggie explained with a sigh. "But I was exhausted, and fell asleep right there on top of the covers. Forgive me."

"Anyone would be exhausted after an evening with
June Riordain," Gladys Chesterton observed. "When
that woman starts talking, there's no end to it. And
mostly foolishness, if I might say so."

Maggie bristled. "I didn't notice any foolishness.
Just warmth and friendship."

"Don't be so sure of that. She has her own reasons
for taking an interest in *you*."

"Pardon?"

Gladys smiled. "June Riordain can't be pleased that
her husband has taken such a personal interest in a
pretty girl like you."

"Gladys!" Eleanor Blake frowned. "We've all taken
an interest in Maggie, and for good reason. She's going to be teaching our children."

"The sheriff doesn't have any children," Gladys reminded her briskly. "And you heard what Mr. Waller
said last night—every man in town is wondering why
a decent girl would travel so far from home unes-
corted. They're all seeing the worst in it." Turning to
Maggie, she insisted, "I told him no one should be
speculating about such things. And I also told him I

was certain you had a good reason for the choices you've been making."

"Thank you."

"I told him I was sure you've had some dreadful misfortune that drove you to seek a new life. Some unfortunate episode with a man—"

"Gladys!" Eleanor Blake gave Maggie an apologetic smile. "The truth is, we all know you'll tell us about your past as soon as we've earned your trust. And we'll never earn your trust if we gossip, so I simply won't allow that kind of talk in my house."

Maggie leveled a stare at Gladys. "You know everything you need to know about me. I have spotless references, from two professional educators and from a well-respected clergyman. I arrived on time; I'm clean and otherwise presentable; and I've been cordial and uncomplaining."

"You've been a pure delight," Eleanor corrected sincerely. "Don't be offended, Maggie. If you never want to tell us a word about your past, it won't matter one little bit."

"That's right," Amos Gentry said. "We've given Coburn that courtesy, haven't we?"

Mamie Lowe nodded. "Amos is right—we owe Maggie the same courtesy we've given Mr. Coburn. And I don't believe your suitors will care one whit about your past, dear. Especially not Mr. Waller. From the way he spoke last night, he'd marry you today, and he's never even met you! Just caught a glimpse of you, walking with the sheriff, and that was enough."

Maggie felt her patience begin to wear thin. Kirk Waller seemed to be everyone's fondest choice for Maggie's future, and she wondered how she could possibly convey to them—and to him—that it was simply out of the question.

Unless, of course, he's willing to hit Mr. Coburn for you, she reminded herself, amused that she had had such a silly thought the prior evening.

As if on cue, Coburn chose that very moment to stride into the kitchen. He was dressed as he'd been the night before, in clothes as black as his thick, wavy hair. Ignoring the group at the breakfast table, he headed for the stove and served himself a cup of coffee, his boots sounding briskly on the gleaming tile floor.

"Good morning, Mr. Coburn." Eleanor Blake scooted out of her chair and went to stand beside him. "Did you sleep well?"

"Yes, thank you."

"Did you want something to eat this morning?"

"Later, perhaps. Thank you."

To Maggie's dismay, the landlady then cleared her throat and announced in a vaguely desperate voice, "The most wonderful thing has happened, Mr. Coburn. Our new schoolteacher has arrived at last. May I present Miss Maggie O'Connor?"

Forcing herself not to cringe, Maggie waited for him to assure Mrs. Blake that he'd already had the pleasure. Would he also inform her that he had made a lewd suggestion to the new boarder, right there in Tobias Blake's library?

Instead, Coburn turned his dark eyes toward the table and gave Maggie a slight nod. "Welcome to Shasta Falls, Miss O'Connor."

She could feel her cheeks blazing with humiliation, despite the fact that there was no hint of mockery in his tone or manner. Managing to find her voice, she thanked him, then dropped her gaze to the table, hoping only that he would go away without any further attempt at conversation.

But Eleanor Blake seemed intent on maintaining a minimum level of cordiality in her home. "Miss O'Connor came to us from San Francisco. Highly recommended, I might add."

"San Francisco?" He studied Maggie curiously. "I thought I heard someplace else in your voice."

"We all have someplace else in our voices, don't we?" Amos Gentry interrupted. "Take Tobias, for example. He came with the first gold seekers, and lived here for almost fifteen years, and yet right till the end, he had only to speak ten words, and you'd know he was from London. Isn't that right, Eleanor?"

"He had the most beautiful voice," the landlady agreed, then launched into a spirited description of Tobias Blake's history—from England to New York to California.

Maggie flashed the gun salesman a grateful smile. Then, because she didn't want Coburn to think she was intimidated by his presence, she looked directly at him, and was surprised to see that he was listening—or at least, pretending to listen politely—to Mrs. Blake's convoluted story of a young man whose education and good looks could not prevent him from falling victim to the vice of gambling.

Taking the opportunity to carefully study Coburn, Maggie didn't much care for what she saw. Even in a moment such as this, there was a troubling lack of warmth in his expression. And while his aristocratic features might have been attractive on another man, they had the opposite effect when combined with Coburn's piercing blue eyes and aloof posture.

How many women have you repulsed or insulted in your travels? Maggie asked him silently. *You do it by choice—that's clear to me now. You could have had*

*so different a life, had you not developed such intense
disdain for the rest of us.*

Again, she reminded herself that she, too, had made
a choice to keep romance and familial bliss at arm's
length, but not because of distaste for the company of
others. Distrust, perhaps—mostly of herself—but only
of the most wistful and apologetic variety.

*And you swore you'd never again compare yourself
to this misanthrope, so stop it immediately! You finally
manage to put Brian and Ian out of your mind for a
day or so, only to find another method of torturing
yourself. Think about your students—they are the only
persons in your life right now who need your concen-
trated attention.*

She smiled with relief at the thought of returning
to the little schoolhouse and continuing her prepara-
tions. June would join her for a while, and perhaps
Angie and the little girls would come again, hopefully
with their brother, or other friends.

And the Lawson boys? Would she see them again
soon? Would they behave themselves?

Grateful that Coburn had been relegated to insig-
nificance so easily, she took advantage of a pause in
Mrs. Blake's story to announce to the group, "If you'll
excuse me, I have quite a bit to accomplish before the
first day of school arrives."

"You aren't going to spend the entire day at the
schoolhouse again, are you?" Mrs. Blake protested.

"I'll be back in time for supper, I promise. I'm hoping more of the children will come around, out of
curiosity. I met eight students yesterday, each one
more darling than the next."

"You can't have met the Lawsons, then," Gladys
interrupted. "Those boys are bad clear to the bone."

"As a matter of fact, I met two of them, and they
were very respectful." She gave Coburn a quick

glance, to see if he would realize these were the same boys who had spied on him, but he had turned away and was staring out the window, completely disinterested.

Relieved, she continued quietly. "Every child in this town—or in the logging camp—is important to me, regardless of his or her perceived faults. If each of you could communicate that to your friends and acquaintances when the opportunity presents itself, I would be very grateful."

"You're making a mistake," Gladys warned. "You don't know how unruly the Lawsons can be. And the jacks' boys? They'll disrupt your lessons, and soon, decent folks will keep *their* children at home. What will you do then? After all, it's the decent folks who paid for you to come here."

"That just shows how little you know about boys, Mrs. Chesterton," said a cheerful voice from the porch.

Maggie turned to beam in Denny Riordain's direction. "Good morning, Sheriff."

"Good morning, missy." He ambled into the room. "As I was saying, Mrs. Chesterton. Those boys'll be angels for our little Maggie. Wanting to impress her, and please her—not from the goodness of their hearts, but because each and every one of them will be secretly in love with her."

Maggie flushed, remembering what Gladys had said earlier about the sheriff's attentive behavior. Would the ill-humored woman take Denny's silly remarks as further proof that the sheriff was "taking an interest" in the new schoolteacher?

Then to her mortification, Coburn made it worse by observing, "Sounds like the boys aren't the only ones falling secretly in love with our Miss O'Connor."

Denny chuckled. "Show me a man who isn't, and

I'll show you a mean-spirited cuss like yourself."
Crossing the room, he pumped Coburn's outstretched
hand. "I heard you were back in town. How was Virginia City?"

"Dusty but lucrative. How's June?"

"She's well—thanks for asking." He turned back to
Maggie. "She asked me to tell you she won't be by
the school till after noon. A neighbor's feeling poorly,
and Junie's going to sit with her for a while."

"I hope it's nothing serious. Is there something I
can do to help?"

"Who is it?" Mrs. Blake interrupted. "Not Alice
again, I hope." When the sheriff nodded, she squared
her shoulders. "I'll make her some soup. That always
cheers her up, even though the poor dear can't seem
to eat more than a bite or two."

"She'd like that, I'm sure."

"Excuse me," Coburn announced abruptly; then he
strode out of the room without further ceremony.

Denny gave Maggie a sympathetic grin. "He's himself. What more is there to say?"

She smiled in return. "I need to be hurrying along,
too. Give June my best, won't you? She needn't come
by the school if she's hasn't the time, although of
course I'd love the company."

"I'll walk with you," he offered.

Maggie noted Gladys's arched eyebrow, and was
tempted to decline. Then on impulse, she reached out
and squeezed the sheriff's arm. "I'll just be a minute
then. I want to fetch June's cape from my room. It
was so thoughtful of her to lend it to me. And now
she's tending a sick friend. No wonder you adore her
the way you do."

"She's the world and more to me," he agreed. "Take
your time gathering yourself together, missy. I'll just
enjoy a cup of Eleanor's coffee while I wait."

After flashing Gladys a triumphant smile that almost shouted *She's the world to him!* Maggie dashed for the staircase, anxious to forget about meddling gossips and brooding bookworms in favor of new friends and loveable schoolchildren.

Four

Four hours and three dinner invitations later, Maggie was in heaven. Never had she imagined that she would find such enthusiasm and trust among the parents of her future students. After all, despite her bold pronouncement at the breakfast table, she was untried as a teacher. At most, she could claim that other teachers had praised her skills as an assistant. But in Shasta Falls, the responsibility rested with Maggie alone.

And while she might have wished the Lawson boys would come by for a visit, she had been thrilled to meet three new children—all girls again, which gave her pause. But as she'd done the previous day, she used the opportunity to both encourage the sisters, and to send a message to the brothers that the first day of school might just surprise them.

At least, she consoled herself, *the parents seem to value education, and so the boys in town have no choice but to come. It's the boys from the camp that are a concern. Will anyone force them to come that crucial first day?*

It occurred to her that she could influence that outcome easily. All she had to do was pay those parents a visit and earn their trust and support. She was certain she could convince Denny to escort her. And she was also certain that, even if his jurisdiction didn't technically extend beyond the town's borders, he was respected throughout the region.

But would June Riordain object? Would she raise an eyebrow at the thought of her husband doing favors for the new, unmarried schoolmarm? Maggie was almost certain she wouldn't, and was pleased when June arrived at noon, picnic basket in hand, and proceeded to laugh helplessly at the idea she might object to the arrangement.

"I can doubt whether summer will be hot, or winter will be cold, but I'll never doubt whether Dennis Anthony Riordain is faithful to me," she proclaimed with a teasing smile. "I suspect it's Gladys Chesterton who made such a ridiculous suggestion. And I have a suggestion of my own for *her.* She should examine her own conscience, since that's where these awful notions originate."

"I agree."

June grinned. "I'll admit, though, if I feared any rival, it would be you. I heard Denny tell Kirk you had the golden hair and emerald eyes of an Irish angel." Her bantering tone faded. "I see an angel, too, but a wounded one. Won't you tell me what happened?"

Maggie flushed. "I can't imagine what you mean. I'm not at all wounded. In fact, I've been worried about *you,* and your neighbor. Denny said her name was Alice, and she has a terrible cough. Is she feeling any better?"

June eyed her with playful reproach. "I learned this game of yours last night. Whenever the subject grows uncomfortable for you, you find a way to change it. That works on the likes of Denny, bless his heart, but not on me. I intend to find out why you ran away from a lovely city like San Francisco, and why you claim you don't want to marry." June's hazel eyes narrowed ominously. "You'll tell me eventually. Why not now? There's an advantage to confiding in me, rather than someone else, because I am truly your friend, whether you realize it yet or not."

Maggie savored a bite of the cornbread June had brought with her before responding. "I know you're my friend. I was raised to believe that friends trust one another. The way Denny trusts Coburn, to be blunt—with no questions about his past. I'm asking you to trust me that way, too."

June arched an eyebrow. "I won't allow you to compare yourself to our wicked Mr. Coburn. His past is undoubtedly filled with evil deeds. Your past, on the other hand, intrigues me. And it intrigues the men, too. Is that what you intended?"

"June—"

"Tell me everything," she persisted. "I have the ear of the town, as you may have guessed. If indeed you have a good reason for rebuffing suitors, I'll be the first to convince them to let you be. If you don't, I'll be the first to introduce you to Kirk Waller, and any other man who promises to treat you with respect." When Maggie didn't respond, June's tone softened. "Trust me, Maggie. I know a wounded soul when I see one. I ache to help you, because I've been wounded myself. But I have Denny, and you have no one. Won't you please allow me to help?"

Maggie felt her green eyes fill with tears. "I don't want the town knowing my business. If I could live with that, I would have stayed in the neighborhood in which I was raised."

"I'll keep your confidence—even from the man I adore—unless your very life is at stake," June promised. "Don't ask for more than that."

Maggie sighed. "My plan was to tell no one, but I can see now I'll confide in you eventually. Not just because I need you to convince the town that I haven't come here in search of a husband, but because . . ." Her voice trailed into embarrassed silence.

"You're lonely?"

"Yes, from time to time," Maggie admitted.

June came around the desk to give Maggie an encouraging embrace. "Not any longer. There's no room for loneliness in Shasta Falls. Denny taught me that, and now I'm teaching it to you."

Maggie cocked her head to the side. "You were lonely before you came here? You mentioned that you've been wounded yourself—"

"There you go, trying to change the subject again." June gave Maggie a sympathetic smile. "It can't be that bad, or you wouldn't be so sweet. And it must be awful, because you're so distressed. Either way, you mustn't keep it to yourself. You see that, don't you?"

"It isn't some dark, terrible secret. Merely a series of misfortunes."

"Terrible enough to convince you never to marry."

"That's true." Maggie nodded slowly. "My father was 'wounded,' as you call it, and my brothers and I paid the price for it. He was a good man, and did his best, but was unable to overcome his bitterness and disappointment."

June perched on the edge of Maggie's desk. "Why was he so bitter?"

"He and my mother had been inseparable from childhood, and had made beautiful plans for raising a family together. But she died giving birth to my brother and me. It broke my father's heart, and in some ways, he never recovered."

"You're a twin?"

Maggie hesitated, uncertain as to whether she could actually find the words for this. She had never told the story to anyone. She had never *needed* to tell it, since everyone in her neighborhood had heard it in intimate detail.

But her audience was waiting, and so, with an apologetic grimace, she began. "It's a complicated story, June, but I'll tell it as best I can. Yes, I had a twin brother. We were remarkably tiny babies, they say, but relatively healthy, which was fortunate because, with Mother dead and Papa beside himself with grief, we were enough of a burden as it was. The doctor who attended the birth suggested to Papa that he hire someone to take care of us. He recommended a patient of his—a young woman named Lettie Price, whose husband had abandoned her. Lettie had given birth to a little baby boy only weeks before we were born. She had abundant milk, and scant resources, and so the arrangement would benefit us all."

"I'm so sorry about your mother, Maggie."

She grimaced again, this time because she knew June had no inkling how much more there was to tell. "As the story goes, Papa apparently spent little time with us those first few weeks. He would come by Lettie's house to make certain we were well, and to pay her. No one knows how long he would have allowed us to live with her, but one day, when I was scarcely six weeks old, Lettie announced that she was leaving Chicago to return to her mother's home in New York. So Papa collected us—me and my brother, Ian—and brought us home at last. Neighbors helped him as best they could, and somehow, we all survived.

"I continued to thrive, despite the loss of my mother, but life was crueler to Ian. He had a variety of ailments, some of them serious, and it was difficult for my father. My first memories of my childhood are of visits by the doctor, and Ian in bed for days on end. Papa was worried, and moody, although I believe, in those days, he found some joy and comfort in us.

And I adored him, of course. At his best, he was an entertaining man, although we rarely saw that side of him."

Maggie moistened her lips, surprised at the slight tremble to her voice, then forced herself to adopt a cheerier tone. "The bond between me and Ian was an amazing one. We shared everything; we played constantly; we could guess what the other was thinking or needed. He was the perfect brother, but in some ways . . ."

"Yes?"

"Well let's just say, he wasn't the perfect son, at least not in my father's eyes. Ian was small and weak, and easily startled. I believe Papa wanted to be patient, but Ian was a disappointment to him. And it was worse when we began attending school, because Ian was constantly teased."

"Poor baby."

Maggie nodded. "I did my best to protect him, and we kept to ourselves quite a bit. We didn't really need the other children's company, since we had each other. But as we grew older, even *I* noticed that Ian's behavior wasn't always appropriate. He would steal things, and lie, and sneak about the neighborhood, making everyone uncomfortable. It embarrassed my father, and finally, he began to punish Ian—first, by confining him, and then, by paddling him. It was a horrible time for all of us, including Papa. And the worst part was, it didn't accomplish anything. Ian simply couldn't behave. But he was so sweet, June. And so well-intentioned, despite the results."

Lowering her voice, she elaborated. "More than once, neighbors caught Ian looking through windows at women dressing. The boys at school taunted him about it, and some of the men lectured Papa on controlling him better. It was all so very mortifying. And so confusing to Ian." Realizing that her voice was trembling again, Maggie paused for a deep, restorative breath.

"Here." June handed her a cup of lemonade. "How old were you when all this was happening?"

"We had just had our eighth birthday when the worst of it began. That was a terrible year around our house. I was still young, but I knew the strain was destroying my father. All I could do was watch Ian closely, try to be a blessing to Papa, and pray for a miracle. But instead . . ."

"Go on."

Maggie swallowed a lump that had formed in her throat. "One day, a friend of my father's—a loveable man we called Uncle Eddie—came calling. I was excited, because we usually had a wonderful dinner and rounds and rounds of storytelling whenever he visited. But this time, he and Papa sat on the porch and whispered so seriously, I was sure someone had died. I did my best to keep Ian out of their way, so he wouldn't aggravate the situation. The next morning, my father announced he was going on an errand and would be home by suppertime. He told us not to go to school, which was shocking. So we sat in the parlor all day long, playing checkers and waiting for him to return."

June's wide eyes were filled with apprehension. "I almost can't bear to hear this. You make it sound as though . . ."

"As though the world came to an end? Believe me, it did. A carriage pulled up, and Papa and Uncle Eddie came up the walk. There were policemen with them, and one of them was holding a boy by the hand. A woman got out of the carriage, too, but she stayed back by the curb."

Maggie's eyes filled with tears. "Then Ian—sweet,

innocent Ian—looked at the new boy, then looked at me and said, 'He looks just like *you*, sissie.' "

When June gasped, Maggie nodded. "It was true. I thought maybe they were relatives, but everyone's expressions were so grim, my heart told me otherwise. Then Papa saw the woman approaching the doorway and said, 'Get the both of them out of my sight,' and then, there was a dreadful scene. Lettie, clinging to the new boy; one policeman carrying Ian out of our house, while the other tried to pry Lettie and the new boy apart. And I was screaming at Papa, trying to convince him to make it stop, and he grabbed me and whispered desperately in my ear, 'That sorry little lad was never your brother. In my heart, I always knew it, girl. Open your eyes, and you'll see it, too.' Then he said, 'We're a family now, at last. You and me and my God-given son.' "

"Oh, Maggie. How horrible for you."

"I pushed Papa away and ran to the curb, begging the policemen not to take my brother from me. But they said they had no choice, so I tried to climb into the carriage with them—Lettie and Ian and the policemen—so I could go, too. Uncle Eddie came and scooped me up, and brought me back to the house. Ian was shrieking my name, over and over, and even when the carriage disappeared from sight, I could hear him."

June's voice was thick with shock and grief. "It's so tragic."

"I didn't know what to do," Maggie admitted. "Neither did the new boy, Brian. It was clear that he missed his mother, but Papa was so patient, explaining over and over that Lettie had done a terrible thing, switching boy babies, so that she could have a healthy, normal son. And it was chilling, because when Brian and

I looked at each other, it was so clearly true, even though we wished it were otherwise.

"I wanted to run away, to try to find Ian, but I didn't know where to go. And I hated Papa—not just for sending Ian away," she explained carefully, "but for not missing him. Not one little bit. Papa was so happy, June." She choked back a sob as she revealed, "I had never, *ever* seen him so happy. So proud. Brian was everything he ever wanted in a son. He kept saying over and over that we were a family at last."

"Was Brian as unhappy as you?"

"I was so absorbed in my own misery, I can't really say. I know he missed Lettie, but he was also very taken with Papa. I suppose he had missed having a father, the same way I missed having a mother. Papa did all the things with Brian he couldn't do with Ian—taught him to box, and took him fishing, and bragged about him to his friends . . ."

Maggie could almost taste the resentment she had felt toward her father in those days. "My uncle took me aside and told me to blame *him,* not Papa. He reminded me that he was the one who found Brian."

"How did that happen?" June asked.

"He said he was crossing the street, on the far side of town, when he saw a boy who looked so much like me, it stopped him in his tracks with wonder. His initial reaction was like mine, that the boy must be a cousin of mine. Then he saw a woman emerge from a shop and take the boy's hand, and it was Lettie, who supposedly had left town while we were still babies. And he knew exactly what had happened. He didn't approach her, for fear she'd run away. He came and told Papa, and when they went to confront her, they took the police with them. According to my uncle, Lettie didn't deny it. She just pleaded for understanding."

"Understanding? She abandoned her own child and stole another!"

"She claimed she thought Ian needed a father more than Brian did, because he seemed so weak."

June shook her head. "How could she do such a thing? Look at all the heartache she caused. It's unforgivable."

"I suppose that's true. But at the time, I didn't blame her. Only Papa. I hated him, and I wanted to hate Brian, too, but . . ." Maggie smiled wistfully. "He was so charming. Funny and kindhearted and smart. I tried to resist him, but he won my heart one afternoon at school, when a boy made a horrid joke about Ian, and Brian hit him in the face. Then he stood over him and said, 'Don't talk about Maggie's brother that way.' "

Tears began spilling from June's hazel eyes. "Oh, dear."

Maggie knew her own eyes were glistening, too. "Brian was such a wonderful boy—the sort who brightened a room just by walking into it. That's what he did to our home. It was impossible not to love him. He used to tell me about Lettie—about what a good mother she was, and how sure he was that she would take good care of Ian. That Ian was better off with Lettie than with a father who didn't love him. And I began to believe it, too, and over time, life became wonderful. Not a day went by that I didn't miss Ian, but Brian was a joy—teasing me and playing games with me. And without Ian to occupy all my time, I made friends with other children, and was able to concentrate more on my schoolwork, which I adored.

"And I began to forgive Papa, because he was so happy. Suppertime, which had been filled with tension, was suddenly the best part of the day. I did all the cooking by then, and Papa always made a fuss about what a wonderful daughter I was. He still had his gloomy moments, missing my mother, but most of the time he was relaxed and content.

"And every night, before we went to sleep, Brian promised me that as soon as he was old enough to leave school and find a good job, we'd send for Ian, and the three of us would live together. If Papa and Lettie wanted to join us, fine, but either way, I would have both my brothers under one roof. He even predicted Papa and Lettie would marry. I knew Papa hated Lettie too much for that to ever happen, but still, I *loved* Brian's story. It was our own personal fairy tale."

"Brian sounds so much like you."

Maggie sat up straight, stunned by the observation. "Pardon?"

"Warm and loving and intelligent, brightening a room just by entering it. That sounds like *you,* Maggie O'Connor."

Maggie flushed. "What a sweet thing to say." She bit her lip before informing June gently, "There's more to this story."

June nodded. "I almost can't bear it, but you must go on. I have to hear everything."

Maggie gave her a grateful smile, then resumed her story. "It was on our fourteenth birthday that it happened. We were having a lovely dinner—Papa, Brian, and I—when the door burst open and Ian came in carrying a gun."

"Oh!" June visibly cringed. "Oh, Maggie, don't tell me . . ."

Maggie's tears had disappeared, replaced by an almost hypnotic need to tell the story with quiet accuracy. "He screamed at Brian, 'Get out of my chair!' then shot him right in the chest. Then he turned, as if to shoot Papa, and I grabbed for the barrel without thinking. It gave Papa a chance to hit Ian—one powerful punch in the jaw—and he crumpled to the floor. Then Papa shouted at me to fetch the doctor for Brian, and I ran until my lungs almost burst. By the time I came back—with the doctor *and* the police—Papa was sitting on the kitchen floor, cradling Brian's lifeless body in his arms. Ian was tied and gagged in the corner, and Papa looked up at the policeman and said, in a dull, lifeless voice, 'Get him out of my sight before I kill him with my bare hands.'

"So, they took Ian away again. There wasn't a trial, really. The judge talked to me alone, and I did my best to explain—about how hard Ian tried to be good, and about Papa being so mean and unloving to him. I was terrified they'd hang him, but the judge promised me it wouldn't come to that. In the meantime, Ian refused to see anyone.

"I finally convinced a policeman to take me to his cell, but he wouldn't look at me or speak to me. It was as if he couldn't hear my voice. But I told him through the bars that I loved him, and that I'd write to him and visit him."

Maggie's lip began to quiver as she remembered what came next. "When we buried Brian, it was as though we buried our hearts with him. I had only known him for five years, yet I couldn't imagine life without him. He was the finest brother a girl could want, and he was my closest confidant and truest friend. And it was so unfair, because he had never once tried to take Ian's place. But of course, poor Ian couldn't have known that.

"And Papa was devastated beyond words. I took care of him as best I could, but all the while my thoughts were with Ian, who had no one to care for him. They sent him to a prison that was more than a day's journey from Chicago, so I couldn't visit the way I wanted. I wrote to him every single week for three full years, but all my letters came back unopened. Twice during that time, I convinced Uncle Eddie to take me to visit him, but each time, he refused to see me. The warden was extremely kind, and did his best to intervene, but Ian was adamant. He wouldn't see me, and he wouldn't see Lettie. And no one else in the world cared about him, so I was sick with worry.

"Papa had no patience with it. After the second time I sneaked away for a visit, he lost his temper, telling me I was a fool to waste my love on a boy who would have shot me dead that terrible evening, but for the grace of God."

Maggie bit her lip, remembering her defiant response: *Is that what you wish, Papa? That he'd killed me instead of Brian?*

Her father had gasped, and all the anger had drained from his face. Then he had insisted in a shaky whisper, *If it was you who took that bullet, no power in heaven or on earth could have stopped me from ripping that murderer to pieces. Don't you know that, Maggie girl? Don't you know you're the light of my life?*

Maggie had stared in disbelief while he explained, *It was only for your sake that I allowed the authorities to deal with the situation. If you hadn't been alive and needing me, I'd gladly have seen to it myself, knowing I'd hang for it in the morning.*

June tapped her shoulder gently. "Maggie?"

"Oh." She flushed and tried to smile. "So many memories."

"I can imagine. It must have been a terrible time for you."

Maggie nodded. "I was sick to death over it—worrying that Ian was being mistreated, or that he was feeling unloved. He wasn't the sort of person who could be alone, and I knew the other prisoners would be cruel to him. I suppose it was a strange sort of blessing when word finally arrived, two years ago, that he had died of pneumonia. But it tore my heart out. We didn't hear in time to bring him home for a proper burial, but at least, I visited his grave at the prison. Papa surprised me by taking me there. He even cried a little at the graveside, although he said the tears were for me, not for Ian."

She paused, remembering how her father had embraced her, and asked her to forgive him for having put her through so cruel a life.

"Maggie?"

She looked up at June and was touched by the warmth and understanding in her eyes. "I'm fine. But perhaps now you understand why I don't want to marry."

June nodded. "You're not ready. I see that now."

"I'll never be ready."

"Of course you will. But not yet. The wounds are still raw."

"That's how they feel," Maggie agreed. "Raw. Jagged—as though they'll never heal. It was worse in Chicago, though. Everyone in the neighborhood had heard the story. I was referred to far and wide as 'the poor little Gleason girl.' There was an infamous cartoon of me in the newspapers, curled up with Brian dying in my lap, and Ian standing over us with a gun." She paused to shudder. "You can't imagine how many people said terrible things about Ian to me, thinking they were offering comfort or support." She flushed and added lamely, "My mother's maiden name was O'Connor. Taking it in place of Gleason was part of the fresh start I wanted for myself."

"Maggie Gleason," June murmured. "That's pretty. One day, when you're ready—"

"I'll never be ready," Maggie repeated firmly. "And I don't *ever* want this town to know the story."

"I agree." June tossed her hair. "It's none of their concern. Can you imagine what Gladys Chesterton would make of it? Don't worry on that account, sweetie. Your secret is safe with me."

Maggie hesitated before saying, "I'd rather you didn't tell Denny either, but if you must—"

"Tell Denny? Are you insane? This story would break that man's heart! *Never* tell Denny. I want your word on that, Maggie Gleason."

"You want *my* word?" Maggie laughed through the tears welling in her eyes. "You're impossible. But you're also a wonderful listener, and I have to admit, I feel better for having told you all about it."

"It's amazing." June's voice was soft and gentle. "Sad, but also just amazing. I loved it when you talked about Brian. So much like my Denny."

"He was a wonderful boy," Maggie agreed. "But Ian was special, too. I know I didn't explain that part well, but—"

"My heart will ache for Ian Gleason until the day I die," June interrupted firmly. "If he were here right now, I'd gather him up in my arms and tell him so. And I'd tell him that none of this horrid mess was his fault."

Stunned by the genuine devotion in June's tone, Maggie buried her face in her hands, and the sobs that had threatened again and again now burst free, racking her shoulders and chest. "Oh, June."

"Here now!" a voice boomed from the doorway, and before Maggie could prepare herself, she had been enveloped against Denny Riordain's powerful chest. "What's this about, missy?"

"It's J-June," Maggie stammered. "She's j-just so sweet."

"Aye, she is that." Still cradling Maggie with one arm, the sheriff asked his wife, "Has something happened?"

June shrugged. "It's Maggie's time of the month, is all."

"What?" Clearly horrified, Denny released Maggie and stepped back, staring at her as though she had two heads, and Maggie burst into laughter that was every bit as gut-wrenching as her crying had been.

"The both of you are scaring the living hell out of me," the sheriff complained. "I thought you'd be a good influence on my bride, missy, but instead, it's the other way round." He turned and stomped toward the doorway, adding over his shoulder, "Mrs. Riordain?"

"Yes, Mr. Riordain?"

"I'll be expecting you within the hour. You'll be needing your rest, after the day you've had." His voice softened as he asked, "How is Alice?"

"I thought I saw some improvement, but the doctor is as concerned as ever. I told her we'd stop by this evening."

The sheriff nodded. "One hour then? As for you, missy—you'll be needing your rest, too. I hear you're having company for dinner tonight."

"Company?"

"Kirk Waller." His eyes began to twinkle. "It's all been decided, as you know. Eleanor and Junie both believe he's the man for you, so there's no point in resisting it."

"You're in too much of a hurry to marry her off, Denny Riordain," June protested. "Haven't you heard a word she's been saying? She wants to concentrate on teaching for a while."

"Huh?" He looked from one woman to the other, then pretended to scowl. "So much for trying to have a sensible conversation. I have work to do, so if there's nothing the two of you need from me—"

"Denny, wait!" June ran to him and draped her arms around his neck. "I'll be down in a while, and we'll go for a stroll."

"I'd like that," he admitted, then he lowered his mouth and kissed her hungrily.

Maggie knew she should look away, as she'd done so many times the prior evening during supper, but somehow, the sight of such pure love now mesmerized her, and so she openly stared instead. And for a fleeting moment, she believed June's prediction: that one day, in a year or so, Maggie might be ready to find this sort of love in the arms of a kind and gentle man.

Then she shook her head and turned away. After all, she'd had such thoughts from time to time when Robert Grimes had romanced her. But always, the chilling reality had reasserted itself, and she had been forced to acknowledge that her childhood hadn't prepared her for the responsibility of raising children of her own. Other women's children were a different matter, and she would find a way to be a successful influence on them. But she didn't trust herself, or her upbringing, or life itself, enough to believe she could have more than that.

Heeding the sheriff's advice, Maggie returned to the boardinghouse well before dinnertime, so that she could freshen up and rest before her would-be suitor arrived. She found Eleanor Blake bustling about the kitchen, clearly thrilled by the prospect of entertaining a guest. "Thank goodness you're home! There's so much to do, and we'll want everything to be perfect. Kirk Waller is going to make some girl a fine husband," she added with a meaningful smile. "One day, you'll thank me for introducing you to him."

"I'll thank you now," Maggie assured her. "If he's half as wonderful as everyone says, I can only hope he finds a bride soon, so he can start having children for me to teach."

When the landlady scowled, Maggie gave her a playful hug. "I know you mean well, but please don't be disappointed if—"

"Yes, yes, I know." Mrs. Blake eyed Maggie's dusty dress pointedly. "You'll change into fresher clothes at least, won't you?"

"Of course."

"Fine. I'll draw a bath for you right away." Without waiting for a reply, she headed for a small, tiled room, directly off the kitchen, that served as bathing facilities for the boarders.

Maggie winced but followed dutifully. The lack of privacy in almost every feature of the boardinghouse was still a challenge for her, although she had to admit this particular arrangement—bathing next to the kitchen—had probably served the Blakes well as they raised their three daughters. The mother had been able to cook with one watchful eye on the little ones as they played in the tub. And even when they were older, they undoubtedly appreciated the warmth from the oven and the reassuring sounds and scents of the kitchen.

And at least it has a real door, so it's ever so much more private than your bedroom, she reminded herself with a smile. *Of course, given the fact that two men live here, a door with an actual lock would be better still. Perhaps in time you can dare suggest it, but for now . . .*

She touched Mrs. Blake on the shoulder and asked as gently as she could, "Is Mr. Coburn home?"

"No. Why do you—oh!" The landlady chuckled. "Believe me, even if he were here, he'd never step foot inside this humble little bathroom."

"Oh? He bathes at the hotel? Or the saloon?"

Mrs. Blake laughed again. "Mercy, no. There's a private bathroom, much more luxurious than this one, adjoining the master bedroom."

Maggie cocked her head to the side and studied the woman in dismay. "You share this with the boarders, while he—" She tried to stop herself but failed, and insisted bluntly, "His lack of gentility mystifies me. Keeping the best to himself, while you—the lady of the house—are relegated to second best."

"I don't mind a bit. The heat from the oven makes this room cozier." The landlady shrugged her shoulders. "I imagine in San Francisco the accommodations are more sophisticated, but—"

"I didn't mean to suggest that." Maggie smiled self-consciously. "In my father's home, there was only one bathroom—a humble affair shared by the entire family. I only meant—well, never mind. A bath sounds lovely. Forgive me if I sounded ungrateful."

"You sounded like my daughters," Eleanor told her. "They claimed they felt like babies when they used this room, and as they grew older, they often used the one in our room. I could ask Mr. Coburn if he minded—"

"Good grief, please don't do that!" Recovering her equilibrium, Maggie managed a sheepish grin. "I'll go and fetch a dressing gown before I say anything else insulting."

"And tonight, you'll wear something feminine and flattering?"

Maggie grinned again, this time at her landlady's unabashed use of guilt to bring her boarder into line with the matchmaking plans. "Something white and lacy, with a matching veil?"

"Mind that tone," Eleanor warned, but her eyes were twinkling, and Maggie guessed that once again, the woman had been reminded of her daughters.

This must be what it's like to have a mother, she told herself as she headed for the back stairs. *It's just what Ian needed—a firm hand, but with boundless love behind it.*

And, she admitted with a wistful sigh as she pushed aside her muslin doorway and gathered up her hairbrush and dressing gown, *I think you needed it, too.*

Five

Maggie bathed with one eye trained toward the doorknob, although she didn't have the slightest idea what she would do if someone other than Mrs. Blake chose to burst into the room. *You'd die of embarrassment,* she assured herself. *Unless it's Mr. Coburn, in which case, you'd actually dissolve into the water from pure mortification.*

Despite her attempt to make light of it, she hadn't been able to rid her mind of Coburn's notorious suggestion that they "adjourn" to his bedroom to indulge in "uncivilized behavior." There had been mockery in his tone, but in his eyes, there had been something else. Something unfamiliar. The man had made her feel as though she'd been virtually undressed—

And here she was, actually undressed!

"But guarded by Mrs. Blake, who may tolerate quite a bit from her well-paying boarder, but who would smash him with a skillet if he came within three feet of that door," she murmured aloud. "So stop being so silly. You spend far too much time thinking about Mr. Coburn when you should be thinking about the children. In particular, the boys. You must find a way to entice them into your classroom. Or rather—" She flushed at the unfortunate choice of words and amended the statement quickly. "You must find a way to draw them into the world of learning."

Young Angie had given her some excellent suggestions: ships and battles and such. She also remembered how both Ian and Brian had loved stories of knights and dragons and bold adventures. There was certainly an element of that in her beloved *Ivanhoe,* but Brian had always claimed it too romantic, despite the fact that such heroic figures as Robin of Locksley and Richard the Lionhearted graced its pages.

Still, she was sure she was on the right course. Warfare and history and drama—what little boy could resist so powerful a combination?

"History, drama, and warfare," she mused, closing her eyes and slipping down until her shoulders were completely covered by warm, sudsy water. "What book combines all of those qualities so perfectly that it will pique the interest of even the most resistant little boy? Something simple, yet compelling, and completely devoid of romance . . ."

Out of nowhere, Robert Grimes's voice echoed in her memory: *Gallia est omnis divisa in partes tres.*

"All Gaul is divided into three parts." The words were indeed simple yet compelling—a military genius introducing his most celebrated campaign, not to dazzle, but to educate, with an economy of style that spoke volumes as to his confidence and character. For Maggie, the book had served merely as a Latin lesson, but to a little boy . . .

Grabbing a fluffy towel off a nearby hook, Maggie scrambled out of the tub and dried herself head to toe in a matter of seconds, determined to plot her own campaign, à la Julius Caesar. Any self-respecting book collector would have at least one copy of that famous general's masterpiece, *The Gallic Wars,* wouldn't he?

"I'm counting on you, Tobias Blake," she warned

in a soft but determined voice. Then she fastened her dark blue dressing gown over her still-damp body and headed for the library.

Secure in the knowledge that Alex Coburn wouldn't return for hours, Maggie hungrily studied the shelves of the Blake library while sifting her fingers through the cascades of tangled hair that hung about her shoulders. It was difficult to concentrate on finding one particular volume, when all of her favorite stories beckoned to her from the spines of the leather-bound volumes. Even worse, there were so many she *hadn't* read—hadn't even known existed!—that she could scarcely resist the impulse to pull one down, sit on the floor, and abandon herself to it.

"It has to be here somewhere, and if you don't find it soon, you'll still be in your dressing gown when Mr. Kirk Waller comes to call," she cautioned herself aloud as she scanned the last of the lower library shelves. But the Julius Caesar classic was nowhere in sight, so Maggie turned her attentions to the higher shelves.

The ceiling of the library was a full ten feet high, and every inch of available space had been used to house books. A solid mahogany ladder stood ready to assist Maggie in accessing the top level, and she had to admit, she was secretly delighted at having an excuse to use it. Sliding the ladder along the shiny brass rail that ran the length of the room, she then climbed carefully up, until she was eye-level with a beautifully bound collection of the works of Nathaniel Hawthorne.

She imagined how much the schoolchildren would enjoy *The House of the Seven Gables,* and resolved immediately to add it to the list of stories she intended to read to them. Not that she would use one of these leather-bound editions, of course. They were clearly too valuable ever to remove from the premises.

And you're forgetting why you're here, she chided herself. *Nathaniel Hawthorne weaves a spellbinding tale, but only a Roman general will do for the first day of school. You simply must find* The Gallic Wars, *and you haven't much time left. Mr. Waller will be arriving in less than an hour.*

As much as she enjoyed her perch, several feet off the ground, she hadn't intended to climb farther in her bare feet and dressing gown, until she noticed another provocative collection, running along the topmost shelf. Bound in handsome maroon leather, the fifteen matched volumes were mysteriously labeled in gold with roman numerals rather than titles. Mesmerized, Maggie didn't even bother to look down before beginning her ascent toward the enigmatic treasures. Three careful steps on the glossy rungs, and finally, the tips of her fingers touched Volume I, which she edged lovingly out of its resting place, holding her breath in rapt anticipation.

Then a furious voice demanded from below, *"What in blazes do you think you're doing?"* startling Maggie so completely that she whirled toward it without thinking. As she did so, her left foot slipped from the ladder's smooth wooden rung, and in a desperate but illogical attempt to steady herself, she clung to Volume I, which slid completely from the shelf and flew out of her hand, missing her face by less than an inch. She shrieked as her right foot lost contact with the ladder, sending her careening toward the floor.

Coburn's strong arm caught her, grappling her roughly against his chest. It might have been a gallant gesture had he used two hands, but he had already used one to snare Volume I. Releasing Maggie quickly, he proceeded to examine the binding, while she in turn backed against the bookshelves to steady herself.

"Do you have any idea how rare this is?" he growled as he tested the book's spine. "Did it not occur to you that it was placed out of reach for a reason?"

Maggie wanted to answer—in fact, she wanted to berate him for daring to suggest that the mishap had been *her* fault!—but the only sound she could make was a raspy one as she struggled to calm her pounding heart and return her breathing to normal.

For the first time, Coburn turned his full attention to her. After a moment's study, he grinned and assured her, "You'll live. You just had the wind knocked out of you."

"By *you*," she managed to retort.

He seemed about to argue, then shrugged instead. "Didn't we have this conversation last night? Yet here you are, roaming the library half naked."

"Be quiet!" she warned between gritted teeth. "You almost killed me."

"You were quite a sight. Unfortunately, I'm not looking for a damsel in distress." Setting the book down, he stepped to within inches of her, then lowered his face toward hers and murmured, "What are *you* looking for, Maggie-Margaret?"

The heat from his breath contrasted eerily with the fire in his eyes—a cold, disdainful fire that stunned Maggie with its terrible brilliance. Never had she seen eyes so blue, and never, ever, had she felt so insignificant or so trapped.

"You're a horrible man," she whispered.

"And yet you keep seeking me out. Why?"

"I wasn't—" She summoned enough courage to give him a disapproving glare. "I was looking for a book. If I were looking for *you,* I'd have started in hell and worked my way downward."

"That's how you see me? As the devil himself?" Coburn chuckled. "Shouldn't a good girl like you learn to stay away from me, then?" Before she could answer, he added dryly, "Be forewarned. The next time I find you in here, I'll consider it an invitation."

Then he allowed his eyes to travel over her, and she knew he was remembering the feel of her through her soft dressing gown. And to her shame, she remembered him too—the taut, steely muscles of his arm; his solid chest, pressed against hers; his hand, almost cupping one of her breasts . . .

"You won't find me in here again," she assured him in a weak, unfamiliar voice.

"Good."

Embarrassed by her inability to stand up to him, she backed a safe distance away, then forced herself to stare directly into his vibrant blue eyes. "This is Mrs. Blake's house, not yours. These books are *her* books. When you're here, I'll stay away because you are a despicable man. But when you're not here, I have as much right to use this room as you do."

"Interesting logic."

She wanted to scratch those mocking eyes from their sockets, but she could hear Mrs. Blake calling to her from the parlor, and for a moment, her anger shifted toward the landlady, who had allowed this ridiculous situation to develop in the first place. Then she reminded herself that the widow had been desperate for money, and thus had fallen prey to Coburn's reprehensible tactics as innocently as had Maggie.

"Run along, Maggie-Margaret," Coburn advised.

"Go to hell," she replied just as coolly, but she knew her words would amuse rather than offend him, so she spun away and bolted out of the room before he could react. Pausing to catch her breath, she stood in the parlor doorway and watched in frustration as Mrs. Blake plumped the cushions of her lavender brocade sofa, completely oblivious to the drama that had just unfolded in the library.

"Mrs. Blake?"

"Oh, Maggie! There you are. Come and tell me what you think of this arrangement. I want everything to be perfect for our guest."

Maggie eyed the older woman with reluctant amusement. Romantic seating arrangements and burnt chicken might not be effective matchmaking techniques where Maggie was concerned, but perhaps Mrs. Blake had unwittingly discovered a way to drive the schoolteacher into Kirk Waller's arms after all—by subjecting her to a fellow boarder so perverse and obnoxious that almost any escape would be a welcome one.

"You haven't even fixed your hair," the landlady scolded. "What have you been doing all this time?"

"I was talking to Mr. Coburn."

Mrs. Blake seemed startled. "Talking? To *him?*"

"About the books. He seems to think they're his personal property."

"Well, in a way, they are."

"Pardon?"

"Not all of them, but . . ." She flashed an apologetic smile. "It's a long story, and we haven't much time—"

"Didn't you tell me it was Mr. Coburn who urged you *not* to sell the books? Are you saying you actually did sell them, and to him of all people?"

The landlady sighed, then sank down onto the sofa and motioned for Maggie to join her. "Mr. Coburn brought some of the books with him."

"Oh, I see. That makes sense." Maggie grimaced

at the thought that the priceless volumes on the uppermost shelf were probably Coburn's. He had been within his rights, then, to want them untouched. But it still didn't justify rude behavior, when a simple request would have worked just as well.

She noticed that Mrs. Blake was fidgeting, and so she asked, "The rest of the books are yours, aren't they? The ones that Tobias left?"

"I'm not supposed to talk about this. Not that it's a secret, but he's just so private." The older woman hesitated, then proceeded bluntly. "I know you think he's selfish and rude, so perhaps it's best if I share this one little detail with you. It's not something he likes to admit, which is that he has helped me financially, beyond simply paying generously for his accommodations."

"Oh?"

"When my grandson was ill last year, I decided to sell some of the books, so that my daughter could take him to New York to see a special doctor. I asked Mr. Coburn to help me with the arrangements, but instead, he bought them himself, with the understanding that the children were encouraged to buy them back from him at any time. He feels strongly that Tobias's collection should be kept intact for as long as possible, in case one of the grandchildren turns out to be a book lover like their grandfather."

Maggie sighed. "I agree completely."

"There have been two other occasions when I've needed funds, and each time, he has insisted on the same arrangement. In my heart, I know he overpays me, but he insists it's just a business transaction that benefits him as well as me."

"You never told me how he first learned about the books. Did he know your husband?"

Mrs. Blake sighed. "They'd met once at a book auction. When Mr. Coburn heard Tobias had died, he came to town to make certain no one was taking advantage of me. Although again, he claims he came in his own self-interest."

She dabbed at her eyes with a corner of her apron. "Sometimes I think Tobias himself arranged for him to come. And now he watches us from heaven as we care for his silly books."

"They say God works in mysterious ways, but I didn't really understand what they meant until now," Maggie mused, half to herself. "It's ironic to think that such a hateful man has been the instrument of good."

"Hateful?" The widow frowned. "That's rather harsh, isn't it?"

"Is it? He wants me to dislike him, and I do. On the other hand, I absolutely adore *you,* Eleanor Blake." She embraced the startled landlady warmly. "And I adore Tobias, too, so to the extent that Alex Coburn has helped you, he has my reluctant admiration."

"He wants you to dislike him," Mrs. Blake agreed, "because he values his solitude. He isn't one to enjoy a good chat, bless his heart."

The thought of Coburn "chatting" brought a grin to Maggie's face. "Believe me, I have no desire to chat with him ever again, so you needn't worry."

"He can be distant—even cold—but he's not usually rude. If you honestly feel he's misbehaved toward you, perhaps I should speak to him—"

"Good grief, no. He didn't misbehave at all," Maggie lied. "He was abrupt, but nothing more."

"He's that way with everyone, so don't give it another thought." The landlady smiled slyly. "If it's pleasant conversation you want, you won't find a better partner than Kirk Waller. And he's attractive, too.

Not handsome like Mr. Coburn, perhaps, but attractive in his own way."

"You're incorrigible."

"And you're barefooted, so run upstairs to your room and put on something stunning."

"I'll try to make myself presentable," Maggie promised. "I assume Mr. Coburn won't be joining us?"

"He asked me to keep some chicken warm for him. That means he'll be out late. Playing cards, I imagine."

"Is that how he makes so much money?"

"People don't *make* money playing cards, dear. They *lose* it."

"Then how— Well, never mind." She jumped to her feet and hurried toward the staircase, annoyed with herself for caring how Coburn earned a living. What did it matter? As long as he used his wealth to make Mrs. Blake's life easier, and as long as Maggie avoided placing herself into compromising positions with him, they could undoubtedly find a way to coexist.

Which means, you need to stay out of the library when he's in town, she told herself grimly. *It's not fair, but it's the only way to prove to him, once and for all, that you aren't "roaming" the house in your dressing gown hoping for a chance to seduce him.*

There wasn't a decent mirror in Maggie's room, so she stopped by the second-floor washroom on her way, just to see how "half naked" she actually had been when she'd fallen into Coburn's arms. The reflection that greeted her was a surprise, and for a moment, she had to admit that her nemesis might have had grounds for misinterpreting her behavior. There was a rosy glow to her cheeks—from the bath? Or the weeks at sea? Or the cold, clear mountain air? In any case, it was unfamiliar and oddly flattering, if only because it accented the green of her eyes. And her hair, so loose about her shoulders! It had been years since she'd worn it this way in front of anyone, least of all a man other than her father! It, too, seemed to have been touched by the weeks at sea, so that the streaks of gold were more prominent—almost wild.

"And your feet and ankles were exposed, and you were climbing a ladder as though it were the most natural thing for a girl in her dressing gown to do. Really, Maggie! You'd best start behaving yourself immediately!"

Out of deference to Mrs. Blake, Maggie wore a pretty blue dress trimmed in lace to supper. It was one of four new outfits she had received from Mr. Braddock, the matchmaker, or more precisely, from his daughter, and Maggie adored them all. For so many years, she had sewn her own clothing, and so these professionally made dresses, while simple and modest, seemed outrageously luxurious to her.

She felt like a princess whenever she donned one of the new frocks, which gave her pause, since she truly didn't want to give Kirk Waller the wrong impression as to her accessibility. She'd done enough of that for one day with Coburn! But her caller proved to be too much a gentleman ever to misinterpret a lady's behavior.

The first thing Maggie noticed about him was his voice, which was soft and gentle, contrasting nicely with his wiry, sun-baked appearance. While he seemed nervous when he first arrived, he and Maggie put one another at ease almost immediately, and she had no doubt that she would have enjoyed conversing with him, had Mrs. Blake and Gladys given them half a chance.

Instead, the two older women chattered endlessly

during dinner, and then again in the parlor. And since the prospective lovers weren't left alone for even a moment, Maggie didn't need to discourage Waller's attentions other than by simply treating him with the detached sort of warmth one might offer to any guest.

It was only when he was saying his goodbyes that he actually dared broach the subject of calling on Maggie again, and she avoided the question by reminding him that they'd see one another the next afternoon at the church picnic. Kirk seemed satisfied for the moment with that arrangement, and there was a charming twinkle in his eye as he bid farewell to the rest of the boarders and ambled on his way.

Mrs. Blake, predictably, was more difficult to discourage, but Maggie was firm, insisting that "he seemed like a nice man, and I've agreed to spend time with him tomorrow after church, but as I've told you more than once, I didn't come to Shasta Falls to find a husband."

"But if you wanted a husband, would Kirk suit you?" the stubborn landlady demanded.

Maggie shook her head in amused warning. "Perhaps I'll take my meals alone from now on, as Mr. Coburn does. I don't see you trying to marry *him* off. If I didn't know better, I'd suspect you don't like having me here at all, and are anxious to rid the place of me."

"Mind that tone, young lady," Mrs. Blake warned. "If Kirk ever saw this side of you, he might run for the hills and never look back."

"Yes, ma'am." Maggie gave her a brisk hug. "The meal was delicious, the company was charming, and I'm exhausted. Would it bother you terribly if I went up to bed now?"

The landlady returned the embrace fondly. "Off

with you, then. Dream about Kirk, and the beautiful babies you'll have with him."

Maggie grinned in defeat, then hurried up to her room, where she shed her pretty new dress, donned a crisp white nightgown, and crawled under her baby quilt. It had been quite a day, she decided wistfully. Telling June about Ian—that had been both painful and cathartic. Falling from a ladder—that really *could* have been painful had she landed on the ground rather than in the beastly but convenient arms of Alex Coburn. And the matchmaking—that had been sweet, she decided. A sweet ending to a rather tumultuous day.

On impulse, she challenged herself with the same question Mrs. Blake had asked: if she were looking for a husband, was Kirk Waller the sort of man she could love the way June loved Denny? Could she surrender herself to Waller's kiss as easily and completely as June surrendered to the sheriff?

"Isn't that the point?" she admitted to herself sadly. "You couldn't surrender to him any more than you did to Robert. Not when you know how painfully love can intertwine with grief.

"That's" what they don't understand," she murmured as she drifted into sleep. "That's what none of them will ever, ever understand."

"Well, Miss O'Connor, you should feel quite proud of yourself. We haven't had this sort of attendance at Sunday service in years, and that includes Christmas and Easter."

Maggie returned the smile of Reverend Jonathan Fletcher. "Your sermon was so inspiring, I'm sure everyone will be back next week for more, picnic or no picnic." Adjusting the brim of her straw hat self-consciously, she confessed, "I borrowed this from Mrs. Blake, and just can't quite make it fit. But everything I brought with me was so somber, and I thought the children would find this more approachable."

"It's charming. And I wouldn't worry about being approachable, the way the children have been crowding around you all afternoon."

"Everyone's so friendly," she agreed. "I was concerned that the boys wouldn't want to meet me, but they've been as darling as the girls."

"You can thank Joey Lawson for that. He's been singing your praises all over town. And according to his brother Patrick, you're the bravest girl this side of the Mississippi, although he didn't give specifics. What exactly did you do to impress them so much?"

Maggie flushed. "It's sweet of them to say nice things about me. Are they here today? I've been watching for them, but so far, they've eluded me."

"Their father's too ornery to set foot into a church, I'm afraid. I've tried to talk to him, but he's virulently anti-clergy. I imagine he's somewhat anti-education as well, so don't be too disappointed if their attendance isn't the best."

"They need to come regularly," Maggie protested. "Finding a way to accomplish that will be one of the most important parts of my job. Of course," she added bleakly, "even poor attendance is better than nothing, which is what I fear will happen with the children from the logging camp."

"There aren't too many of them," the minister assured her. "Most of the jacks leave their families back where they came from, except, of course, if they have a son old enough to help with the work. You won't get them into school for that very reason."

"We'll see."

He chuckled at the determination in Maggie's quiet statement. "If you convince them to come to school, perhaps they'll start coming to church, too."

"Or perhaps we could combine the two? I intend to spend each Saturday out at the camp, but if the older boys need to work then, they could come into town on Sunday for your service, and I could tutor them in the afternoon. Surely they aren't expected to work on the Sabbath, so what harm can there be in that?"

Reverend Fletcher shook his head. "Shouldn't you safeguard Sunday for your personal life? I've heard you're dedicated, but there are limits to dedication, especially for a pretty young woman."

Maggie flushed at the prospect of more matchmaking, which seemed to be the pastime of every citizen of Shasta Falls. Apparently, June Riordain had not yet had time to spread the word about Maggie's unavailability.

Fortunately, a family approached at that moment, to say goodbye to Maggie and the reverend before heading home, and she took the opportunity to walk along with them until they reached the edge of the churchyard. She waved until they were out of sight, then turned back toward the throng of picnickers, but decided against returning right away, in favor of exploring a nearby cemetery.

To her wistful delight, the first tombstone she encountered was carved to resemble an enormous book, and she knew before she read the inscription that she had happened upon Tobias Blake's resting place. Fresh roses from the boardinghouse garden adorned the spot, and Maggie took a moment to honor the memory of a man who had loved books so completely.

Then she carefully threaded her way through the headstones, recognizing almost every surname, thanks

to the myriad introductions that had been made at the
picnic. When she noticed the resting place of a woman
named Martha Lawson, "beloved wife and mother,"
she exhaled in soft sympathy for the boisterous lot
Martha had left behind.

Then two tiny tombstones, apart from the others,
caught her eye, and she moved toward them, intrigued
by the fact that they were so delicately chiseled, each
in the shape of an angel kneeling in prayer. These were
clearly the graves of children, yet nothing could have
prepared Maggie for the stab of recognition she felt
when she read the simple word "Riordain" carved at
the base of each, along with a date—a different one
for each child, but for each, only one day, rather than
a span of days, or months, or years, as appeared on
all the rest of the headstones.

"Oh, no." Maggie dropped to her knees, her eyes
filling with hot, disbelieving tears. "Please, no." She
scooped up a bouquet of wildflowers that had been
placed on one grave and clutched it to her chest, as
though somehow she could cradle the infant that way.
Then she reached for the second bouquet and inhaled
its poignant scent.

She thought of Denny, with his huge, loving smile.
One of her first impressions of him had been that he'd
make a glorious father one day, but instead, he had
been cruelly tested. And June! Had Maggie dared burden that sweet woman with her sad story, when June
had been through so much—perhaps more than Maggie herself could ever have survived?

She remembered Coburn's simple question: *How's
June?*

And Denny had said, *Fine. Thanks for asking.*

And Maggie had thought it odd at the time, but now
she understood that even a coldhearted man like Alex

Coburn had been touched by the trials this loving couple had endured.

"Miss O'Connor? Maggie?"

"Oh!" She wiped hastily at her tears and rose to greet Kirk Waller. "I didn't hear you approach."

"It's a shame, isn't it?" he asked quietly. "Such fine folks, to suffer so harshly."

"I didn't know about it until just this minute."

"They been through hell twice," Waller confirmed. "The last time, she almost made it to the end, but . . ."

Maggie buried her face in her hands, overwhelmed at the thought of June's anguish. "You'd think she'd be bitter, or guarded. But instead, she's always smiling and laughing. Or at least, that's the face she shows the world. And Denny! It must have been so hard for him."

Tell Denny? Are you insane? This story would break that man's heart . . .

"They have each other," Waller reminded her. "I envy them that source of strength. Every man needs someone to cling to. Every woman, too, don't you suppose?" Before Maggie could stop him, he continued eagerly. "I'd like to get to know you, Maggie. I'd like to know if you and I might be able to have what the Riordains have one day."

Maggie touched his arm. "June was going to explain something to you, for me."

"About the heartache you've known? She told me to be patient, but that you were worth the wait."

"Oh, for heaven's sake." Maggie shook her head, then tucked her arm through Waller's. "Let's walk for a bit, shall we? Perhaps I can explain it all more clearly than June did."

As they strolled back toward the church, Waller insisted upon detailing his qualifications for marriage, touching Maggie with his humble persistence.

Finally, she assured him, "Anyone would be fortunate to have you for a husband. Are you certain there aren't any girls in Shasta Falls who might do?"

"Only the schoolteacher."

She felt her cheeks warm. "If I were interested in marriage, sir, I assure you, I would take your interest as both a compliment and a blessing. Unfortunately—"

"There's another fella?"

Maggie sighed. "No."

"Well, then . . ." He was clearly trying not to grin. "That's fine news. I mean . . ." He caught himself and added solemnly, "Whatever heartache you've known, it'll pass. It always does."

"I want something different from life than most women want. I want to teach. I don't want children of my own, Kirk. Surely that alone is enough to discourage you."

"You don't want children? Why? They're such a blessing, and you'd be so lovely a mother."

Maggie thought about June's angels and shook her head sadly. It was a particularly bitter irony to think that the Riordains wanted children so desperately, yet couldn't have them, while Maggie had the temerity to proclaim she would simply forgo the privilege. No wonder June had to believe that Maggie would change her mind one day. Anything else would be incomprehensible, given the circumstances.

"I didn't mean to offend you, or to pry," Waller insisted. "I'm willing to wait for as long as you need. And if you don't want children, I suppose—"

"Don't be silly." She blushed again. "You'll find a girl soon, Kirk. One who'll love you the way June loves Denny, and who'll want dozens of little Wallers running around the house. You deserve no less than that."

"Back east, it might have happened. But here?" He shrugged his shoulders.

"Have you considered . . . ?" Maggie hesitated, then continued bluntly. "There are companies that arrange matches, did you know that?"

Waller was clearly stunned. "I didn't think a decent girl like yourself would approve of that sort of doing."

"I might have been shocked by it, had I not had occasion to hear wonderful things about a particular company. A particular man."

Waller seemed receptive, so she continued. "Have you heard the sheriff refer to Father James?"

"Sure. He's the priest who found you for us."

"That's right. When I was visiting Father James, a few weeks before I came here, he and I had occasion to discuss a mail-order bride company that's flourishing in San Francisco. I asked him if he approved of a man making a living that way. And he said, in this particular case, the proprietor was doing God's work. Then he told me some stories about the way this particular company had arranged matches—matches built on respect, that grew quickly into love. It was quite a tribute."

Her pulse began to race. "You could write a letter, and we could send it to Father James, to pass along to the matchmaker. And I could write a letter, too, vouching for you. So that they would see you were a worthy candidate. Is that agreeable?"

"I'll have to think on it." He shook his head, amused. "Girls coming through the mail, like a package from a dry goods catalogue. What'll they think of next?"

Maggie laughed lightly. "I'm beginning to understand why June and Mrs. Blake enjoy matchmaking so much. I hope you'll decide to pursue this, Kirk.

And if you do, perhaps you could do something for me in the meanwhile."

"Anything," he assured her. "What is it?"

Maggie smiled. "Don't mention any of this to Mrs. Blake. If she realizes you're no longer courting me, she'll invite someone else to take your place as my primary suitor."

"You want me to *pretend* to court you?"

Regretting the suggestion, Maggie said quickly, "I'm being unfair, of course. Please forget I made such a ridiculous suggestion."

"I'll tell you what I'm going to do. I'm going to tell her you've asked me to wait a while—to let you adjust to this town, and to unresolved business from your past—before I start courting you in earnest. How's that?"

"That's perfect," Maggie admitted. "It will give me time to show the town I didn't come here to find a husband. And it will give *you* time to consider using the services of the Happily Ever After Company."

Waller flashed a mischievous grin. "Of course, if I decide against using the matchmaker, I might just turn my attentions back to you again. You can't choose to be alone forever."

"Yes, I can."

"That would be a sad, sad decision, Maggie O'Connor."

"I agree," she murmured, half to herself. "Unfortunately, I've already made it."

Six

To Maggie's delighted relief, Alex Coburn left on one of his "adventures" while the rest of the household was at the picnic, and from that moment forward, wonderful things began to happen for the young schoolteacher. First, she managed to find not one but two copies of the elusive *The Gallic Wars*. One magnificent edition—leather bound with gold leaf pages, containing both the Latin and the English versions on facing pages—was clearly priceless, and she handled it more carefully than she would a newborn baby, for fear it belonged to Coburn.

The other copy had apparently been used by Tobias Blake as a schoolboy, with earmarked pages and an occasional scribble in the margins. While this book was also priceless in Maggie's eyes, she felt comfortable asking her landlady if she could borrow it, and was humbled when that kindhearted woman tried to make a gift of it.

"Tobias would have wanted you to have it, you loving books as much as he did," Eleanor Blake told her.

But Maggie knew Coburn was correct about one thing—a grandchild could appear one day who would be enraptured by this charming bit of his or her grandfather's past. It had to remain with the collection, for a while longer at least, but she would borrow it with confidence and gratitude, knowing that Tobias really would be pleased that it was being used to inspire another generation of schoolchildren.

To Maggie, finding the book was an omen that the first day of school was bound to go well. And from the moment Denny appeared to escort her, to the moment the Lawson boys—not just two, but three!—bounded into view, her wishes for that morning continued to be granted. And while Julius Caesar made the hoped-for impression, it was the new teacher herself who seemed to capture the imagination of each and every student.

In fact, they were so curious about her that she decided to use it as an opportunity to address one particularly troublesome issue, and so she informed the attentive audience quietly, "I've been very impressed by each and every one of you today, and I have no doubt that you'll continue to behave wonderfully and to make me proud. Still, I believe it bears mentioning, right from the start, that I don't tolerate bullying in any form. If I see that sort of behavior, in this schoolroom or in the schoolyard, I fully intend to deal with it quickly and sternly."

Mary Ellen Deighton spoke up immediately. "What will you do?"

Maggie shrugged. "I have a number of possible remedies, depending upon the circumstances. They're effective, I promise you. But as I said, I'm confident everyone will behave, so there's no reason to dwell on this."

"Are you going to send us to the sheriff?" Joey Lawson asked. " 'Cause we're not afraid of *him*."

"Oh?" Maggie arched an eyebrow for a long, challenging moment, then smiled. "I'll keep that in mind. Are there any other questions? This time, please raise your hand so that I can call on you."

Mary Ellen's little hand shot up immediately, and when Maggie gave her permission to speak, she demanded brightly, "Have you ever kissed a boy?"

Maggie waited for a burst of laughter to subside before scolding gently, "That's not the sort of question I was talking about. Do you want to know anything about this school? About my rules, or what we'll be learning?"

"Why should we learn *your* rules?" a new voice asked. "Everyone says you won't be our teacher for long."

"Oh?" Maggie turned to Junior Lawson, the oldest of the three brothers, and met his gaze directly. "Why do you say that?"

"You're just here to get a husband. Everyone knows that."

Maggie saw that the comment made the children squirm, yet they also seemed curious, so she sighed and perched on the corner of her desk, a tentative smile on her lips. "I keep hearing that myself. And even though it's not really a proper topic for a schoolroom, I'm going to tell you all something: a secret that might just convince you that rumor isn't true."

Their eyes widened, and she had to struggle to keep her tone solemn in the face of such an adorable sight. "I came here from a big city—"

"San Francisco!" several students shouted out proudly.

She cleared her voice and studied them until they had settled down, then she continued softly. "Back home, I knew a very nice man. The kind of man any girl would be proud to marry. And in fact, he did me the great honor of proposing marriage to me. I was flattered, but I said no, because I wanted my life to take another path—the path of teaching."

She scanned the anxious faces, then asked them

simply, "Why would I come all this way just to find a husband, when I had a perfectly nice prospect right at home?"

Mary Ellen raised her hand and waved it eagerly.

"Yes, Mary Ellen?"

"Did you kiss *him?*"

The other students laughed wildly, and Maggie had to grin as well. "You're persistent, aren't you? Yes. I kissed him several times."

"Did you let him—"

"I kissed him on the front porch of my father's house, with my father sitting right inside—undoubtedly with a loaded shotgun close at hand."

The children laughed again, and Maggie waited until they'd finished before explaining, more soberly, "I had two brothers when I was your age, but both of them died as children. My mother died when I was little also. The only part of my life that was very, very safe and very, very certain, through all the heartache, was school. As a consequence, I loved school very dearly. And so I decided to become a teacher. Does that make sense?"

Joey Lawson raised his hand but didn't wait for her to acknowledge him before asking, "Did your father die, too?"

"Yes."

"So you don't have anyone but us?"

Maggie nodded. "I only told you about this so you'd believe me when I say I'm not here looking for a husband. I don't blame the adults in town for misunderstanding, or for doing a little matchmaking. But it's important for *you* to know the truth. And now . . ." She flashed an apologetic smile. "I think that's enough serious talk for the time being. How does a little fresh air sound?"

When they immediately began to swarm out of their

seats, she asked coolly, "Shall I take that to mean you're ready to be excused?"

They froze in position, sheepish expressions on their faces, and she arched her eyebrow for a long, meaningful moment, then smiled and waved her hand toward the door. Within seconds, the room had emptied, and the new schoolteacher found herself standing on a narrow porch, awash with midmorning sun, and watching in quiet wonder as her children began to play.

With her first successful day behind her, Maggie knew she should go straight to the boardinghouse and rest, but she had one loose end to an otherwise perfect life, and she couldn't put it off any longer. She hadn't been able to find a moment to talk to June alone, and hadn't dared raise any serious subjects with Denny on the walk to school that morning, but the knowledge of their loss weighed heavily on her, all the more because she had so cavalierly burdened June with the tale of Brian and Ian.

And so, as soon as the last child disappeared from sight, Maggie headed along the ridge until she came to the Riordains' blue-and-white cottage, where she found June digging energetically in the vegetable garden.

"I'm so glad you're here!" The auburn-haired bride jumped to her feet, wiping her hands quickly on her apron before pulling Maggie into a brisk hug. Then she studied her face and demanded, "Don't tell me the children misbehaved? After Denny and the parents threatened them so often? It's unbelievable!"

"They were darling," Maggie assured her. "I couldn't have asked for a more perfect start to my teaching career."

June cocked her head to the side. "Why the long face, then? You look as though you've lost your best friend."

"Not lost her, but hurt her. Unintentionally, and I'm so sorry." Amazed that her eyes were already beginning to fill with tears, Maggie waved her hands helplessly in the air. "I don't know what I was thinking, burdening you with my grief, when all the while—"

"That's enough," June insisted. "Let's go inside and have some lemonade, shall we?" She took Maggie by the arm and urged her gently toward the kitchen steps. "Some lemonade and a good cry. How does that sound?"

"June . . ."

"I know. I saw you in the cemetery, visiting my angels. I would have come right over and explained it all, but I could see Kirk was doing a lovely job of it, so I thought we'd just wait until later."

They had reached the doorway, and she motioned for Maggie to sit at the table. Then she fetched two glasses and an earthenware pitcher and joined her, a sympathetic smile on her face. "I should have told you about the babies, I suppose. But you're so softhearted, I kept putting it off. Forgive me?"

Maggie patted her hostess's hand. "You have nothing to apologize for. And I think in your own way you did tell me, when you said you've been wounded, too. I'm so, so sorry, June. How painful and unfair it's all been for you."

"There have been moments of pure heartbreak and despair," the young wife admitted. "Horrible moments, when I was sure neither Denny nor I would ever smile or trust again. But because we had each other, we've been able to do both. I think that's why your story broke my heart. Because you had no one to help you. And you were just a child, especially the first time they took Ian away."

"I don't want to talk about that," Maggie interrupted gently. "If it's not too painful, I'd like to hear about—well, about your angels, as you call them."

June sighed. "There's so little to tell—I suppose that's a blessing. The first time . . ." She bit her lip, then admitted, "Denny and I were deliriously happy. It never occurred to us that something might go awry. It happened early that time—before the doctor could even determine if it was a boy or a girl that I'd lost. It didn't hurt physically, but my heart . . ."

Maggie jumped to her feet and came around the table to embrace her friend tearfully. "How horribly unfair. I'm so sorry, June."

The young bride nodded, her hazel eyes bright with misery. "I thought I could never dare take a chance again, especially because of how difficult it was for Denny. But in time, we regained our confidence, and our hope. Neither family had a history of these sorts of problems, and the doctor was guardedly optimistic, and so we tried again. It was a boy for sure this time. We knew because—well, because almost six months' growing told us so."

"Oh, dear."

"I spent days in bed, with my face turned to the wall, not wanting to live. Denny took care of me during all that, and I was so selfish, I didn't really think about *his* poor heart, until I started feeling a little better. That's when I realized too late that his despair was blacker, and more abysmal than my own. He made me promise we'd never try again. Can you believe that?"

"I suppose I can," Maggie mused. "Are you saying . . . ?"

"That *I'm* ready?" June smiled through her tears.

"Denny says I must be insane to even consider it, but what I said earlier is true: there's no history of this in either family. It's a tragic and cruel coincidence that we've been asked to endure this sort of misery twice, but that doesn't mean it will happen again."

Maggie moistened her lips, wary of the optimistic attitude. "What does the doctor say?"

"He felt so guilty, for encouraging us last time, he doesn't dare say a word. And even if he did, Denny wouldn't listen. That man is so stubborn," June added ruefully. "I've done my best to reassure him, and when that didn't work, I did my best to seduce him, but he's bound and determined never to try again."

Maggie stared in disbelief, remembering all of the lusty kisses she'd seen in just one short week. "Are you saying you and he don't . . . ?"

June burst into laughter. "We most certainly do. For heaven's sake, Maggie, are you as innocent as all that? You believe Denny Riordain is willing to live like a monk, and that I'd allow it, even if he were? Denny's stubborn, but he's a healthy man with healthy needs—"

"Fine." Maggie felt her cheeks turning to crimson. "There's no need for details."

"Apparently, there is," June countered gleefully. "You're such a prude, Maggie Gleason! How can you decide against marrying when you don't yet have all the necessary information?"

"I have all the information I need."

"Apparently you don't. Have you ever even kissed a man?"

Maggie scowled, wondering how many times she would be expected to tell this particular story before Shasta Falls accepted her decision as final. "You're as bad as the children, and I'll tell you what I told them: I was courted once, by a very nice, attractive man.

And yes, he kissed me, more than once. I have all the information I need—"

"From a kiss?" June giggled helplessly. "I doubt that. But at least you admit he was attractive. Did he make your heart skip a beat?"

"I don't remember. And I don't want to talk about it anymore."

"Did you blush every time he flirted with you, the way you do with Denny?"

"Pardon?" Maggie stared in dismay. "What makes you say such a thing?"

"My husband is a flirtatious man—do you think I don't know that? And every time he flirts with *you,* you blush—which means you enjoy the attentions of men. But apparently—" she sniffed as though slightly offended—"you only allow them from men you can't have."

"That's not true!"

"You think you *can* have Denny?"

Maggie gasped, then noticed the twinkle in June's eyes and declared wearily, "I'm going home."

"Stay for supper. I promise I won't tease you any more."

Maggie grinned. "Don't make promises you can't keep. And I appreciate the invitation, but Mrs. Blake said she's going to make something special, to celebrate my first day as a teacher." With a mischievous smile, she suggested, "I'm sure there's enough for you and Denny, if you'd like to join us. She complains that the two of you never come to supper anymore."

"I adore Eleanor, but that food of hers." June pretended to shudder. "How do you tolerate it?"

"It was a shock at first, but I'm getting used to it. The Lowe sisters and Mr. Gentry actually seem to like it, so I imagine it's an acquired taste."

"Unless it kills you first."

Maggie smiled. "I've had so many dinner invitations from my students' parents, I doubt if I'll dine at the boardinghouse more than three times a week for the indefinite future." She added impishly, "If I were a man, I could do as Mr. Coburn does, and pretend to eat Mrs. Blake's cooking, but secretly eat at the hotel or the saloon."

"He does that?"

"According to Mr. Gentry, he does. And I imagine he eats well when he travels, too. Did I mention he left town again already? I almost feel responsible, as though having a stranger in the house drove him away.

"He's such an odd man," she added, half to herself. "Mamie and Francine seem to agree with Mrs. Blake and Denny—that he's a good person, deep inside. But Mr. Gentry agrees with you and me, and I believe Reverend Fletcher does, too. Still," she added quietly, "I hate to think he left town because of me."

"You couldn't drive a fly away, much less a brute like Coburn," June assured her. "He comes and goes constantly, Maggie. Don't take it personally. We can only hope one day he'll leave and never come back."

"He'll come back. He can't resist that library, and neither can I." Maggie felt her pulse race at the very thought of having that wonderful room all to herself again after dinner, and she jumped to her feet and gave June a quick hug, adding on mischievous impulse, "Give my love to that flirtatious husband of yours."

True to Maggie's prediction, she rarely ate two meals in a row at the boardinghouse during the next month, due to the plethora of invitations from the families of her students, and her weekly meal with the Riordains, which quickly became a Thursday night ritual. It wasn't long before Maggie decided she truly had stumbled upon paradise, consisting of days with her students, evenings with friends, and late nights with Tobias Blake's book collection.

She wasn't sure what Kirk Waller had said to Mrs. Blake, but it certainly seemed to have an effect on her landlady's matchmaking schemes. Although single men, young and old, still appeared in the parlor after dinner, their hostess no longer tried to encourage anything but friendship between the visitors and the schoolteacher. "Because she still believes it will be Kirk," Maggie told herself, but she also hoped that, during this time, Mrs. Blake would learn to accept the fact that Maggie simply wasn't interested in marriage.

In the meantime, nothing could compare to the moment, each night around ten-thirty, when the rowdy commotion from the parlor faded into quiet; Maggie curled up under her baby quilt by a small fire she tended herself, and Tobias Blake's room enveloped her. She even pretended sometimes that Tobias was there with her, sitting in Coburn's chair, paging through a book of sonnets with the air of a man who had found the secret to happiness that had eluded so many men before him.

Of course, every time she tried to explain all that to June Riordain, her efforts were greeted with disgust.

"You're having an affair with a dead man," June declared one cloudy Saturday afternoon as the two women finished their latest project: lining the path to the schoolhouse with posies transplanted from June's garden.

"Don't tell Eleanor," Maggie replied evenly. "At least I'm not making eyes at *your* husband anymore."

"True." June grinned. "If they could see you now,

none of them would have you. There's more dirt on your face than on the ground."

"You're something of a mess yourself," Maggie assured her with a laugh.

"But I already have a husband, so it doesn't matter." June pursed her lips thoughtfully. "Have you ever thought about having an affair—not with dead men like Tobias, but with someone young and handsome and amorous?"

"That's a wonderful idea. Find me a young, handsome lover and I'll run off with him."

"You've changed," June complained. "Six weeks ago, I could make you blush and stammer and take offense without any effort at all. Now you're maddeningly serene."

"It's this town. The children. My friendship with you. And the library. Honestly, June, I can't bear the thought of Coburn coming back one day soon and robbing me of my most treasured pastime."

"Denny says he won't be back for weeks."

Maggie cocked her head to the side. "I thought Denny didn't know where he went."

"I didn't say he did. He just knows it's far away, so it stands to reason he'll be gone for a while longer."

"Far away? Do you think he went to another country? Do you suppose he's in Italy?" she added, annoyed at the fact that Coburn could so easily go to places Maggie could only dream of seeing. "Or Greece? I don't think I could bear *that*. It's so completely unfair."

June sat back on her heels and studied Maggie closely. "You're obsessed with him, you know."

"Pardon?"

"You're having an affair with a dead man and you're obsessed with a brute. Yet you claim you have no room in your life for a man."

"I'm having an affair with the library, and I'm obsessed with keeping it to myself."

"No. You don't speculate for hours on end about the library. It's Coburn, Coburn, Coburn."

"That's not true."

June adopted a singsong voice. "Coburn, Coburn, Coburn. How does he make his money? Where does he go? How can a man who loves books be such a beast? I wonder how many languages he speaks, who his favorite authors are, why he dresses all in black. If I didn't know better, Maggie Gleason, I'd believe you were secretly in love with the man!"

Maggie gasped, then caught the glimmer of mischief in June's hazel eyes and glared in disgust. "You were determined to goad me until I lost my temper? Honestly, June."

"You should have seen your expression!"

Maggie had to smile at her friend's gleeful boasting. "I'm going home, and you should, too, before Denny starts to worry."

"Too late." June gestured toward the bottom of the hill, and Maggie saw that Denny Riordain was on his way to the school to check on his bride.

She waved toward the sheriff, then eyed June with a teasing smile. "Has he seen you covered in dirt before? It's very becoming."

"He'll take me home and bathe me. If only Coburn were in town, he could do the same for you."

"Don't tease me about him anymore," Maggie protested. "If you knew some of the things he's said to me, you'd never make light of that particular subject again."

June frowned. "What sort of things?"

Maggie glanced toward Denny, but he was still a safe distance away, and so she decided to confide in her friend, if only to keep her from making jokes about Coburn at Maggie's expense in the future.

"It's about time you knew just how despicable he is," Maggie said finally. "Don't tell Denny a word of this, but, well, Coburn actually suggested to me that I might want to go to his bedroom with him! And you should see the way he looked at me, as though—"

Jumping to her feet, June wailed toward her husband. *"Dennis Anthony Riordain!"*

Maggie stared in speechless dismay as her irate friend whirled and ran down the path toward her husband, babbling angrily about Coburn's "attempts on Maggie's honor."

"What are you talking about?" Denny demanded, catching his wife by the shoulders and scanning her expression carefully. "Is this one of your jokes?"

"You told me he was trustworthy," June retorted. "Every time I said I didn't like the idea of an innocent girl living with a beast like Alex Coburn, you assured me he wouldn't come within five feet of her, let alone attempt to molest her. But you should hear what he's done to her! Right under *your* nose. Some sheriff you turned out to be!"

Denny released June and hurried to Maggie, an expression of abject concern on his face. "What's this about, missy?"

"Nothing. I swear it, Denny. June's just—well, she's just being June." With a smile that she knew looked more like a wince, she added, "Don't the flowers look lovely? We've been working so hard, we completely lost track of the time. I'm sorry if we worried you."

The sheriff rested his hands on Maggie's shoulder. "June says he molested you. If that's true . . ." He seemed to choke on the words, and had to shudder slightly before beginning again. "If it's true, just tell me. I'll see to it that he never bothers you—or anyone else—again."

"It's nothing like that," Maggie promised, although to herself she muttered that it actually was something like that. His tone, his manner, his repeated suggestions that she was interested in finding a man—those words had both offended and intimidated her, to the point where she could barely stand the idea of ever again being in the same room as the man.

"What did he do?"

"It's not what he did, it's what he said. Or rather," she corrected lamely, "the way he said what he said."

"Words?" Denny murmured. "Did he touch you?"

"Touch me?" She struggled to remember—she certainly had *felt* touched!—then she shook her head. "I fell, and he caught me. But he was rude about it. That's all," she admitted. "He's rude. And he made two very pointed suggestions that reflected badly on me."

"Huh?"

"He implied that *I* was pursuing *him,* and offered to—well, never mind."

"He implied you were pursuing him, and offered to take you up on *your* offer?" Denny was clearly trying not to chuckle. "Would it make you feel any better if I told you he wouldn't have done it, even if you had agreed?"

"I beg your pardon?"

"Really, Denny," June interrupted. "What an insulting thing to say to Maggie! If Maggie asked Alex Coburn to take her to his bedroom and do unspeakable things to her, I'm sure he'd be delighted to oblige her."

"June!" Maggie shook her head, then turned to Denny and insisted, "You have to admit, it *was* an odd thing to say."

"He's an odd fellow," Denny reminded her with a gentle grin. "Most men would love to spend time with you, doing whatever you wanted to do, but not Coburn. He told me so himself. That's why I can assure you he'd never molest you in any way."

Ignoring June's gasp, the sheriff continued ruefully. "I had misgivings of my own, when they talked about your living at the boardinghouse. Coburn's my friend, but there are aspects to him I know nothing about. I mean, I know he spends a little time with women at the saloon, but they've never complained about his conduct."

"Such a relief!" June glared. "If he's good enough for a whore, he's good enough for Maggie? Is that what you're saying?"

Maggie flushed. "Go on, Denny. You had misgivings of your own . . ."

"Right. So I asked him about it. He said he didn't have any interest in a relationship, proper or otherwise, with a decent woman. He promised he'd keep his distance from you—said he'd be in the library, and you'd be in the parlor, and that would suit him just fine. But then you started trying to build a friendship—"

"I did not!" Maggie caught her temper and added grimly, "I didn't want a friendship. Just a civil acquaintanceship. A polite word or greeting from time to time. And shared use of the library. Nothing more."

Denny nodded. "Shared use of the library—that might have been what did it."

"Did what?"

"Made him decide to make you want to keep your distance."

"You're saying he made suggestive remarks to Maggie just to frighten her away? That's ridiculous."

Denny shrugged. "He said ignoring her wasn't enough, so he made himself distasteful."

Maggie was intrigued. "Why didn't he just explain all this to me?"

"Would you have left him alone if he had?" Denny eyed her knowingly. "He figured you'd find his attitude intriguing. You'd want to know more, and the questions would be endless. It was easier just to make you run away."

"He's even more despicable than we guessed," June declared.

Maggie held up her hand to silence her friend, then asked carefully, "You're certain, Denny? He looked at me with such a disrespectful smirk, and suggested that if I was looking for male companionship—"

"You ought to try the logging camp?" Denny grinned reluctantly. "So I heard."

Maggie knew she should be appalled, or disgusted, but instead, she was flooded with relief. He *was* a recluse after all. A hermit, and like any good hermit, he used any tool at his disposal to scare away the world when it tried to encroach on his solitude.

And of course, June was correct: it was despicable. But not lustful. Not depraved. He hadn't been staring at her body because of need to have her, but rather, from need to make her go away!

"He knew it offended you, but he figured it was the fastest way to make you keep your distance. And since I don't particularly want you near him myself, that suited me just fine."

Maggie squeezed his arm and insisted, "I thank you for telling me, Denny. And when your friend returns, give him a message for me, won't you? He needn't worry anymore that I'll invade his solitude. I'll use the library when he's off on his adventures, but when he's in Shasta Falls, he won't catch a glimpse of me there."

"That isn't fair!" June's eyes blazed with disgust. "You have as much right to be in that library as he does."

"Perhaps," Maggie said soothingly. "But he has nothing else. Fortunately, I can seek comfort from my students and my friends as well as from the library. But it's all Mr. Coburn has. Don't you see?"

June shook her auburn curls. "You tell me endlessly that you dread his return because it will separate you from your precious library, and now, it's fine?"

Maggie nodded. "Now that I understand—now that I'm not staying away from the library because I fear his attentions, but because I respect his bizarre need for solitude—yes. It's fine."

Denny's blue eyes twinkled. "And it's not a book she's needing at the moment, it's a bath. And you're in need of one yourself, Mrs. Riordain."

June brightened instantly. "Will you join me, Mr. Riordain?"

Maggie groaned. "Go on, both of you. I'll finish up here."

She could hear them cooing and giggling as they departed in one another's arms, and to her surprise, she found that she was laughing a bit herself. *You really have changed, just as June said,* she told herself happily. *It's as though their friendship—and their provocative example—have taught you more about romantic love than all the books in all the libraries you've ever visited.*

The more she learned about love, the more she weakened in her plan to live her life alone. She had even considered finding a kindhearted widower who already had children for her to adore and raise. Because while she was reconsidering her decision not to marry, she was steadfast in her determination that she mustn't have babies of her own—knowing that her own mother had died in childbirth, and knowing how sorely her children would miss her if the same happened to her.

June's idea is a better one. Find a handsome young lover, she teased herself as she scurried through town, anxious to reach the boardinghouse's bath before anyone saw her. The children would be aghast at the sight of their teacher in such a grimy condition, and the parents would wonder if they'd entrusted their youth to the right person!

She managed to reach the back steps of Mrs. Blake's house without incident, and laughed when she heard her landlady's voice exclaiming "Mercy sakes alive!" from the kitchen window. Entering sheepishly, she explained, "I was gardening with June, and I'm sorely in need of a bath before dinner, as you can see."

Mrs. Blake glanced toward the tiny tiled room. "I'm dying fabric in the tub."

"Pardon?"

"We've decided to make a quilt from the scraps I've been saving, and Mamie wants it to be blue, so . . ."

Maggie smiled. "Don't worry. I can wait a while, if you can stand the thought of such a disheveled boarder. I'll sit in the backyard, under the peach tree, and read until the fabric is a lovely shade of blue."

"Nonsense. It's not as though it's the only bath in the house. You stay right there, and I'll find you a change of clothing—"

"Wait!" Maggie stared at the woman, wondering if she had completely lost her mind. Then, in a tone that was at once forceful and fraught with panic, she demanded, "Are you suggesting I take a bath *in Mr. Coburn's room?*"

Seven

Maggie stared at her landlady in complete amazement. "I simply couldn't, Eleanor. I can wait—"

"The fabric has to be rinsed twice. And the Fletchers are coming to dinner at six-thirty."

"But—"

"It isn't Mr. Coburn's bathtub, it's mine. Isn't that what you always tell me? I use it myself when he's gone, you know."

"You do?" Maggie narrowed her eyes and scanned the landlady's expression. "Honestly?"

"Of course. It's a delightful room, with an enormous tub. You'll love it."

I'll hate it, Maggie assured her silently, then asked aloud, "Does Mr. Coburn know you use it when he's gone?"

"Do you suppose I need his permission to use my own bath?"

"In other words—"

"In other words, it's all settled." Mrs. Blake arched an eyebrow in warning against further discussion.

"Well . . ." Maggie bit her lip, remembering what June had said. Coburn wouldn't be back for weeks, and as long as no one told him—

"You won't tell him I used it, will you?"

"Mercy, no. He'll be none the wiser."

"And if he comes home unexpectedly . . ."

"He won't. He said he'd be gone for months, and it's been only weeks."

"But *if* he comes home while I'm in that tub—" Maggie paused to flash her landlady a grin—"I want your word that you'll shoot me right there, dead in the water."

Mrs. Blake chuckled. "Wouldn't it be better if I shot *him?*" Before Maggie could agree, she waved her away with a cheerful "I have a bath to draw, dinner to cook, and a hundred other things to do before the Fletchers arrive. Go on upstairs and take off those filthy clothes. Bring them to me and I'll wash them tomorrow."

Knowing better than to argue, Maggie hurried up to her room, reminding herself how fortunate she was. Along with all the other blessings that had been heaped upon her these past months, she actually had someone in her life who insisted upon doing her laundry! She had protested at the beginning, assuring Mrs. Blake that she had done the household wash since the time she was old enough to reach the washstand, but her landlady had insisted that it was all part of the service she provided in exchange for the town's payment, and she'd feel like a criminal if she didn't earn every penny.

Maggie tried to remind herself of all that, but her nervousness over invading Coburn's lair won out, and she paced back and forth in her tiny room, wondering if she shouldn't just use the second-floor washroom to freshen up.

What would Mrs. Blake say to that? At this very moment, she was drawing a steamy, decadent bath for her, and Maggie had to admit, it sounded wonderful. If only Denny hadn't told her about Coburn's confession: that he was so intent on preventing any contact whatsoever between himself and the new teacher that he had feigned lust to drive her away!

What would he say if he ever found out Maggie had been in his rooms? Touching his personal possessions, seeing his bed, his dresser, his private domain . . .

"But he *won't* ever know about it," she whispered suddenly. "So where's the harm? And you have to admit, Maggie Gleason, you're dying of curiosity! He doesn't spend much time in there, but still, it will give you more clues to his past, his character, perhaps even his livelihood, than you've ever had!"

Her imagination began to dance at the thought, and she wriggled out of her dirty dress and into a soft pink robe that Noelle Braddock had given her. Then she grabbed her hairbrush and flew back downstairs, intent on exploring every inch of Alex Coburn's sanctuary.

But when she reached the doorway to his room, her conscience caught up with her enthusiasm and she sighed in defeat. She wouldn't "explore" at all. In fact, she'd do her best not to see anything, other than the tub. She wouldn't violate his privacy, not just because it was wrong to do so, but because to him, more than to ordinary men, it would be the ultimate invasion.

And if the situation were reversed, and he ever dared enter *her* room, or look at *her* personal possessions, she'd feel exactly the same way, wouldn't she?

"Maggie?" Eleanor Blake bustled out of the bathroom and came to take her boarder by the hand. "You really *are* afraid to come in here, aren't you? I thought you were just being polite."

Maggie grimaced. "I know I'm being silly, but he's such a private man."

"Every room in this house belongs to me. And it's not as though you're going to sit at his desk or sleep in his bed—oh, gracious! I didn't mean to suggest *that*."

Maggie laughed lightly. "You really would have to shoot me then, wouldn't you?"

The older woman eyed the younger with stern disapproval. "That's enough nonsense for one afternoon. Come now, and see what I've done."

Maggie trailed dutifully behind her, trying not to notice Coburn's huge bed, despite the eye-catching brown-and-red Navaho blanket that adorned it. The only other notable pieces of furniture were a massive oak armoire and an uncluttered desk and chair. Not a clue in sight, and Maggie had to admit, it was a relief.

Then she entered the spacious bathroom and smiled with delight at the blue-and-white tiles that lined the floor and walls. And in the tub—the largest she'd ever seen—were armloads of fragrant bubbles.

"It's so inviting!"

"I save this soap for special occasions, or for when I'm missing Tobias," Mrs. Blake explained. "It's dreadfully expensive, but I had a feeling it would put you at your ease."

Maggie leaned down to bury her nose in the bubbles. "Gardenia? How blissful."

"I'll leave you to it, then. In a while, if you'd like, I could bring a cup of tea, and you can soak to your heart's content."

"You've done more than enough already."

"Mint? Or cinnamon?"

"Cinnamon, please." She gave her benefactress a grateful hug and murmured impulsively, "Your daughters were so blessed, to have someone like you to spoil them this way."

"What a lovely thing to say." Mrs. Blake wiped at her eye with the back of her hand, then she briskly instructed Maggie to enjoy herself and hurried out of the room, closing the door firmly behind herself.

After ensuring that the crisp, white curtains were fully drawn over the room's only window, Maggie slipped out of her robe and hung it carefully on a hook behind the door. Her landlady had draped a thick white towel on a rod within inches of the tub, and had placed a small mat on the floor. On the far wall was a mirror large enough to reflect Maggie's image from the top of her head to her knees, and she curtseyed to it playfully, then loosened her long, gold-tinged hair from its knot, allowing it to spill about her bare shoulders and down her back.

"What would Mrs. Blake say if she knew you were admiring your naked body like a strumpet," she teased herself. "And what would Coburn say! If half of what Denny told you is true, he'd faint dead away at the thought of it."

Smiling broadly, she eased herself into the hot, sudsy water, allowing her senses to be engulfed along with her body. Once her muscles had relaxed, she slid completely under the water so that her thick hair could become thoroughly drenched. When she surfaced, she took another moment to study the pretty room, then closed her eyes and eased back, lounging in decadent surrender.

"To think you tried to resist this," she chided herself. "From now on, you should always bathe in here when Mr. Coburn is on an adventure. It can be an unspoken clause in the agreement: custody of the library *and* the bath will be yours when he's gone, and in exchange, you will stay out of his path when he's here."

She inhaled deeply, then blew the air out, pleased with the way it made a cluster of bubbles take flight.

Does Mr. Coburn enjoy this lovely tub, she wondered idly. *Does Mr. Coburn enjoy anything at all?*

Books, she reminded herself. And perhaps, the girls at the saloon? Probably not. If he enjoyed *them,* it would mean that he found value in a fellow human being, and if that were true, he wouldn't be so quick to reject a possible friendship—correction, acquaintanceship!—with a fellow bibliophile.

He simply uses the saloon girls to meet his basest needs. Just as he uses Mrs. Blake's poverty to gain access to the library. And his friendship with Denny? What use is that to him?

But Denny had explained it, hadn't he? "He watched my back, and I watched his . . ." The simple needs of a man whose love of books forced him to live in a town, rather than a cave in the middle of nowhere.

That's probably the truth of it, she decided with a yawn. *He needed one male friend in town, in case there's ever trouble. And who better to choose than a big, strong sheriff who wouldn't make any demands on their friendship? Yet even then, he couldn't be polite to June . . .*

Maggie had to smile again. A man who valued privacy and had no need for human interaction—if Maggie's tentative overtures had threatened him, June's vivacious curiosity must have absolutely overwhelmed the poor hermit! What was it June had said? That he actually ran away before his meal was finished, muttering something under his breath?

For some reason, the image tickled Maggie's fancy, and she laughed aloud, then lifted a handful of bubbles and sent them into the air with a slow, steady breath. "Fly away, little bubbles. Just like mean Mr. Coburn flew away from June."

As much as she longed to lie back and relax for

hours, she knew it would soon be time to leave this hideaway and return to her cramped little room to dress for supper, so she lathered her hair, then dunked herself under the water for a quick rinse.

The bubbles will be gone soon, and the water will cool, she reminded herself as she surfaced again, so she wiped a soapy film from her eyes, then began to wring some of the water from her hair. Her fingers worked expertly, untangling the locks with gentle efficiency. Then she piled the whole mane on top of her head and slipped down into the water again, but this time only up to her shoulders, making sure that her long tresses stayed outside the tub, where they could begin to dry.

"Comfortable?" a gravelly voice demanded from the doorway.

Shrieking softly, Maggie spun to face Coburn while simultaneously cringing farther under the water in a futile attempt to hide her nakedness from his narrowed eyes.

"It is beyond my comprehension," he informed her quietly, "that you dared to come in here, after all I've said to you."

"Y-you c-can't—" She stopped herself and tried to take a breath, but she inhaled water instead of air, and to her mortification, began to cough roughly. Desperate, she grabbed for the towel, but while the rod was within easy reach of a person *sitting* in the tub, it hadn't been designed for a person cowering within it.

"Allow me," Coburn drawled, stepping right up to the side of the tub, then reaching across Maggie to grab the towel off its rack. He then stepped back and spread the towel wide, as though inviting Maggie to stand up and step into it.

"Give it to me!" she wailed, and with a desperate thrust of her arm, she managed to snare an edge of the towel and pull it into the tub. Molding the drenched fabric to her breasts and torso, she pleaded, "Get out!"

"I'm not the intruder here," he reminded her.

Maggie stared past him at her robe, hanging on the back of the door. Did she dare try to jump out of the tub and dash for the garment, knowing that the towel would cover only a portion of her body?

Idiot! He's already seen every inch of you! she taunted herself mercilessly. *You don't even know how long he's been standing there. What if he watched you blow bubbles, and giggle, and wash yourself? You put on a show for him, and you're still doing it! You can't lie here quivering under a towel, with your arms and legs naked to the world, forever. Do something!*

Daring to look him in the eye, she noticed that the anger had faded from his face, and she blessedly remembered the truth—that he wanted this to be over as desperately as she did. Behind those midnight blue eyes, twinkling with contempt, there lurked the soul of a hermit who wished only that this "intruder" would be gone from his life forever.

Silently thanking Denny for explaining it all to her, she summoned her courage and announced, "If you'll just turn around for a minute, I'll be gone before you know it."

The statement brought a grin to his handsome face. "So, you found your voice? I'm impressed, Maggie-Margaret. *Very impressed,*" he added, allowing his gaze to travel over her with methodical thoroughness.

He's pretending to lust after you, to frighten you, she reminded herself, trying to quell the panic that his ploy was successfully inducing. *Please don't let him manipulate you so easily.*

She could scream for Mrs. Blake, now that she'd "found" her voice. Or, she could stand up to this bully, once and for all. One time, to show him that his silly game had lost its effectiveness, and then he'd never bother her again.

And so she forced herself to respond to him in kind, by allowing her own gaze to travel slowly, from his dusty boots, up his long, lean legs, along his torso and finally, up to his chiseled face. Then she locked eyes with him and repeated, "Turn your back."

He was quiet for a moment, then to her relief, he did as she'd asked. Elated, she began to exit the tub, kneeling first, so that she could securely wrap the towel about her chest and hips. It was almost impossible to climb gracefully with both hands gripping the soaked fabric, but she managed finally to negotiate the slippery side of the tub, and to plant her feet firmly on the bath mat.

She was about to dart past him and grab her robe when he turned abruptly, then smiled at the sight of her standing there in her towel. "Do you remember what I told you the last time we met like this, Miss Gleason-O'Connor?" Stepping closer, he murmured, "I said that if it happened again, I'd consider it an invitation."

"Don't be tiresome," she replied, her voice more even than she had dared hope it could be under the circumstances.

He grinned, clearly surprised. "Tiresome? I'm losing my touch. That was supposed to arouse you, not bore you."

Maggie eyed him sternly. "It was supposed to frighten me, but it didn't. Because I now know the truth about you, and I'm no longer frightened by your tactics."

"I beg your pardon?"

"Sheriff Riordain told me everything."

"I see. And what is the 'truth' about me?"

She forced herself not to tug at the towel, despite the fact that it was beginning to slip lower on her breasts. He would see any such gesture as a sign that she was intimidated, and she had made too much progress to allow that to happen.

And so she locked eyes with him again and explained, "You have no interest whatsoever in associating with me, carnally or otherwise. In fact—" she stood straighter, more confident by the second, and informed him with a condescending smile—"if I were to try and seduce you at this moment, you would be grievously confused and dismayed."

"Is that so?"

She jutted her chin toward him, pleased that her fear of him had turned so easily to defiance. "Mrs. Blake suggested that I use this tub because she was dying fabric in the other one. I doubt if it will ever happen again. The library, however, is another matter."

"Oh?"

She nodded. "Don't expect to have it to yourself from here on out. There's more than enough room in there for both of us. I won't disturb *you,* and you won't disturb *me,* but we *will* co-exist."

"I see." He stepped closer, and then to her confused disbelief, he rested his hands on her hips. "It's fascinating to me that you believe a man—even a man like me—could resist this luscious body of yours. Shall we test your theory?"

She searched his eyes for any sign that he was bluffing, but saw no hint of discomfort. Instead, there was mockery, and behind that, a blaze of desire that danced like a blue flame before her. And to make matters worse, the pressure of his hands on the towel was straining against her own hold on it, whether by his design or just her sudden run of dismal luck.

She opened her mouth, fully intending to try one

last time to scold him, but no sound emerged, and she saw a flash of victory in his eyes that made her humiliation complete. Mortified, she wrenched herself away from him, then lunged for her robe, but the puddle that had formed at her feet from the dripping towel made the tile floor too slippery for such a move, and her feet began to sail out from under her.

"Careful there." He caught her easily, one hand under each of her arms, and steadied her as he'd done the day she'd fallen from the ladder. Only this time, rather than thin fabric, his rough hands contacted her skin, and the sensation confused her almost as fully as did his blue eyes.

"You're going to kill yourself one of these days, and then have the nerve to blame it on me," he was complaining with an irreverent grin.

"I hate you," she whispered, her voice now as weak as it had been strong.

She tried to wriggle away, but his grip tightened unexpectedly. "If you hate me, why do you keep undressing for me?"

"Be quiet!" She tried to pulled away again, and again he stopped her, his grip like iron.

Just when she was about to truly panic, he released his hold on her, then turned and retrieved her robe, handing it to her with a gesture of clear dismissal. "Run along, Maggie-Margaret, before Mrs. Blake finds out that she's housing a seductress."

It took her a minute to realize that he wasn't going to do anything to her, other than send her away. She was half-naked and vulnerable, and for an instant, she had actually been aroused by his magnetic eyes, yet he had no intention of taking advantage of the situation, because . . .

Because what Denny said was true. This man has no interest in you at all!

She wanted to gloat, or at least, to tell him she was no longer afraid of him, but her towel was slipping again, and she wasn't sure how long this renewed surge of confidence would last, so she clasped her pink robe to her chest and backed away from him until one foot contacted the wooden floor of the bedroom. Only then did she feel safe enough to do what she needed to do, so she summoned a no-nonsense tone and informed him, "Feel free to join me in the library this evening, if you're not too fatigued from your travels."

Then she turned and bolted away, past his bed, into the library, and up the back staircase, not pausing, even to catch her breath, until she was in her room again.

If only she had a door to slam, and a lock to turn, she might have been able to truly relax, but as it was, she had to force herself to breathe evenly as she sat on the edge of her bed and waited for her heart to stop pounding.

But at least she could smile. In fact, she was grinning from ear to ear! Because she had seen something in that second before she turned and ran from him. She had seen the flash of surprise in those vibrant blue eyes of his when she'd issued her bold invitation to join her in the library.

Bullies, she whispered in amused disgust as she donned her robe and fastened it securely into place. *They're never as tough as they seem.*

"Maggie?"

"Oh!" She laughed at herself, wondering when her nerves would settle down, and called out brightly, "Come in, Mrs. Blake."

The landlady gave her a sheepish smile as she pushed aside the curtain and proffered a cup of tea. "I was out of cinnamon, believe it or not, so I had to dash over to Gladys's, and she and I started chatting, and I forgot all about you. I told her you'd probably turn into a prune, but I can see you had sense enough not to wait for me."

Maggie resisted an impulse to scold the woman for having left her alone in a man's bathtub. Instead, she accepted the beverage and sipped it gratefully, glad for the comforting warmth. "This is delicious. Thank you."

"You'll never guess what's happened."

"Oh? What's that?"

"Mr. Coburn has returned. Isn't that the strangest coincidence? Thank goodness you weren't still in the bath when he walked in."

As Maggie stared, the landlady added brightly, "Can you imagine? That would have been quite a scene, wouldn't it?"

Without warning, Maggie started to laugh, gently at first, and then, as the full absurdity of the situation dawned on her, with such force that she almost spilled her tea. "Yes, that *would* be quite a scene."

"It really isn't funny, dear," Mrs. Blake scolded.

"I was just trying to imagine who would be more distressed—Mr. Coburn or myself."

A hint of a smile tugged at the corners of the landlady's mouth. "Some things are best not imagined, especially where men are concerned."

"And most especially where Mr. Coburn is concerned?"

"He's just a man like any other."

"Really?" Maggie grinned. "Does that mean you wouldn't mind fetching my hairbrush for me? I left it in his room."

When Mrs. Blake blanched, Maggie eyed her with playful disapproval. "He's just a man, for goodness sakes. Just explain to him that you were using the other tub for dying fabric. And remember to tell him that *you* use his tub frequently when he's gone."

The landlady's eyes began to twinkle. "He's out in the back, talking to the sheriff. Maybe I can sneak in and get it before he notices it. By all rights, I should make you get it yourself, since you're the one who left it there, but—"

"But I haven't time. I'm not even dressed, and the Fletchers will be arriving momentarily."

"The reverend! I'd forgotten all about—well, never mind. I'll be back in a moment with your brush, and I expect to see you wearing something other than a robe, young lady."

Maggie watched in fond amusement as Mrs. Blake bustled away, then her mood sobered. In a few short hours, she would be confronting Coburn again.

And this time, he would be expecting her.

Between her nervousness over the impending showdown in the library, and Reverend Fletcher's long-winded style of exhortation, Maggie was scarcely able to follow the conversation during dinner. Instead, she fidgeted and tried to think about more cheerful subjects, such as the progress her students had made, and the affection they had heaped upon her.

The situation grew even worse when the party moved to the parlor, where the loud "tick, tick, tick" of Eleanor Blake's ornate anniversary clock seemed to be taunting Maggie. Just when she thought it best to excuse herself and run upstairs for some panicked pacing, the subject of the Lawson boys came up.

Gladys Chesterton made the usual insulting remarks, and Maggie was saddened when even the reverend and his wife reluctantly agreed with the assessment, although the kind minister was quick to add, "As a community, we bear some responsibility in all this. We turned our backs on Jed Lawson in his hour of need, didn't we? He was always a mean fellow, but it was only when his wife died that his heart hardened completely, and those boys really began running wild. I've always wondered—"

"If *we* could have redeemed him?" Gladys shook her head in disgust. "What is it we should have done? Offered sympathy to him on her passing, knowing it was he who killed her?"

"We know no such thing."

"But really, Reverend." Mrs. Blake sighed in exaggerated disagreement. "I saw her once, right before the end, and both her eyes were bruised. She tried to hide it, but—well, you'll never convince me her death was an accident. Not with the history between those two."

Maggie shuddered. "You're saying the whole town believes Mr. Lawson killed his own wife?"

"That's right."

"But there's no proof," Reverend Fletcher added.

"Proof?" Gladys gave him a reproachful glare. "How much proof does a body need?"

"The sheriff said it was inconclusive," Mrs. Fletcher reminded her. "I agree with my husband. We all made judgments, based on our prejudices rather than facts."

"Do *you* believe it was an accident?" Mrs. Blake demanded.

Mrs. Fletcher hesitated before shrugging her shoulders. "We'll never know, will we? I'm just saying, it wasn't our place to judge him."

"She died three years ago," Maggie mused, remembering the dates she'd seen on Martha Lawson's headstone in the church cemetery. "Did he whip the children even before that?"

"Not to the extent he does now," the reverend replied. "He's been hardest on little Joey—probably because he looks so much like his mother."

"It's so distressing." Maggie chose the next words cautiously. "You say the town turned their backs on him when he needed community support? Has anyone tried since then?"

It was Mrs. Fletcher who answered. "We've invited them to dinner several times, but Jed just snorts and says he doesn't have any use for our kind. *Or* our God."

"Gracious sakes alive," Mrs. Blake whispered. "It makes it hard to feel pity for him, doesn't it?"

"We'll keep trying," the reverend said. But Maggie could see from his expression that he held no hope for success. Her heart went out to him, knowing that his concern for Jed Lawson was sincere, as were his fears for the boys' futures.

She shared those fears, especially in light of this conversation, and as she'd done so many times over the past weeks, she struggled to imagine how she could best help.

"We've upset Maggie," Mamie Lowe scolded the group.

"I'm not upset. Just a bit preoccupied, I'm afraid. I haven't finished preparing tomorrow's lesson. In fact, if you'll all excuse me, I'd really best take care of that right away. I've enjoyed this visit immensely."

"You spend too much time alone in that tiny room of yours," Francine told her gently.

"Actually, I plan on spending the next few hours in the library, not my room."

"But, Maggie . . ." Mrs. Blake eyed her with clear surprise. "Aren't you forgetting? Mr. Coburn has returned."

"Yes, I know. He and I had a nice chat about it,

and he agrees with me that we can share the library in companionable silence. Isn't that nice?"

"You chatted? When exactly was *that?*"

Maggie tried to smile despite her own growing doubts. "We spoke briefly before dinner. I'm surprised you didn't notice."

"So am I. You're saying he actually agreed to this?"

"How could he not?"

"How indeed?" Reverend Fletcher smiled. "I'm sure he's secretly delighted at the prospect of sharing the library with an intelligent and beautiful girl. What man wouldn't be?"

"Well, I wouldn't go so far as to say he's delighted," Maggie said with a rueful smile. "But he couldn't really refuse, as I said. So if you'll all excuse me?"

"Certainly." The Fletchers rose and each embraced her in turn, with the reverend assuring her, "I meant what I said earlier, Maggie. The parents rave about you constantly, and the children have never seemed happier. You've brightened the life of each and every member of our town."

"And now, you can brighten Mr. Coburn's," Mamie said with an impish grin. "You must be sure to tell us all about it at breakfast."

Maggie suppressed a laugh, suspecting that the elderly woman knew exactly what was going on, despite her foggy behavior. It would be fun to talk to her about the whole silly business one day, far into the future, when the incessant confrontations with Coburn had finally died away. But for now, she needed to gather her wits about her, summon her most confident smile, and hurry to the library before she lost her nerve completely.

Eight

"Good evening, Mr. Coburn."

"Miss O'Connor."

He didn't looked up from his book, and his tone was dismissive, but Maggie was too relieved to feel slighted, so she quickly took her seat on the sofa and opened her lesson book without glancing again in his direction. The only sound in the room, aside from the crackling of the fire, was the occasional rustle of pages as the two bookworms pursued their solitary quests.

Then to her surprise, he was on his feet. Taking two steps toward her, he murmured, "Have a nice evening, Miss O'Connor."

She opened her mouth to speak, but no sound emerged, and then he was gone. She tried to feel victorious, or at least relieved, but instead, her every instinct told her to run after him—to offer to leave in his stead, so that he could reclaim his rightful place by the fire.

Why? she asked herself in confusion. She had as much right as he to the library, yet deep inside, she knew it meant more to him than to her. It was Coburn's refuge from something—something horrible, perhaps—or, more likely, just from loneliness. And while it was a refuge for Maggie, too, she suspected his need was infinitely greater.

She even walked over to his bedroom door and stood there, her knuckles poised to knock, for a long, indecisive minute. But what would she say to him?

Forgive me, Mr. Coburn. I had no intention of ruining your evening. Please don't retire on my account. I'm leaving now, and I shan't burden you again with my unwelcome presence.

You're a fool, she chided herself suddenly. *Do you suppose that speech will touch or reassure him? More likely, he'll laugh in your face. Or worse, he'll accuse you of coming to his bedroom with sinful thoughts on your mind!*

She could almost hear his mocking tone, and feel his disrespectful gaze traveling over her. It was true— he would use the opportunity to humiliate her, as he'd done every other time they'd been alone together.

"I'll not make it easy on you, sir," she informed him proudly under her breath as she dropped her hand to her side and backed away from his door. Then, with a defiant toss of her head, she returned to the sofa and lost herself in her reading.

The following evening, the drama replayed itself, although this time, when Coburn left after only five minutes, bidding her a quiet "Good evening," she managed to smile and reply in kind, her tone cordial but distant. On the third evening, he surprised her by greeting her as soon as she entered the room, although his tone was absentminded and he still didn't lift his gaze from his reading. She was even certain he stayed a bit longer, by a matter of minutes, than he'd done on the previous evenings.

Like a wild stallion . . .

She was beginning to see the truth in Denny's analogy—Coburn, the magnificent lone animal, needing no one, and suspicious of even the slightest overture. Yet the library was his pasture, and Maggie had proved that she was willing to keep her distance, and so bit by bit, he was learning to accept her presence.

One day, perhaps he'll even take a lump of sugar from your hand, she teased herself on the fifth night of their new arrangement, as she watched him add a log to the blazing fire. *Perhaps he'll even allow you to pet his mane!*

It was a silly thought, and somewhat naughty, too, she had to admit. Coburn's jet-black hair was so wavy and lustrous, she felt slightly giddy as she imagined how it would feel to sift it through her fingers.

If he knew you were having such thoughts, he'd run off to his room and you wouldn't see him again for weeks.

Or would he? She couldn't help but wonder, remembering the feel of his hands on her hips that confusing afternoon in his bathroom. Hadn't there been a moment when his eyes had blazed, and his fingers had tightened their grasp, and she had been certain he was about to pull her naked body flush against his own? And the afternoon when he'd caught her in his arms when she fell from the ladder—hadn't that provoked something from him? His eyes had blazed that day, too—

"Stop it," she pleaded with herself, and to her mortified surprise, she realized she had spoken these last two words aloud.

Coburn turned from the fire and studied her with evident curiosity. "I beg your pardon?"

"Nothing. It was just . . . well, I was so deep in thought, I forgot someone else was in the room."

He grinned. "Interesting trick. I wish you could teach it to me."

She knew he had just insulted her, but at least he was smiling for the first time since her invasions had begun, so she decided not to object, and returned instead to her reading. She was almost certain she heard him chuckle softly, and to her embarrassed delight, the sound sent a shiver through her body. Desperate to keep her gaze fixed on the pages of her book, she was nevertheless dying to know if he was staring at her with those magnetic blue eyes. Perhaps he, too, was beginning to have harmless fantasies about this new acquaintanceship!

"The fire should last for a few hours now. Enjoy your book, Miss O'Connor. I'll see you tomorrow night."

"Oh! You're leaving?" Again she locked gazes with him and, without thinking, she insisted, "You needn't—at least, not on my account. I'm willing to be the one to leave tonight, if you'd like."

She knew instantly that she had made a crucial mistake. His expression hardened, and there was almost a sneer in his voice as he assured her, "I have an appointment, Maggie-Margaret. Would you like to know with whom, and for what purpose?"

"Of course not. I'm sorry I said anything."

"Apparently, you can't help yourself."

"Apparently not," she agreed with an apologetic smile.

A familiar twinkle lit his eyes. "If you're asking me to stay, perhaps you'd care to offer some incentive?"

"That's enough." She arched an eyebrow in warning. "Go to your appointment, or stay and read. But please don't be tiresome."

He chuckled, then strode to his bedroom, returning

in less than a minute with his long coat draped over his arm, his holster and hat in hand. "You're welcome to come along to the saloon if you'd like. The jacks would love a chance to meet you. You're all they talk about these days—did you know that?"

Maggie yawned. "Are you going to shoot someone?"

"My appointment is with a woman, and if she pleases me, I'll let her live."

Maggie yawned again, determined not to let him see that his teasing was having an effect. "You mustn't keep her waiting, then. Good night, sir."

"Good night, Maggie-Margaret."

Maintaining her cool expression until she heard the sound of boots clambering down the back steps, she then closed her book and stared into the fire he'd built for her, sighing loudly as she considered the peculiar choice both she and Coburn had made—to spend their nights alone with a roomful of books, rather than in the company of a lover.

"Of course, he *has* a lover," she reminded herself, but she knew he didn't have more than a passing affection for the woman. Or rather, the women—a houseful of them, if Denny's reports were accurate.

In any case, Maggie was glad he had reminded her about his illicit relationships. Now she wouldn't need to feel so sorry for him anymore. He wasn't quite as lonely and cut-off from the rest of the human race as she had feared. In fact, he probably had everything he needed or wanted: books, solitude, money, women, and a friend—a sheriff, no less—to "watch his back."

"But not love," she mused. "I suppose that's the difference between males and females. For a man, physical pleasure can be quite enough, even without depth of commitment or shared dreams."

And for the first time in her life, she found herself

seriously wondering if it could be enough for a
woman. Was June right? Should she consider taking
a lover one day?

Banishing the scandalous thought, she forced herself to return to her reading, although the room was
now uncomfortably warm, thanks to Coburn.

Maggie couldn't get the Lawson family out of her
mind, and was determined to find a way to draw them
slowly back into the Shasta Falls community. After a
week of careful strategizing, she realized that the so-
lution was right in front of her eyes. She had been
invited for dinner at the home of every one of her
students, other than the Lawson boys, hadn't she? Why
not take matters into her own hands and invite herself
to their place? Of course, Jed Lawson might not take
to the idea as quickly as she might like, so she decided
to arrive unannounced.

But not empty-handed, and so she rushed home
from school one beautiful spring day, intent upon bak-
ing Sugar Berry Pie, a tender-crusted delicacy that her
father and brothers had always adored. The recipe had
come from a cookbook her mother reportedly used as
a young bride, making the dessert even more beloved,
and therefore, perfect for this all-important "dinner
with the teacher."

Locating Mrs. Blake in the kitchen, she noted with
relief that the oven was free, and asked breathlessly,
"Would you mind if I bake a pie? I'll make two, in
fact, so there's plenty for everyone here, too, and I'll
clean up everything until it shines. Please?"

"If you'd like pie, dear, just ask. I'd love to bake
one. The peaches aren't quite ready, but there are ap-
ricots."

"It's not for me. I'm joining the Lawsons for dinner

tonight, and I thought I'd bring dessert. Something I made for them myself." Alarmed by the landlady's ashen face, she added quickly, "I shouldn't have suggested it. It's your kitchen, and of course you don't want anyone usurping it. I'll just bring them something else."

"It's not the pie, dear. I simply can't believe you'd consider going to that awful man's house. Haven't you heard what a brute he is? We told you all about it last week—he killed his own wife! And he beats those boys of his—"

"Yet we all allow them to eat supper with him every night," Maggie reminded her. "And yes, I've heard all about him. It's time I saw for myself, so I can try to help the boys. Mr. Lawson won't harm me. He has no reason to do such a thing."

"Jed Lawson doesn't need a reason. I forbid it, Maggie."

Maggie smiled and gave the landlady a quick peck on the cheek. "You're sweet. But I'll be fine. I shouldn't have mentioned it."

"Maggie, please—Oh! Mr. Coburn! Thank goodness you're here. Maybe *you* can talk some sense into her."

Maggie spun toward Coburn, who had just entered by the back door and was already scowling, presumably because of his landlady's attempt to involve him in domestic politics. He arched an eyebrow in tentative warning. "I beg your pardon?"

"Maggie's intent on going out to the Lawson place for supper. I've tried to tell her it's dangerous, but—well, you of all people know how stubborn she can be when she gets her heart set on something."

Maggie winced. "Mrs. Blake, please. There's no reason to involve Mr. Coburn. I apologize, sir. You have my assurance that the subject is closed."

To her surprise, Coburn began to laugh. "It's ironic, isn't it, Eleanor? You've been filling the parlor with polite, gentle suitors, only to discover the truth: our Miss O'Connor is attracted to danger and excitement. And so, Jed Lawson—"

"Be quiet!" Maggie ordered.

He grinned again and assured Mrs. Blake, "I was teasing, of course. And I agree with you completely. Miss O'Connor can't go up there alone." Turning to Maggie, he added simply, "If you're intent on meeting the murderous bastard, take Sheriff Riordain with you for protection."

"That's a wonderful idea," Mrs. Blake said with an enthusiastic smile. "You always know just what to say, Mr. Coburn."

Maggie shook her head. "The sheriff and Mr. Lawson don't get along. And I didn't take a lawman to any of the other dinners I've had with my students. It would be an insult to the Lawsons, and completely uncalled for."

"Then take Waller with you. From what I've heard, he's love-starved enough to consider even *this* a romantic rendezvous."

Maggie glared again. "I appreciate the advice, Mr. Coburn. Don't let us detain you."

Coburn laughed. "I won't be home for dinner either, Eleanor. While Miss O'Connor tries to tame a beast, I'll be doing the same with a she-cat."

"Mr. Coburn!" the landlady said with a gasp. "What's gotten into you this afternoon?"

"Spring, I suppose. And having someone like Miss O'Connor around to keep us amused. Good afternoon, ladies." With a mocking bow, he headed for his bedroom.

Mrs. Blake stared after him. "I've never seen him in such good spirits."

At my expense, Maggie replied in silent disgust.

"He's right, you know, dear. Kirk would be happy to escort you anywhere, even to the Lawson cabin."

"I'm going alone. And I'd appreciate it if you didn't mention it to anyone else. Especially not the sheriff. If you do, I'll be very hurt and offended." Eyeing the older woman coolly, she added, "A person should be able to confide in her landlady—her friend—without it becoming the talk of the town. And *don't* tell Gladys."

"I won't. I promise."

Maggie pulled her into a reassuring hug. "He has no reason to hurt me. And the boys will be there to protect me. And if he is the least bit insulting or threatening, I promise I'll leave immediately. Now . . ." She gave her landlady a hopeful smile. "Are we going to bake pies, or aren't we?"

Years earlier, Maggie's brother Brian had insisted she learn to ride a horse, and while it had been quite some time since she'd done so—and never alone!—she decided to approach the owner of the livery stable in the hopes of securing a gentle beast and a sidesaddle. As happened constantly in Shasta Falls, the man cooperated enthusiastically, although he wouldn't hear of taking money from the schoolteacher.

To her delight, a pretty brown quarter horse named Buttercup proved to be the perfect mount, and with the simple directions Mrs. Blake had provided, Maggie soon found herself at the Lawson cabin. Everything was tidy, she noted with quiet satisfaction. Not the premises of a madman or butcher after all. Exhaling sharply, she realized she'd been terrified, and with a toss of her braided hair, she rebuked her landlady and Coburn for having made her so wary.

Sliding off Buttercup, she tethered her to a fence rail just as the door to the cabin burst open and little Joey came careening toward her, his arms opened wide and his face glowing. "Miz O'Connor! You're visiting me!"

"I most certainly am." She dropped to her knees and embraced him. "I wasn't sure if I'd be welcome, but just look at you. I think my heart's going to burst."

"Burst? Do you need a cup of water?"

Maggie laughed lightly. "It's just an expression, sweetie. Here, give me another hug, then climb up there on my new friend Buttercup and see what's in that package."

"A present?"

"A pie."

"Pie?" He spoke the word reverently. "That's better than a present. We never have pie, 'cept when the reverend makes us visit him."

"Well, then . . ." Maggie rumpled his hair. "Does this mean I can stay for dinner?"

"Here? With us?"

"If it's not too much trouble."

"It might be trouble," the boy told her solemnly. "Pa doesn't like company. And today's worser, 'cause he got in a fight with some jacks, and it put him in a bad mood."

"Oh, dear. It does sound as though I should come back another time. On the other hand . . ." She studied him anxiously. "Wouldn't it be nice if I could cheer him up a little? Nice for you boys, I mean?"

She watched him struggle with the concept, wishing she could tell him the truth: she wanted to stay to protect him and his brothers. *Come back another time?* Not likely. She was here, she had a pie, and she was staying. Unless of course, Jed Lawson threw her out.

The door opened again, and this time, it was Patrick

who approached, at a much less frantic pace than his younger brother had. "Howdy, Miz O'Connor."

"She's here for supper," Joey explained. "She brought pie. I told her Pa was in a bad mood—"

"Pa says you should come on inside."

"Oh?" Maggie exhaled sharply. "Well, that settles it, then. I've been looking forward to meeting him, and it seems the sentiment is mutual."

"Huh?"

"I'd love to come inside and meet your father. Shall we?" She crooked her arms impishly, and was pleased when each blushed and took hold of an elbow, leading her straight up to the threshold, where they paused and exchanged wary glances.

"It will be fine," she assured them in a whisper. "You have my word."

Patrick gave her an apologetic smile. "If Pa talks mean to you, it's just because his ribs hurt."

"And his face," Joey added. "And his gut. And most all the rest of him, too."

"Pardon?"

"Those jacks hurt him real bad."

"Oh, dear. It sounds dreadful."

"It's hard for him to breathe," Patrick explained carefully. "But it keeps him from yelling, so that's good. For you, and for us."

"Has the doctor been here?"

Patrick shook his head. "Junior wanted to send for him, but Pa said not to."

"I see." Maggie straightened her shoulders, prepared for the worst, and pushed open the door, then stepped into the cozy main room of the small cabin.

It was cleaner than she had expected. Immaculate, in fact. And nicely decorated, with bright yellow gingham curtains at the window, and some lovely needlepoint samplers on the walls. Junior was at the stove, frying something in a pan—although his gaze was trained in Maggie's direction. There was a message in those big brown eyes of his, and while she didn't want to over-dramatize the situation, she was fairly certain he was telling her to run back to town.

On the far side of the room, in front of a smoldering fireplace, sat a man in a rocking chair. Creaking, back and forth, while studying Maggie through eyes swollen from the recent beating. It was clear that no part of his face had gone untouched, and while he sat fairly straight in his chair, she remembered what Patrick had said about his ribs, and imagined that the effort was painful.

"Mr. Lawson? I'm Maggie O'Connor, the boys' teacher."

"If I could stand, I would."

"Yes, I'm certain of that." She moved closer and murmured impulsively, "You must let me send for the doctor. Or at least, let me have a look—"

"Keep your distance!"

She jumped back. "I didn't mean to intrude. I'm just so furious that those awful jacks did this to you."

"They look worse than I do, so save your sympathy for someone who needs it."

"Bullies," Maggie said in quiet disgust.

"And cowards, right, Pa?" Joey asked.

"Shut up," the father advised dryly.

"Miz O'Connor brought pie," Patrick interjected. "She wants to eat with us. Can she, Pa?"

"She can do what she pleases. Serve her up some of those eggs, Junior."

"And then we'll have the pie," Patrick agreed. "It smells real good, Pa."

"I'm not hungry. Just get the dangblasted meal over with so I can get some rest."

The tension in the room was growing by the second,

and Maggie knew the boys wouldn't be able to eat under such conditions, so she summoned her cheeriest smile and announced, "Your father is absolutely right, boys. The last thing you need now is company. I'm going to go back to the boardinghouse so he can get his rest. And once he's all better, perhaps you'll invite me back. In the meantime, I hope you like the pie. And, Mr. Lawson? I'm so very, very glad to have finally met you. You have three wonderful sons, and I love having them in my class."

Lawson eyed her with suspicion. "They don't give you trouble?"

"Never. In fact, they're my unofficial protectors. I feel very safe when the Lawsons are around. And they work hard at their studies. You should be very proud of them."

"I don't need you to tell me what I should think and feel."

"That's true. Get some rest. I'll say a prayer for you."

"Don't." He had snapped the word out, and now seemed to regret it. "It looks worse than it is. Save your prayers for someone who needs 'em."

"Now *you're* telling *her* what to think, Pa," Joey observed cheerfully. "After you just told her—"

"It's just an expression, darling," Maggie interrupted, fearful that the boy would draw his father's infamous wrath. "Walk me to the door now, won't you?"

"Wait," Lawson ordered her, then turned his attention toward the kitchen. "Junior, you go with the teacher. See she gets home safe, then get right back here."

"Sure, Pa." Junior seemed delighted, whether because it gave him a chance to get out of the cabin and away from the tension, or because Maggie—the source of the tension—was finally leaving.

"Well, then . . ." Maggie dropped to one knee and pulled Joey into a quick embrace. "I'll see you tomorrow." Standing, she rumpled Patrick's hair. "You, too."

"We can't go to school tomorrow, Miz O'Connor. We've gotta stay here and take care of Pa," Patrick objected.

"Oh, I see." Maggie gave Jed Lawson a hopeful smile. "Perhaps they could take turns?"

His nod was so stiff, Maggie knew it caused him pain, whether in his swollen jaw or, more likely, the shoulder he held at such an odd height, as though it was not quite in its socket.

Those cowardly jacks, she reminded herself, suddenly furious. *Why must there be so many bullies in the world?*

Then she remembered that Jed Lawson was the biggest bully of all. And the irony of his beating at the hands of other louts was that, for the next few weeks, he wasn't going to be able to whip his own sons as efficiently as usual.

That, at least, was a relief, and so Maggie was able to smile as she again bade farewell to the two younger boys, then followed Junior back out into the yard, where Buttercup was patiently waiting.

Later, as she curled up on the library sofa and tried to read, she couldn't get Jed Lawson out of her mind. Having met him under such unusual circumstances, she couldn't really judge him, but considering the fact that he'd been in severe pain, he hadn't been uncommonly rude to Maggie, who, after all, had shown up uninvited, expecting to be fed and entertained.

He tried to be civil, she decided finally. *At most,*

he was curt. Which either means he isn't as bad as everyone says, or the pain was so intense, he couldn't muster the strength to be his usual self.

Either way, she decided to take it as a blessing. The boys, at least, had been glad to see her, and would probably enjoy the pie. And while Junior had been silent on the short ride together, he hadn't seemed unhappy or apprehensive. Just preoccupied, which made sense in light of his father's serious condition.

"So?" a voice boomed from the doorway, interrupting her reverie.

Maggie jumped, then arched an eyebrow in reproach as Coburn ambled into the room without bothering to take off his long, dusty coat or his black leather gloves.

"Good evening, sir."

He grinned. "Don't keep me in suspense. How was your romantic rendezvous with the town bully?"

"That's quite enough."

"No wedding bells?"

She glared, then turned her attention back to her reading.

"It's ironic, isn't it? You throw yourself at malevolent strangers who aren't interested in a pretty little virgin. But the parade of gentlemen who would die for you leaves you cold."

Apparently, he wasn't going to stop teasing her, so she closed her book and sighed. "You know very well I'm not interested in Mr. Lawson, or any other malevolent strangers. I went to that cabin because I'm concerned for my students' welfare."

"And? Did he live up to his reputation? Did you witness any whippings firsthand?"

"That isn't funny," Maggie told him quietly. "And the truth is—"

"Go on."

She grimaced but continued. "You'll enjoy this, given your love of irony. Mr. Lawson himself has been the victim of a rather vicious beating, and so, for the next few weeks at least, the boys shan't be touched."

Coburn cocked his head to the side. "Did the older boy do it? It was only a matter of time before he stopped letting his old man treat him like a dog."

Maggie inhaled sharply. "Junior would never do such a thing."

"Why not? It would be self-defense, wouldn't it?"

"I don't know. It's inconceivable. A boy, hurting his own—" She gasped again, this time because she had suddenly remembered a warm summer's night, a birthday celebration, and a boy so bitter and twisted that he actually pointed a gun at the head of the man who had raised him.

Brian's blood had been all over the table, and all over Maggie, and she had lunged for that pistol, believing for that instant that anything, even the shattering effects of a bullet, would be better than being alive. Either way, she had known she would be in eternal pain from that moment onward. And Brian was gone, and Ian was lost, so what reason was there to live?

"Maggie?" Coburn touched her shoulder. "Is something wrong?"

She flinched, uncomfortable with the feel of his gloved hand, and even more uncomfortable with having let him witness her distress. "It's nothing. I was just remembering Mr. Lawson's bruised face. It's not something Junior could do. In fact, it took a gang of men to do it. Brutish, cowardly lumberjacks who have probably never had a fair fight in their lives."

"So? Lawson was the victim of brutes? And you tended his wounds? Romantic."

"That's enough." She shook her head, then explained softly, "In his own way, he was rather gallant. He insisted on having Junior escort me home."

"And that passes for gallantry in your imagination? You, who reads *Ivanhoe* with such rapt enjoyment? I suppose that fits. He's the injured knight, and you're his nurse. Which one, though? Rowena or Rebecca?"

It surprised her to know Alex Coburn actually paid attention to what she was reading, and she realized with a start that he was behaving completely out of character. He had even tried to comfort her when her thoughts had turned to Ian! Without thinking, she said, "I've never seen you in such good spirits. Has something happened? I don't mean to pry," she added quickly.

"You have a right to know, since you're the cause of my good spirits."

"I am?" She flushed. "In what way?"

"You've turned your romantic attentions toward Lawson, and now I can read and bathe in peace without fear of molestation."

"Oh, for goodness sakes!" She knew her cheeks were crimson. "Either go sit in your chair and read, or go to your room. I have lessons to plan, and no time for foolish insults."

He grinned, completely unrepentant. "My room it is, then. Enjoy your evening alone, Maggie-Margaret. I'll see you tomorrow."

As soon as he had closed the door to his bedroom, Maggie jumped to her feet and began to pace, furious and confused. What sort of bizarre relationship did he have in mind now?

The silence that had permeated their first few nights of sharing the library had been uncomfortable, but bearable. This, on the other hand, was completely unacceptable. Rather than developing a morsel of genuine regard for her, Coburn had apparently decided to use her as the object of his heartless, soulless wit.

To him, the thought of you out there, in the cabin of a brute, is comical! Lawson beats his sons, and may even have murdered his own wife, yet Coburn finds it all amusing. At your expense!

She tried to settle herself down, reminding herself that a great measure of what she was feeling was simple embarrassment. She had been flattered that he'd noticed her love for *Ivanhoe,* and had believed for a moment that he was beginning to regard her as a friend.

Is that what's really bothering you? she accused herself. *After all he's said and done, do you actually harbor hopes of becoming friends with him? How very foolish of you, Maggie. Or should I say, Maggie-Margaret?*

Chagrined, although mostly with herself, she scooped up her books and headed for her room where, for the first time in weeks, she allowed herself to think about Ian, if only because she knew such thoughts could distract her completely from the memory of Coburn's laughing face. And Lawson's bruised face. And Joey, his eyes wide with disbelief at the sight of her.

So many new faces, and to her amazement, she couldn't push them out of her mind, no matter how hard she tried. Even the image of Ian, bursting into the kitchen that dreadful evening, could not dominate her imagination for long.

It was an oddly comforting discovery, confirming for her that her decision to come to Shasta Falls had been a wise one. She had wanted a new life, filled with new memories to chase away the old ones, and apparently, she had found herself an abundance of them!

All in all, she had nothing to complain about, so she snuggled under her baby quilt and soon managed to find herself sweet dreams.

Nine

Maggie's faith in the healing powers of Shasta Falls continued to grow over the next week, as she watched the reverend and his wife organize a campaign to ensure that the Lawson family was well fed during Jed's convalescence. Mrs. Blake and June, among others, put aside their prejudices and rallied to their neighbor's aid, and the effects were evident to Maggie almost immediately.

The boys, who took turns coming to school as promised, seemed lighter of spirit than usual, especially Junior. And Joey confirmed her observations by telling her, "Pa acts different."

"Oh? In what way?"

"Well, he can't hit us, 'cause his ribs are busted and his shoulder's all swoll up. But I don't think he even wants to."

"Oh?"

"Yeah. I guess he likes us 'cause we're taking care of him, and not acting bad. Yesterday, he said I was a good boy."

Maggie struggled not to let him see how much his words had affected her. "That's good, Joey."

"Yeah. He's surprised about all the food. So are we. It's real good. But not as good as your pie," he assured her quickly.

"Did he ever let the doctor look at his injuries?"

"Nah. Pa hates Doc Hudson."

"Oh? Do you know why?"

"He says if the doc had took better care of Ma, she'd still be alive. But that's what some folks say about Pa, so I figure . . ." He paused, then told her simply, "No one should say that about no one, 'cause it's mean, and I don't think it's true."

"People should be very careful what they say about others," Maggie agreed. "I'm sorry you had to learn that this way, but it's a valuable lesson."

"Yeah. I'm learning a lot. 'Cause of you."

"Thank you." She kissed his cheek. "Go run and play with the others now, sweetie."

He grinned—a semi-toothless grin that made her heart ache—and then raced toward the larger of the oak trees, which he climbed expertly. Maggie stared after him for a while, then sighed and turned her attention back to the lesson she was planning for the afternoon.

When she opened her lesson book to review her notes, a small, folded piece of paper slipped out of the pages and onto the floor. She picked it up, intrigued by its rough edges. Then she smiled as she read the sing-song verse that some unknown hand had recorded there for her to find.

> I like watching you
> I hope you like me to
> Don't be cross
> Don't be scared
> Just be mine, all the time

Maggie tried not to grin too broadly, in case her poet-admirer was watching from afar. Apparently, one of her students had become infatuated with her, and while she knew it was silly, she found it amazingly flattering.

Her brother Brian had developed a similar passion for a piano teacher, and while Maggie had teased him mercilessly, she had also been impressed by the magnitude of his devotion. Was one of her students feeling that same queasy, giddy, confused euphoria? If so, she certainly hadn't noticed it.

Vowing to be more observant, she reread the poem and decided that it was impressive, given the young age of the anonymous writer. And while she knew she shouldn't waste too much time on such foolishness, she couldn't help going down a list of her male students in her head, trying to guess who had become enamored of her.

Joshua Deighton was a definite possibility. Quiet, reserved, adorable, and just the same age Brian had been when he'd been hit by Cupid's little arrow. But she'd heard a rumor that Josh was madly in love with the daughter of Randall Simmons, the owner of the logging camp. The daughter, Julia, attended boarding school in Boston, but from all accounts, had sworn herself to Josh, and he to her, the previous summer.

One of the Lawson boys? That would be both flattering and heartbreaking. And it would be important for Maggie to handle it just right, especially given the family's current circumstances.

That's enough foolishness, she scolded herself finally. There would be time enough to solve this mystery in the wee hours of the night, when she needed a distraction from Coburn's moods.

Not that he'd been annoying these last few days. In fact, he had reverted to his old habit of ignoring her. But at least he didn't seem to object to her company. He rarely retired before midnight, and hadn't left abruptly on any other "appointments," or at least not

Introducing Ballad,
A LINE OF HISTORICAL ROMANCES

*A*s a lover of historical romance, you'll adore Ballad Romances. Written by today's most popular romance authors, every book in the Ballad line is not only an individual story, but part of a two to six book series as well. You can look forward to 4 new titles each month – each taking place at a different time and place in history.

But don't take our word for how wonderful these stories are! Accept our introductory shipment of 4 Ballad Romance novels – a $23.96 value – ABSOLUTELY FREE – and see for yourself!

*O*nce you've experienced your first 4 Ballad Romances, we're sure you'll want to continue receiving these wonderful historical romance novels each month – without ever having to leave your home – using our convenient and inexpensive home subscription service. Here's what you get for joining:

- *4 BRAND NEW Ballad Romances delivered to your door each month*

- *30% off the cover price with your home subscription.*

- *A FREE monthly newsletter filled with author interviews, book previews, special offers, and more!*

- *No risk or obligation…you're free to cancel whenever you wish… no questions asked.*

Passion-
Adventure-
Excitement-
Romance-
Ballad!

*T*o start your membership, simply complete and return the card provided. You'll receive your Introductory Shipment of 4 FREE Ballad Romances. Then, each month, as long as your account is in good standing, you will receive the 4 newest Ballad Romances. Each shipment will be yours to examine for 10 days. If you decide to keep the books, you'll pay the preferred home subscriber's price – a savings of 30% off the cover price! (plus shipping & handling) If you want us to stop sending books, just say the word…it's that simple.

A $23.96 value – **FREE** No obligation to buy anything – ever.
4 **FREE BOOKS** are waiting for you! Just mail in the certificate below!

BOOK CERTIFICATE

Yes! Please send me 4 Ballad Romances ABSOLUTELY FREE! After my
introductory shipment, I will receive 4 new Ballad Romances each month to
preview FREE for 10 days (as long as my account is in good standing). If I decide
to keep the books, I will pay the money-saving preferred publisher's price plus
shipping and handling. That's 30% off the cover price. I may return the shipment
within 10 days and owe nothing, and I may cancel my subscription at any time. The
4 FREE books will be mine to keep in any case.

Name _____

Address _____ Apt. _____

City _____ State _____ Zip _____

Telephone (___) _____

Signature _____

(If under 18, parent or guardian must sign)

All orders subject to approval by Zebra Home Subscription Service.
Terms and prices subject to change. Offer valid only in the U.S.

DN042A

Passion...
Adventure...
Excitement...
Romance...

Get 4
Ballad
Historical
Romance
Novels
FREE!

ll..l...lll....lll.ll.l.ll.l.ll.l.l.lll.l.lll..l

BALLAD ROMANCES
Zebra Home Subscription Service, Inc.
P.O. Box 5214
Clifton NJ 07015-5214

PLACE
STAMP
HERE

to Maggie's knowledge. Companionable silence—that had been the sum total of their second week in the library.

If only Maggie could have returned the favor and ignored *him,* but she was woefully unsuccessful in her efforts. He fascinated her with his ability to concentrate completely on whatever he was doing. She could often tell from his expression just how deeply moved he was by something he was reading, and sometimes, when he was jotting notes in his worn leather journal, she knew for certain that he was a million miles away, completely unaware of the fact that another human being was in the room.

At some point, she had been forced to admit to herself that he was the handsomest man she'd ever seen in her life. And even in her imagination, Ivanhoe notwithstanding, she hadn't ever dreamed a man could have so intense a physical effect on her from clear across the room.

And June Riordain had made matters worse, with her constant talk about men. If she wasn't trying to dazzle Maggie with some romantic moment she'd shared with Denny, she was expounding on her newest inspiration: if Maggie was dead set on never marrying, she should at least take a lover.

According to June, Maggie could travel to San Francisco, on the pretense of visiting Father James, and find herself a handsome, wealthy widower—"not too old, mind you, but experienced in pleasing women"—and begin a lifelong affair that could accommodate the proclivities of both participants.

Maggie secretly enjoyed the fantasy, especially as June told it. She was slowly beginning to regard June as the sister she had never had, the friend she had never allowed. She even suspected that images of Ian had become less haunting because June had so graciously allowed her to tell the story in all its unhappy detail. And then, wonder of wonders, June hadn't judged Ian harshly!

But to Maggie's amusement, Coburn was not accorded the same privilege. The mere mention of the handsome recluse's name sent June into conniptions, and so Maggie refrained from telling her how, more and more, night after night, she had begun to see Coburn as the epitome of masculinity. The fact that he could wield a gun, yet also give himself over to a love sonnet—and that either experience made his blue eyes blaze—had captured Maggie's imagination.

A poet-warrior of the Gaelic tradition, she had decided wistfully. She had heard her father and his friends tell of such men—in hushed tones, only half-believing, but fervently hoping that somewhere in the past, such men had traveled the length of Ireland, imbuing the land itself with power and mystery.

Of course, they probably treated women with a bit more courtesy, she complained to herself as she studied her inattentive companion late one night. *Some poet-warrior—he's just a beast with a love of books. If you want poetry, you must turn to your secret admirer for sustenance.*

She searched through her belongings until she found the love notes. The second had arrived that very afternoon, and this time, had been accompanied by a deep red rose, pressed into the pages of her lesson book along with the letter, which read:

> I love looking at you.
> When I don't see you
> I'm not me.
> When I see you
> I'm me.
> That's why I love looking at you.

Maggie sighed. As much as she enjoyed these little notes, she had to admit that this one bothered her just a bit. In some ways, it seemed too sophisticated for a child, but since it had presumably been written by one of her students, and her oldest male student was fourteen, she had to assume it was simply someone advanced for his years.

Unfortunately, while she had many bright children in her class, none actually fit the description "advanced." Did that mean one of her students had a sophisticated talent for poetry, but Maggie was not astute enough to recognize, much less nurture, it?

"What's that?"

Maggie looked up, startled by the sound of Coburn's voice, and by the concomitant attention. "Pardon?"

"You're staring at that piece of paper. What is it?"

She coughed lightly—an excuse to study the situation for a moment. Had he been watching her? Why? Perhaps she had underestimated his awareness of her? Or, more realistically, perhaps he had glanced up for a moment, and had been annoyed to see that she was puzzling over a simple piece of paper.

She was about to scold him—to suggest he return to his own reading and not bother himself with the private business of others—when it occurred to her that he knew much more about poetry than she. Countless times, over the last two weeks, she had noted that he was reading sonnets, or other collections of verse. Not that she'd been paying inordinate attention to his reading habits, of course, but . . .

She took a deep breath, then dared to attempt a full-fledged conversation. "Could I ask you something?"

"That depends."

Maggie grimaced. "It isn't personal."

To her delight, the assurance made his eyes twinkle. "Let's hear it, then."

"Well . . ." She was determined to choose her words carefully, to avoid any misunderstanding. "You've had more than a little formal education, and so—"

"What makes you say that?"

"Pardon?"

"You assume that, because I enjoy reading, I've had a formal education? That's presumptuous, Maggie-Margaret. And an insult to self-taught men everywhere."

She had offended him again, presuming to know something about him, his habits, or his precious past. Ordinarily, she might have apologized, but instead, her patience began to fail her, and she demanded, "Are you suggesting you're wholly self-educated?"

Before he could answer, she added dryly, "You needn't take offense, either on your own behalf or that of self-educated men everywhere. You asked me what I was reading, and I was foolish enough to think I could answer you without initiating a tiresome diatribe. As usual, I overestimated you."

"Tell me what it is."

"No."

"Don't make me come over there and see for myself, Maggie-Margaret."

She ordered her cheeks not to redden, despite the silly surge of excitement his suggestion had elicited. She had to think of some new tactic quickly. He was more than capable of crossing that room in two short strides and wrenching her love letter from her hands.

"This is one of the essays my students wrote today," she bluffed finally. "This particular one is a nice effort, but unremarkable. However, one of the other children did raise an interesting point that I thought you might be able to help me with."

"And?"

As Maggie folded her love note and slipped it back into her lesson book, she silently thanked Joey Lawson for the precocious remark he'd made earlier that day. "I asked the children to write about civic responsibility. The assignment was inspired by the rather phenomenal response Shasta Falls has made to Jed Lawson's injuries. Are you aware of any of that?"

"Enlighten me," he suggested dryly.

"Everyone's sending food, and notes of encouragement, and small items for the boys. It's as though they've been waiting for an excuse to welcome the family back into the community. All this, despite the fact that, as you know, there were some harsh judgments made when Mrs. Lawson died."

"Sheriff Riordain tells me Jed murdered her."

"What?" She recovered her equilibrium and asked quietly, "Based upon what? The way I heard it, there was no proof."

"Not enough proof for a conviction. That's not the same thing, Maggie-Margaret."

"Stop calling me that!"

He arched an eyebrow, then shrugged. "Sometimes there isn't enough evidence for a conviction, but the investigator knows in his heart that the person is guilty."

"And sometimes the evidence is overwhelming, but one knows in one's heart that the person is innocent," she countered, thinking of Ian and the unfair price he'd been asked to pay.

"I beg your pardon?"

Maggie scowled. "Are you planning on traveling any time soon, Mr. Coburn?"

He burst into laughter. "Not soon enough to suit

you, I suspect." When she didn't smile, he coaxed her gently. "You wanted my advice on the essay, didn't you? Civic responsibility is our topic, if I remember correctly. What exactly did you want to know?"

She wanted to know if he had a heart, but didn't dare ask that, so she proceeded more logically. "I told the children to write about their duty to their neighbors. And they wanted to know if *you* were their neighbor."

Something flickered behind his blue eyes, but his voice was flat as he asked, "What did you tell them?"

"I told them 'yes,' you are their neighbor."

"You were wrong."

Maggie moistened her lips, intrigued by the hint of defensiveness in his tone. "I thought about that encounter you had with the Lawson boys in the livery stable. In some ways, you have more of an influence on them by being aloof than you would if you simply kept to yourself, but without seeming so disdainful."

"I don't disdain this town."

"You don't? Then, what *do* you think about it?"

"I don't think about it at all."

Maggie searched his expression in vain for a trace of feeling, but there was nothing. "Doesn't it bother you that some of the town's children fear you?"

"I *want* them to fear me."

"Why? Because it keeps them away? Don't you see it simply makes you more intriguing?" She flushed and added quickly, "I mean, to the boys, of course. They see your guns, and your stallion, and your stern expression and they wonder . . ."

His eyes narrowed. "What?"

Her voice was unexpectedly steady as she answered, "They wonder if you'll hurt them."

"Good. I *want* them to wonder that."

"Then I congratulate you, sir." She gathered up her

papers quickly and headed for the doorway to the
kitchen. It was best just to leave, but silly, too, so she
turned to bid him good night, expecting to see a triumphant grin on his face.

Instead, he was clearly puzzled. "Did I offend
you?"

"No. I'm just tired." Realizing that it was probably
true—she *had* had a long and taxing day—she smiled
as an apology. "Good night, Mr. Coburn."

"Good night, Miss O'Connor. And, Miss O'Connor?"

"Yes?"

"Try not to take me so seriously."

"I'll do my best," she promised, then before he
could mock her further, she turned and ran toward the
stairs.

Her heart was still pounding when she reached her
room, so she forced herself to take several deep
breaths, reminding herself of his last words.

Try not to take me so seriously.

Wasn't that the problem? She paid far too much
attention to the man, scrutinizing his every word,
every action or inaction, for some clue to his true
opinions and character.

"But his every word and action is calculated to mis-
lead you," she reminded herself. "He as much as told
you that. He wants the children to fear him. He wants
them—and you—to think he might do harm. That's
how he keeps the world at bay. Denny explained it all
to you weeks ago, but you keep forgetting it."

It was true. Coburn had made suggestive remarks,
and placed his hands on her hips, to frighten her into
thinking he might molest her, so that she would keep
her distance. He carried weapons, and dressed in omi-

nous black clothes, to instill fear in any curious observer. And yet, he had not made one genuine attempt at seducing Maggie, despite limitless opportunities. And it was logical to assume that he also had never actually harmed another human being.

"Some warrior," she decided with a fond smile. "And you were such a goose, for thinking that a man who loves books and poetry as much as Coburn does, could also roam the countryside, armed and ready to take lives as needed. It's all an illusion, created by him to protect his privacy."

And when the illusions were swept aside, there was really only one thing Maggie knew for sure about the man: that books were his refuge. In some ways, that was really all the information she needed, wasn't it?

He came here for the same reason you did—to bury himself in a carefully orchestrated world—one in which his heart and soul were completely protected from his past. Only in your case, June Riordain intervened. She forced you to share your secret with her, and the simple telling of it, to a sympathetic soul, set your own soul free.

And Maggie ached with unexpected ferocity to do the same for Coburn. To show him that a trustworthy friend could be a refuge, too. She would prove herself to him, night after night, until the moment came when he could admit the truth to her—that his gunbelt and scowl were artifices, designed to distract onlookers from seeing a gentle and harmless bookworm.

And will you miss the warrior, just a bit? she asked herself gently.

The answer was simple: yes, the warrior had aroused her. There was no denying that. But she had had enough violence in her life, and so she would gladly say goodbye to Coburn's dark side. She would embrace the poet—not literally, of course, but—

"You're doing it again, Maggie-Margaret," she scolded herself suddenly. "Didn't he just warn you not to take him so seriously? Are you going to stay awake all night imagining what can and cannot happen in that library?"

Her gaze fell on the two love letters that she had piled, along with her books, on the dresser. Was there a boy out there in the moonlight, having just such a jumble of conflicting thoughts about Maggie at that moment? A hopeless romantic, like Brian had been. Like Maggie apparently was.

And Coburn? She'd probably never know. And she wasn't going to waste one more moment of thought over it. He had his mistresses across town, after all. And Maggie had her secret admirer. Wasn't that all any hopeless romantic needed?

She had grown so protective of her nights in the library that she rarely lingered at the homes of her students when she accepted dinner invitations. She even grew restless on Thursday nights at the Riordains', although she was careful to conceal it, for fear of one of June's relentless interrogations.

On one such occasion, the alert hostess did in fact demand to know why Maggie seemed so preoccupied. Glad at least that Denny wasn't in the room to overhear the question—what if he mentioned it to Coburn!—Maggie confided that she had a secret admirer, albeit a juvenile one. June was captivated. And blessedly distracted. And as soon as Denny returned, Maggie insisted that he take her home so she could plan the next morning's lessons.

Of course, once she was comfortably settled in To-

bias Blake's library, it was Coburn, not history or
arithmetic, that absorbed her attentions that evening.
It had been weeks since he'd last gone out on an "appointment," and she suspected the women at the saloon missed him terribly. Of course, he probably
visited them in the daytime, she told herself with a
mischievous smile, remembering Denny's innocent observation: *The girls don't complain about him.*

No, a woman wouldn't complain about Coburn as
a lover. Those strong, rough hands; those startling
eyes; windburned cheekbones; long, lean thighs—

"Something on your mind, Maggie-Margaret?"

"I can't imagine what you mean," she said with a
sniff, although it was a ludicrous response, considering
that she had just been staring at him.

He shrugged and returned his attention to his work.

At first, Maggie had thought he was writing in a
journal, but the book in his hand was not the worn
leather volume in which he usually wrote. This one
was the size of a sketchbook, and from the long,
sweeping strokes he'd been making, she was positive
he was drawing something.

She wondered if he had talent, then decided he almost certainly did. He wasn't the sort of man to do
anything badly, and so, if he spent time sketching, it
was because he was at least passably good at it.

He glanced up at her again, and scowled. "You're
staring again."

She wanted to remind him that he, too, seemed to
be taking more than his share of peeks across the room
this particular evening, but it would just lead to more
superficial banter, and she decided they'd had enough
of all that. If and when he was ready to have a meaningful conversation with her, he'd do so. Until then, it
was best just to read in silence.

She didn't look up at him again, but had the distinct

feeling *he* was looking at *her,* again and again. When the truth finally fit her, it was with the force of a thunderbolt.

Alex Coburn was sketching *her!*

Ten

Shock gave way to apprehensive delight, and she
ordered herself not to blush or wriggle or otherwise
alert him. Still, she was flattered, and tried her best
to imagine how she looked to him at that moment.
Her hair was loose; she was wearing an unremarkable
gray dress; and her feet were curled up under her. Her
lesson book was open in her lap, and several other
books were piled on the sofa beside her. All in all, a
rather lackluster image, she decided ruefully. Why
would he want to record it?

She wanted to stay still, but was now so aware of
her body that she felt an overwhelming need to stretch
her legs. Did he expect her to sit like this all night?
If he wanted to practice on a subject, why not just ask
her?

Because he doesn't ask favors of anyone, she reminded herself. *That would be a sign of weakness. Or
worse, friendship.*

But wasn't it a sign of friendship that he was sketching her at all? He was choosing to look at her, to study
her, to appreciate her with an artist's eye, and as Maggie pondered the implications, she felt her pulse begin
to race. Was he attracted to her? When had *that* begun?
Not at their first meeting, of course, when he had proclaimed her 'homely,' but perhaps when she'd fallen

into his arms? Or when she'd stepped out of the tub, clad only in a towel . . .

Her cheeks began to burn, and she knew he would notice. Unwilling to be humiliated so easily, she decided to cover her arousal by making *him* uncomfortable, so she raised her head and looked directly at him.

He was staring, just as she had suspected, and it was easy to ask, in a soft, innocent voice, "Are you by any chance sketching me, Mr. Coburn?"

"Actually, I'm sketching the mountain."

"I beg your pardon?" She tried to read his expression, but it told her nothing. "The mountain?"

He arched an eyebrow. "Look over your shoulder, Maggie-Margaret."

"Oh!" She didn't have to turn around to understand that he was referring to an amateurish oil painting by Tobias that hung on the library wall. "Oh, I see."

"It's a logical mistake," he assured her with uncharacteristic magnanimity. "Your head and shoulders were in my line of vision—"

"You should have asked me to move," she retorted, then she regretted the tone and offered lamely, "I could sit in the other chair, just for tonight."

"That's not necessary." He closed the sketchbook and shrugged to his feet. "I finished just a minute ago. So, if you'll excuse me, I'll say good night and be on my way."

She jumped up and smiled apologetically. "I feel as though I've ruined your evening. Please stay? Couldn't we just—well, couldn't we just relax with one another?"

"I beg your pardon?"

His tone warned her to be quiet, but instead, she suggested desperately, "We could have a conversation. A normal one. Wouldn't that be refreshing? I could

tell you about my day with the children, and you could
show me your drawing, and we could—" She stopped
herself, acutely aware of the fact that she was babbling, and tried again. "I know I'm not making much
sense. I just don't want you to leave on my account.
Not after all the progress we've made. I've begun to
think of you as a friend," she continued breathlessly,
"and I was hoping you felt that way, too. Unless it's
all my imagination, of course, which is admittedly
possible. My father always told me I expected too
much from people—and that's *my* failing, not yours—
but I honestly thought we could be friends."

He was staring at her as though she'd been speaking
a foreign language, and she realized he didn't know
what to say, so she assured him unhappily, "I promised
you from the start that I wouldn't bother you. That we
could just share this room in silence. Please forgive
me for breaking that promise. And please, say something."

He looked directly into her eyes then, and said gently, "Your father was correct."

"My father? What does that— Oh . . ."

"Good night, Miss O'Connor. Pleasant dreams."

She stared after him until he'd disappeared into his
bedroom, then she sank onto the sofa, struggling to
make peace with his last remark.

Your father was correct.

In other words, she *did* expect too much of people.
Her expectation that she and Coburn could be friends,
for example. He had just told her, clearly and without
his usual mockery, that that would never happen.

And the very fact that he hadn't teased her told her
even more: he felt sorry for her, for being so needy.
She needed a friend—someone with whom to talk
about her day, her students, her hopes and her dreams.
Someone to sit across from her at night and sketch

her. For some foolish reason, she had given him the impression that she wanted him to be that man.

And in that moment, she had ruined everything. Never again would he tease her mercilessly about her supposed attraction to dangerous men. It was no longer a joke, but rather, a pitiful reality in his eyes. And while she had been stung by the moments of disdain and dismissal he had inflicted on her in the past, nothing could have prepared her for this—the knowledge that he now felt sorry for her.

There was one sure remedy for the mortification she felt, so she moved to the bookshelves and located Tobias Blake's copy of *Ivanhoe*.

At least, I don't expect too much of you, she told the book as she curled back up on the sofa. *Coburn's been right all along—books really are the only reliable refuge. I shan't forget it again, no matter how many blue-eyed warriors I meet in real life.*

For the first time, Maggie drifted into sleep right there on the library sofa, and didn't awaken until a faint glow of light from the kitchen windows finally made its way into the dark-paneled room. She stirred, and was sheepishly pleased to realize that she had slept with *Ivanhoe* clutched to her bosom. No wonder her dreams had been so sweet!

Someone had covered her with a wool blanket, and she allowed herself the luxury of snuggling under it for just one more minute before officially starting her day. Who was it who had taken care of her? she wondered. Mrs. Blake? One of the other boarders? Coburn?

First, you think he's sketching you; now you think he's looking after you, she teased herself. *The poor man does his best to discourage you, but you truly are hopeless.*

With a sigh, she rolled to her feet and began to fold the blanket, her eyes on the dreadful painting of Mount Shasta. If Coburn could transform that sight into an attractive sketch, she would have to give credit to his talent. On impulse, she moved to his chair and sat down, trying to see the mountain through an artist's eyes for a moment.

"Your head and shoulders couldn't possibly have been blocking his view," she told herself with confused fascination. "Why on earth would he say such a thing? To make you uncomfortable? Surely he realized you were already mortified. After all, you were foolish enough to accuse him of sketching *you.*"

Cuddling the folded blanket against her chest, she allowed herself to entertain a daring thought—what if he *had* been sketching her, and had simply claimed otherwise to distract her from the truth and its implications? One of those implications being, of course, that he had some small measure of interest in her.

In any case, she hadn't been blocking his view. And to the extent he'd been looking directly at her, he hadn't been looking at the painting—the angle was simply not a direct one.

Mrs. Blake was humming in the kitchen, and Maggie wandered over to join her.

"Well, look who's awake! You fell asleep right there on the sofa."

"Yes, I know. Thank you for covering me."

"I didn't. I assume it was Mr. Coburn. Didn't I tell you he was a gentleman, in his own way?"

"You were right, as always." Maggie tried to keep her tone casual. "As soon as he comes out, please let me know, so I can come down and thank him."

"He already left for the day."

She tried not to grin. "Oh, what a shame. I'll just put this blanket back on his bed then, shall I?"

The landlady hesitated, then shrugged. "I don't see the harm in that."

No harm at all, Maggie assured her silently. *And if I happen to accidentally open his sketchbook and see what he was last working on, what harm could there be in that either?*

Her burst of bravado notwithstanding, Maggie's heart began to pound the moment she crossed the threshold to his bedroom. Everything was just as she remembered, and as she tiptoed over to his bed and set the folded blanket on one corner, she scolded herself for being so skittish. Even if he returned unexpectedly, she'd hear him in time to put the book away. At least this time, she had the perfect excuse for being in his room, didn't she?

More importantly, if she *did* find proof that he'd been sketching her, it would be *his* turn to be embarrassed and tongue-tied! Wouldn't that be a refreshing change?

There were a dozen or so leather-bound volumes on the shelf above his desk. The smallest was the journal she'd seen him with so often, and she congratulated herself for having the strength not to page through it for even just a moment, despite the secrets it certainly contained.

There were two sketchbooks, and she selected the larger of the two because it appeared to be the newer. Glancing backward to confirm that she was alone, she set the volume on the desk and opened it.

But it wasn't a sketchbook at all, or at least, he hadn't used it for that purpose. It was more of a keepsake album, with various papers glued to its pages.

Maggie scanned them, and as she did so, a queasy
sort of revulsion welled up inside her.

WANTED posters. Page after page of WANTED posters.
For murderers, robbers, swindlers—each with a price
on his head. And for each poster, a scribbled notation
in the corner. Always the same: a sum of money, and
a brief description of the criminal's disposition. And
while that disposition was often trial and incarceration,
it was just as often death, either by the hangman or,
more expeditiously, at the hands of the bounty hunter.

Sickened, Maggie forced herself to close the book
and shelve it carefully, so that he wouldn't know it
had been disturbed. Then she leaned on the corner of
the desk, struggling with a wild array of confusing
images. Brian's blood, Ian's cell, the prison cemetery . . .

*Sometimes the evidence is overwhelming, but one
knows in one's heart that the person is innocent. . . .*

No wonder that statement had intrigued him!

Mrs. Blake's voice, calling cheerfully from the
kitchen, helped Maggie regain her composure, and she
hurried into the library. Ordinarily, the sight of so
many books would have offered solace, but all Maggie
saw was the fruits of Coburn's mercenary ways.

*He kills men, then uses the money to buy books.
Blood money! There's your poet-warrior, Maggie
Gleason. He's neither, and you're a fool.*

"You'll be late for school, young lady," Mrs. Blake
warned her from the kitchen. "Come and have a cup
of coffee—that'll help you wake up."

"No, thank you. I need—well, I need to get ready."
Maggie gathered up her books and took the steps two
at a time until she was safe behind her muslin curtain;
then she wrapped her arms around herself and held
tight, afraid that she might actually start shivering.

June saw it, clear as can be. And Denny—Denny

has known it all along! That's what he and Coburn talk about! The WANTED *posters arrive at the jail, and Coburn saunters over there and studies them, deciding just whom he'll kill this week. He doesn't travel, he hunts! Hunts human beings, because to him, they mean nothing. Only books matter, and how fitting that he's found so convenient a way to accommodate both his prejudices.*

Tobias Blake would roll over in his grave, she told herself, then she remembered what Eleanor had said, that very first day: books had been one of her husband's vices. And Maggie had naively insisted that books weren't a vice . . .

And what was it the landlady had said to that? *Anything can be a vice, if it's done beyond the bounds of common sense.*

"You're so wise, Mrs. Blake," Maggie murmured sadly. "And I've been so very, very blind."

She was miserable over the disheartening turn of events, and would have allowed herself to wallow in her misery indefinitely, but her students were too boisterous for such self-indulgence. And while most of their mischief was innocent, the third letter from her secret admirer was anything but that.

For the first time, the anonymous writer didn't bother to put his thoughts into verse. Instead, he poured them onto the paper in a wild rush of ill-chosen words, describing Maggie from head to toe, with particular emphasis on her bosom. Interspersed with dubious compliments were some rather raw descriptions of the boy's own needs, and to the extent Maggie could make sense of them, they made her flush with embarrassment and concern.

It was difficult to believe that a child—even an

older one—had written such words, but the handwriting was clearly the same in all three notes. Had there been any doubt about that, she would have taken the third letter to the sheriff immediately, for fear that a grown man was having such thoughts about her, and worse, daring to communicate them.

"You're as bad as the women who complained about Ian," she scolded herself nervously. "Can't you see that this child is struggling with feelings he can't understand? You've done everything possible to earn your students' trust, and now you would betray it by going to the sheriff?"

But the alternative, of allowing it to continue, seemed equally unacceptable. For one thing, it was only a matter of time before someone other than Maggie realized that a troubled child lived among them. She knew all too well what would happen then.

And so, when she made her latest list of possible "admirers," she forced herself to be thorough: her students; the boys she'd met on her Saturday excursions to the camp, especially those who avoided her lessons, choosing instead to gawk at her from a distance; the young men, too old for school, but not yet settled down with a wife and children; and while she told herself it was unfair, she also included other, older bachelors and widowers.

A tremor of foreboding came over her when she recorded Jed Lawson's name on her list, but she told herself she was being foolish. He hadn't shown any interest in her that evening at his cabin, had he? And he was hardly capable of writing the innocent lines that had captured her heart in that very first note.

The sheriff tells me he murdered his wife, Coburn's voice insisted upon reminding her.

But Coburn was a killer, too, wasn't he? Yet she didn't suspect *him* of writing the notes, nor should she suspect Mr. Lawson. The letter writer was a child—a disturbed but well-intentioned one who loved Maggie too much ever to harm her.

So why, she wondered, did she feel so all alone and vulnerable?

"You've spent so much time in your room this past week, it's as though you don't live here at all," Mrs. Blake chided her one evening during supper. "You bolt your food and run upstairs before we have any chance to talk to you."

"I've missed you all," Maggie said with a forced smile. "But my responsibilities to the children come first."

"But not tonight, at least," Mrs. Blake said firmly. "Tonight, you'll join us in the parlor."

Maggie sighed. It had been almost two months since she'd participated in parlor activities. For a time, of course, she had been spending her evenings in the library with Coburn, but ever since her glimpse into his personal life, she had avoided both the library and Coburn himself.

It hadn't seemed to bother him, either. While they had exchanged perfunctory greetings when they encountered one another, usually when he came to the kitchen for his morning coffee, neither of them had made any effort to converse.

She had been grateful to him for that—for not gloating, or interrogating her. It had proved conclusively that all he wanted was to be left alone. And now, thanks to the WANTED posters, he had his wish.

Still, the sight of him could confuse her when her guard was down, and so, when he strode into the kitchen just as she was formulating an excuse for not joining the others in the parlor, she was momentarily speechless.

Fortunately, Mrs. Blake greeted him warmly enough for all of them. "Don't tell me you're going to dine with us! What a lovely surprise."

He shook his head. "It smells delicious, but I ate at the hotel."

"I don't know why you do that, when there's plenty of good food here, and better company."

"It's my way," he reminded her gently. "But I'd appreciate a cup of coffee if you have any left."

"Of course." The landlady hurried to the stove. "Shall I bring it to you in the library?"

"Yes, thank you." He seemed about to leave, then looked at Maggie and asked quietly, "How are you this evening, Miss O'Connor?"

"She's as stubborn as ever," Mrs. Blake assured him. "I'm sure you've noticed that she spends all of her time in her room these days."

Maggie flushed. "I find I can prepare my lessons best up there, where there are no distractions. I don't mean to be unsociable, though. I—I hope no one takes it that way."

"Well, tonight, you're joining us in the parlor. Ted Aronsen has memorized another long speech from a play he attended in San Francisco. Which one is it, Amos?"

"Hamlet," the gun seller replied. "The famous 'to be, or not to be' soliloquy, I believe. And as an encore, the scene he did for us the week Maggie first arrived—the one from *Romeo and Juliet.*"

Maggie tried to keep her face expressionless, but wondered if it wouldn't be better to just admit, rudely but practically, that she couldn't bear the thought of another Aronsen performance. In addition to the aforementioned *Romeo and Juliet,* he had massacred scenes from *King Lear* and *Dr. Faustus,* horrifying the purist in Maggie with his bizarre interpretations.

"You'll have to do without Miss O'Connor tonight," Coburn interrupted. "She promised me a game of chess, and I intend to hold her to it."

Maggie's jaw dropped, but she recovered before the disbelieving eyes of the other boarders who turned to stare in her direction. She even managed a weak smile as she hastily weighed her options.

But the rescue was so unexpectedly considerate of Coburn, and Aronsen's performances were so abysmal, the choice proved simple. Turning to the bounty hunter, she murmured, "I've been looking forward to it myself, sir. I'll join you in a few minutes."

"I'll set up the board."

She waited until he'd left, then eyed the others cheerfully. "Is something wrong?"

"You and he play chess? We thought you just read and ignored one another. And lately, you haven't even done that."

"Because I've been otherwise occupied. But I've been wanting to sharpen my chess skills, and Mr. Coburn was kind enough to offer to help."

"Didn't I tell you?" Mrs. Blake's expression was triumphant. "They've become friends, slowly but surely. You all think he's so rude, but here he is, treating Maggie quite gallantly."

"Because she's a beautiful girl, and he has no scruples," Amos Gentry muttered.

"Mr. Gentry!"

Maggie intervened hastily. "Mr. Coburn has been a perfect gentleman. On the other hand . . ." She reached across the table to pat the gun salesman's hand. "I adore you for watching out for me. Enjoy your evening with Mr. Aronsen, and tomorrow, I shall make a point of joining all of you in the parlor. I could use some entertainment, and everyone knows, Eleanor Blake's parlor is the best place for that in Shasta Falls."

It seemed to mollify the group, and Maggie was left to finish her meal in relative silence, while the others chatted about the upcoming dramatic presentation.

Then her plate was empty, and Mrs. Blake was refusing her offer to help with the dishes, and there was simply no choice—it was time to join Coburn in the library.

He was seated when she entered, but to her surprise, he jumped to his feet. "Good evening, Miss O'Connor."

"Good evening." She didn't know whether to walk toward the sofa or the chess table, so she crossed to the middle of the room. "It was very kind of you to come to my aid, Mr. Coburn."

To her relief, he flashed her a genuine smile. "I've had the misfortune of hearing Aronsen perform at the saloon, in front of a captive audience."

"Mrs. Blake adores his work."

"Mrs. Blake is a woman of many and varied tastes," he observed wryly. "Some of them frightening."

Maggie bit back a smile. "Well, in any case, I'm grateful."

"Grateful enough to stay for a few minutes while I explain something to you?"

Maggie caught her breath. Explain what? The fact that he was a bounty hunter? Did he know she'd snooped in his room? If so, wasn't he furious?

He surprised her further then, by moving to a sideboard and pouring liquor into two short crystal glasses. Then he was back, handing one of the drinks to Maggie, his expression more unreadable than ever.

She accepted the glass, but didn't drink from it. Instead, she simply stared at him, trying to ascertain what he could possibly be about to say.

Just when she was about to confess herself, Coburn rescued her again, this time by stating simply, "I owe you an apology."

"An apology? For what?"

"For making you uncomfortable the other evening."

Maggie winced. "I can't imagine what you mean. If anything, you made me very comfortable. If I remember correctly, you covered me with a blanket."

He seemed surprised, then shook his head. "I was referring to the sketching."

She coughed gently, and took a small step backward. "You have every right to draw the mountain."

"If I wanted to draw the mountain, I need only step outside any day of the week," Coburn reminded her with a chuckle. "Why would I rely on Tobias's handiwork, interesting though it may be?"

Maggie tilted her head to the side, intrigued. "So? You admit you were sketching me?"

"Isn't that why you've stayed away?" Before she could answer, he added, "I know I've been difficult these last few months. I resisted the suggestion that we share this library, and I did my best, at first, to chase you away. But I assure you, I wasn't drawing you to make you uncomfortable."

Then why? she demanded silently, but aloud, she heard herself say, "You had every right to chase me away. After all, you are the owner of many of these books, are you not?"

He scowled. "Eleanor told you about that?"

"Yes. It helped me understand why you were so—

well, so protective of them." She swirled her drink, then insisted, "You should have told me yourself."

He shook his head, still scowling. "This is the very reason I *didn't* tell you. You insist on seeing everything in its most romantic light. Do you suppose I bought these books to save Mrs. Blake? The truth is, I paid next to nothing for priceless editions. That makes me a scoundrel. Don't see a hero where there isn't one."

It was Maggie's turn to scowl. "Why were you sketching me, Mr. Coburn?"

He was clearly startled, then grinned approvingly. "Nice move."

"I'm learning a lot from you," she admitted. "And from June Riordain."

Coburn burst into laughter, then waved his hand toward her and advised, "Sit down and finish your whiskey while I explain myself to you."

"I prefer to stand," she retorted, but sipped at the drink as he had requested. The heat surprised her, but the aroma was intoxicating, and so she sipped again, then gave him an expectant stare. "I'm waiting."

"Fine." He tossed back his own drink, then began. "My reasons for drawing your picture were completely honorable. I intend to make a present of it to your future husband."

Maggie belatedly sank to the sofa, staring in disbelief. "Whatever are you talking about?"

Coburn smiled. "I know you mean it when you say you'll never marry, but the truth is otherwise. A fine young man will eventually break down your defenses, and you'll have a home of your own. Children of your own. You'll cook and clean and care for them, cheerfully and unselfishly.

"You need all that to be happy. But you need this too." He swept his arm around to encompass the book-lined walls. "I wanted him to see you here, absorbed in your reading. To understand how it nourishes your soul. I felt that if he could see you this way—see the peaceful expression on your face—he'd understand, and make certain that you always had books around you."

Maggie stared in misty delight. "That's the loveliest thing anyone has ever said to me."

Coburn's eyes narrowed. "As always, your reaction is laughably romantic. I'm beginning to think you should be in the parlor with Aronsen!"

"And miss our chess match?"

"Huh?"

Maggie grinned. "Your tactics are obvious, sir. You're trying to inebriate and insult me, all to gain a tactical advantage. Are you so very afraid of being defeated by a woman?"

Coburn had clearly been caught off his guard, but rallied quickly. "Unlike yourself, I am not a patient teacher. You'd do better to find another instructor."

"In other words, you're afraid to play me."

"Maggie . . ." He switched tactics quickly. "I enjoy winning as much as the next man, but I have my limits, and I'm not about to crush you just to prove a point. Let's just say, we decided we weren't well matched, and leave it at that."

"You forfeit? Then let's just say, I won." She flashed a confident grin. "I had a wonderful mentor, Mr. Coburn. A master of the game. I'd love to see you face him, but since that will never happen, allow me to give it a try."

He grinned reluctantly. "You're serious?"

"Absolutely."

"You think I'll hold back, because you're a woman?"

"On the contrary, sir. I believe you'll use every trick

at your disposal, for fear of being defeated by a mere female."

Coburn laughed. "Fine. But no tears when you lose, understood? And *no* sulking."

"I intend to hold you to that rule as well."

He laughed again. "You're in a feisty mood tonight, Miss O'Connor. I haven't seen this side of you before."

"You're more comfortable with the bookworm?"

"She knows her place."

Maggie started to retort, then realized he was goading her, in hopes she'd lose confidence and concentration. Grateful for having had brothers to familiarize her with such tactics, she eyed Coburn coolly. "Are we going to talk, or play?"

Eleven

Coburn flashed a deadly smile, then moved to the chess table and began to set up the pieces. Maggie joined him, enchanted by Tobias Blake's finely crafted ivory collection. The knights on horseback were particularly spectacular, she decided, and her pulse began to quicken at the thought of putting Robert Grimes's lessons to the test.

"After you," Coburn said, holding her chair with a flourish.

Maggie seated herself, then smiled up at him, hoping for a confident expression. "Thank you, sir." She waited until he'd settled across from her, then reached out toward her queen's pawn. Her fingertips were a hair's width from it as she paused in feigned indecision, then she grasped it and moved it as though she had no doubt that she'd outmaneuvered him. And in truth, she had no doubt at all, since she had never seen Robert Grimes open with any other move.

Without bothering to look at her, Coburn made an identical move with instantaneous, methodical precision.

Maggie tried not to grin. Typical. Correct, but typical. Now she had two choices: another typical move, to secure the center, or a more exciting second move she'd seen Robert make from time to time. The latter would not only be more of a challenge for Coburn, but would also allow her to touch her handsomely carved knight again.

Still, she hesitated, unsure of whether it was the queen's knight or the king's that Robert had used in the past. The queen's, she decided finally, and made the move without further hesitation.

Coburn glanced up at her, and in that instant, she knew she'd made an error, despite the lack of expression on his face. He moved his bishop, again without expression or hesitation, and Maggie grimaced. She had hoped to frustrate him just a bit, and decided it was ungallant of him to behave so dismissively.

"Your move," Coburn reminded her.

"Yes, I know."

"Would you like another whiskey?"

She glared, then turned her full attention to the board, trying desperately to remember what Robert had taught her. Finally, she moved her king's pawn one space, then sighed with relief when Coburn moved his queen's bishop's pawn two spaces, virtually sacrificing the piece. She didn't care if he'd done it out of charity or to gain a future advantage. She was simply glad to make the first capture, although she was careful to show no emotion as she did so.

In the meantime, she couldn't help but notice that his pieces, particularly his bishops, seemed to have unobstructed paths across the board, while her pieces were locked in place. Worse, she had no presence at all in the center of the board.

And so it began, with Coburn moving freely, while Maggie resorted to a new strategy, trying to duplicate his moves. Unfortunately, when she moved her knight as he had done, he took it cleanly with his bishop.

"Your move."

"Yes, I know," she snapped.

"Now would you like another drink?"

"That's enough." She raised her eyes to his, and tried to ignore the laughing blue fire. "Perhaps you're the one who should have another drink. It might make you less tiresome."

He chuckled fondly. "Your move."

"Yes," she repeated through gritted teeth. "I know that."

She needed to bring her bishops into the game, and so she edged a pawn forward to make a path, trying desperately to plan her next few moves. *That's all you need,* she assured herself. *Some semblance of a strategy. After all, you never really believed you'd win. But you must try to give him a challenge, however hopeless.*

"We agreed that there'd be no sulking, did we not?"

"Yes, why do you—oh!" She glared in disgust as he took her bishop.

"I apologize."

"Be quiet." She caught her temper and asked quietly, "Do I have any chance at all?"

"I'll win in five moves, assuming you don't make any more mistakes."

Maggie grimaced. Not exactly a safe assumption under the circumstances. Why had she always thought of chess as a game that lasted for hours? It appeared this one would be over in less than five minutes!

She considered conceding, knowing that he would be magnanimous about it. After all, defeating her at chess meant nothing to him, so he could afford to forgo the teasing. And he still felt guilty over having made her uncomfortable with the sketching. So why not?

Maggie sighed. For some reason, she had an overwhelming need to protect her queen from him, almost as though an assault on that particular piece would be an assault on Maggie herself.

Maybe that should be your strategy, she advised herself. *Redefine the game. He wants your king, so let him have it. If your queen survives, you'll have secretly won, despite what this bully believes.*

Then she made the mistake of looking up at him, and almost melted under his vibrant blue eyes. If only she knew what he was thinking! He seemed calm enough, but wasn't it possible that his heart was beating just a bit faster than usual, knowing that at any minute, their hands could brush against one another across the board? Or their toes could touch under the table. Or he could assault her queen . . .

The mere thought brought heat to her cheeks and she dropped her gaze to the board, reminding herself of the new rules. Protect her queen at all costs. So she moved her remaining knight into the path of his own.

"Interesting move," Coburn murmured. "Care to explain it?"

"Just play," she advised.

He grinned and rested his fingertips on his bishop. "There's still time for that drink, Maggie-Margaret."

She wanted to give him a cool, confident glare, but had noticed too late that the bishop could take her. Or rather, could take her queen, which had suddenly become too symbolic for comfort.

She steeled herself for the loss, then frowned when nothing happened. What was he waiting for? she wondered. Then she raised her eyes to his, and knew that he'd wanted *this*—to see her expression, before he took her with a clean, decisive stroke.

Determined not to appear weak, she held his gaze until he'd knocked her queen aside, then she jumped to her feet and announced too loudly, "Congratulations, sir. Thank you for the game."

"Miss O'Connor?"

"What now?" she asked, not bothering to censor the edge from her tone.

"The game isn't over."

"Oh." She flushed and sat back down, then told him quietly, "I concede."

"Why?"

"Don't be tiresome." She caught her temper and explained sincerely, "I honestly thought I could give you a bit of a challenge, but I was wrong."

He picked up her queen and ran one fingertip over its smooth, feminine curves. "These pieces are exquisite, aren't they? Such attention to detail."

"Give me that!" She snatched it from his hand, then glared when he burst into laughter. "I wish Mrs. Blake could see you now. She's so sure you're a gentleman."

"And you're so sure I'm not?"

Maggie threw the piece onto the table and stormed over to the fireplace, where she folded her arms across her chest before staring into the flames with disgust. "I don't know why I bother trying to have a civilized relationship with you, sir."

"Neither do I." He walked up behind her and rested his hands on her waist. "Don't blame me for your defeat. Blame the man who taught you. He should never have claimed to be a master of the game."

Her anger disappeared in an instant, and all that was left was a wave of confusion engendered by his touch. Every finger seemed to be laying claim to her, and she stood perfectly still, despite an urge to either pull away, or sway backward against him. What would he do then? she wondered in giddy confusion. Would he pull her hard against himself and murmur something sinful in her ear?

Then she remembered that he had insulted Robert, and so she forced herself to respond. "I assure you, he *was* a master. I wasn't a very good student, I suppose."

"Do you know what I think?" Coburn turned her to face himself, then looked down at her, his eyes blazing. "He was in love with you, and it clouded his ability to criticize or instruct you. He saw perfection in your every move, the poor fellow. Whatever became of him?"

"I don't know," Maggie murmured. Her heart was pounding so fiercely, she wondered how Coburn could hear her words, even standing as close as he was. "I wish I'd been able to give you a better game."

"Under the circumstances, I think you did just fine."

Her throat began to tighten, and she wondered if he was about to kiss her. Then he stepped backward and flashed a playful grin. "Did your teacher tell you that the loser has to put the game away?"

Maggie flushed and nodded.

"Then you won't mind if I say good night? I'm late for a card game on the other side of town."

"A card game?" She turned away quickly, hoping he hadn't noticed the dismay in her voice. Trying for a lighter tone, she added, "Don't you want to stay and gloat? I promise I won't sulk."

"I'm restless," he explained. "I'm doing you a favor by leaving, believe me."

"By all means, then," she said with a sniff. "Go."

"Still feisty, I see."

"No." She smiled apologetically. "I suppose I'm a bit restless myself."

To her chagrin, he burst into laughter. "I have two pieces of advice for you, Miss Gleason-O'Connor.

Never leave your queen unprotected, and *never* tell a strange man you're feeling restless."

"And I have some advice for you!" she told him angrily. "The next time Mr. Aronsen comes to perform in the parlor, don't bother rescuing me. I vastly prefer his antics to yours."

"Fair enough." He disappeared into the bedroom and reemerged almost immediately with his coat and hat. "Good night, Maggie-Margaret. Enjoy the library."

She turned away and began to stuff the chess pieces back into the table drawers without bidding him good night in return. Why should she? He was being intentionally insufferable, as always!

And that quip about her queen and her restlessness—hadn't those been the remarks of a reprobate? Not that she hadn't initiated that silliness by placing such unnecessary emphasis on his capture of her queen, but still—

As soon as his footsteps on the back porch faded, she hurled the remaining chess pieces to the floor, then glared at the thick carpet that kept them from causing a suitably loud commotion. Apparently, she couldn't do anything right anymore!

And the truth is, you did initiate that silly business, so don't blame Coburn for seeing the humor in it. And as for your so-called restlessness, well that's true too, isn't it? There was a moment during the game, and another when he stood with you by the fire, where you were ready to throw yourself right into his arms!

Dropping to her knees, she began to gather up the ivory figures again, while continuing her volley of self-recriminations. *You're the most restless female in all of Shasta Falls, Maggie Gleason! Dreaming of Coburn, imagining how he feels, letting him touch you whenever he pleases—*

She stopped herself, allowing the figures to drop to the carpet again, although this time more gently. "Letting him touch you whenever he pleases . . . And it pleased him tonight. That, at least, wasn't your imagination."

She picked up the queen and studied it intently, remembering how his finger had stroked it. How would that feel? she wondered. More importantly, how had it felt to him? What had it all meant?

"You know very well what it meant," she told herself softly. "Playing that game with you made *him* as 'restless' as it made you. And that's not all! He was sketching you the other night—for your future husband, perhaps, but still, he wanted to capture your image. And what about those things he said about Robert? That Robert must have been in love with you, and . . ."

. . . and it clouded his ability to criticize or instruct you. He saw perfection in your every move . . .

She trembled at the thought of what it all could mean. Not that Coburn was in love with her, or she with him. Yet that naughty little tingle—that restlessness!—she felt whenever she thought about him for long was almost as wonderful as true love. Better, in fact, because it wouldn't lead to unnecessary complications. Instead—

"Instead, it could lead to an affair in San Francisco, for one month every year, just as June recommended," she told herself. "He'll take you in his arms, and make love to you so passionately—so expertly—that you'll think you're in heaven. And for the other eleven months, he'll sit across the room from you, reading his books. And occasionally, your eyes will meet, and you'll wish you could rush into one another's arms, but you'll remember that what you have is unique, and mustn't be mistaken for anything more than it is.

"But isn't it so much more than you ever intended to allow yourself? Just appreciate it, and don't ask for more. He's a bounty hunter, after all—not the sort of man you'd choose, even if you did change your mind about marriage."

Her thoughts flashed back to the sketch, and she knew, suddenly and conclusively, that that drawing could tell her what Coburn would not: how he felt about her. Did she dare go rummaging in his room again? Could she ever fall asleep if she didn't?

Without giving herself a chance to change her mind, she scurried into his bedroom. Once again, she resisted the temptation to read his journal. Instead, she reached for the second sketchbook—the one that hopefully didn't contain WANTED posters—and began to page through it.

So many of the sketches depicted Mount Shasta in all its snow-capped glory, from every angle and in every season. In contrast to Tobias Blake's work, these were exquisite, both in detail and effect. There were also drawings of horses, and redwood groves, and bubbling brooks, but no human subjects, until she reached the last of the drawings—a fanciful depiction of a young woman, curled up on a graceful settee in an alcove lined with books.

A wave of warmth washed over Maggie as she sank onto the foot of his bed and wistfully studied the drawing. Was it possible he saw her this way? So delicate and innocent and appealing? The girl in the drawing was nothing short of captivating, from her serene expression to the graceful manner in which her stocking feet were tucked up under herself. Her hair flowed loosely over her shoulders, spilling onto her bosom in rich, luminous curls; a hint of lacy petticoat, unlike anything Maggie owned, peeked out from under her skirts; and her lips were slightly parted—as though she was mesmerized by something she was reading in the small volume she held.

Time ceased to exist as Maggie drank in the image, her heart both humbled and overjoyed. To draw this, he had to feel something special for her. It was so idealized—so flattering—so unlike the sturdy, practical young woman she'd always seen herself to be.

She felt herself smiling—softly at first, and then, as the implications came in greater force, she was positively giddy. She almost couldn't bear to reshelve the sketchbook, but knew that she mustn't risk discovery at this point in their fragile relationship.

You must be scrupulously careful, she warned herself as she left and took the back stairs toward her room. *Remember what Denny said: he's a wild stallion, and you don't want to overwhelm him. And in truth, you don't want to be overwhelmed, either! What if he suddenly wanted to pull you into his arms? Are you so certain you'd allow it? It may take weeks, or months, or even years—it may never happen at all! So be patient. Be the girl in the drawing. And one night soon . . .*

A tremor of need shot through her, and she didn't even try to dispel it. Instead, she slipped out of her dress and into her little bed, then allowed her imagination to dance with thoughts of the blazing-eyed master who would undoubtedly be making love to her before the end of the year.

Maggie overslept the next morning, and barely had time for a bite of toast before racing out of the boardinghouse and up the hill to the schoolyard, where the children waited, their eyes twinkling at the sight of "Miz O'Connor" so flustered and disorganized.

At least, she told herself with a rueful smile, *they*

will attribute the glow in your cheeks to this dash in the fresh mountain air, rather than memories of a romantic chess game and a flattering drawing.

Putting aside the regular lessons, she lectured the children on subjects that suddenly seemed infinitely more important: romance through the ages; the power of an artist to capture emotion, and to inspire hope; and last but not least, the history and rules of chess. And she also returned to a theme from a previous lesson: there was good in everyone, and one mustn't judge a person too harshly, but rather, should look beyond a few bad acts, lest true value be missed. The first time, she had been referring to Ian, and to a lesser extent, Jed Lawson, although she hadn't mentioned names. Now, the name she didn't mention was Alex Coburn, who had tried so valiantly to make the children, and Maggie, fear and dislike him.

She hoped that her secret admirer was in the classroom that day. Perhaps he would learn a bit about the true nature of love, so that his prose could ascend to a higher plane, rather than the base and juvenile level that had made his latest note so disturbing.

But when she dismissed the children for the day and gathered up her books, she was frustrated to discover that her admirer had left another folded page for her. She was even tempted not to open it, for fear of ruining her wonderful mood. Then she reminded herself that the first two poems had been charming. Perhaps this would be more of the same. And in any case, she would now do what she'd tried to do earlier that month, and show the notes to Coburn. His insights—into the child's talent, and an appropriate response by Maggie—would be doubly welcome in light of the fondness he felt for her.

Settling back down at her desk, she unfolded the paper, then gasped at its lurid contents. Across the top,

in large block letters, was the title "Beloved Maggie."
The rest was a juvenile drawing of a naked woman,
spread eagle on a bed, her hair wild and full around
her face. The woman's breasts had been drawn with
exaggerated detail, and there was a huge smile on her
face that should have sent a chill down Maggie's spine.

But the horrified teacher's eyes looked beyond such
trifles, fixated instead on the quilt on which the female
was lying. A series of squares, each with a letter. M
in the top left corner, Z in the bottom right.

A jumble of frantic, half-finished thoughts exploded
in her head. Who? How? Had he been in her room?
Why? *When?* What should she do? Which child could
possibly see her this way?

Stuffing the drawing into her lesson book, she hurried out onto the schoolhouse porch to gulp some
sweet, fresh air. A few of the children lingered in the
yard, either climbing trees or playing with tin soldiers
in the dirt, and she almost cringed to think that one
of them might have left the notes. Worse, one of them
might have sneaked into her bedroom and looked at
her belongings through a haze of misguided interest!

She was sickened by it. Worse, she was frightened,
and while she didn't honestly believe one of the children would ever harm her, she also knew that, child
or not, this could not be allowed to go further.

*This is how those women in Chicago felt, when they
realized Ian was looking through their windows,* she
told herself shakily. *You were so quick to judge them,
but now you know the truth. They had every right to
protect themselves, and so do you. In fact, you must,
for the child's sake as well as your own. He can't be
allowed to have these thoughts, do these things—it
can only lead to something worse.*

Her first temptation was to tell Denny and June,
but she suspected that the sheriff might overreact. And

even if he didn't, he would have to take official steps, because of his position. As much as she wanted this to end, she also wanted it handled delicately, and informally.

Talk to Coburn, she advised herself, and almost immediately, a familiar warmth began to flood her, chasing away the chill of the child's transgression. The memory of the bounty hunter's idyllic sketch was strong enough and loving enough to drive the child's drawing out of her mind, or at least, to render it harmless.

Coburn would help her sort it out—the poetry, the disturbing images, the trespass into her room. She shivered again at the thought that an intruder, even a young one, had touched her baby quilt with prurient intent. What if he came back while Maggie was there? While she was asleep, or undressing!

Coburn has a gun, and he knows how to use it, she reminded herself, unashamed of the violent thought. If she could keep the authorities out of this, she would, but this boy was a strange person, and she needed to be sensible. To protect herself, and to allow Coburn to protect her.

With a quick wave of her hand toward the children, she made her way down the hill. Her panic had subsided in the wake of one simple, reassuring thought: despite her plan to spend her life alone, she had a man—a big strong warrior-poet—to advise and protect her.

As she neared the boardinghouse, she smoothed her hair, and began to imagine what this meeting would be like. He'd be protective—of that she was certain. But what else? Would there be a moment between them, when their eyes first met? Was he feeling giddy, too, at the possibility that they had found more than companionship during their chess game?

"You're being silly," she scolded herself, but still, she smiled to think that this harmless little crisis might be just the sort of push into romance a man like Coburn—a wild stallion—needed.

"Mrs. Blake? Is Mr. Coburn in his room?"

The older woman looked up from her sewing and beamed. "Good afternoon, dear. How was school?"

"It was fine." Maggie stepped into the parlor and kissed Mrs. Blake's cheek. "How are you?"

"Fine, thank you."

"Do you know where I can find Mr. Coburn?"

"He left. About an hour ago."

"Oh." Maggie glanced toward the staircase, but couldn't bring herself to go to her room alone. "I'll just wait for him in the library for a while."

"It will be a long wait," Mrs. Blake said cheerfully. "He said he might be gone a month or more."

"You're saying he left town?" Maggie stared in dismay. "Just an hour ago?"

"Yes, dear." The landlady flashed her an understanding smile. "He only said goodbye to me because I was in the kitchen. If you had been here, I'm sure he would have said it to you, too. You know how he is."

"He could have waited an hour," Maggie murmured. "He knows what time I come home." She caught herself, embarrassed to have spoken such thoughts aloud, and added quickly, "At least I'll have the library to myself for a while."

"That's right. And I'll make you a cup of tea—"

"No! No, thank you. I—" She grimaced. "I wasn't quite honest when I said my day was fine. It was exhausting, actually. Forgive my mood, won't you?"

"Of course, dear. Go upstairs and rest until dinner. Everything will look brighter after a good meal."

"That's good advice." She kissed the older woman's cheek again, then went into the hall and began to trudge up the stairs.

She felt like a fool. She also felt hurt, and angry, and embarrassed. *Mostly angry,* she tried to tell herself, but it wasn't true. Overshadowing all else was the painful knowledge that he didn't care—that she hadn't touched his heart, or his soul, as he'd touched hers; that he hadn't spent any sleepless moments over her.

Thank goodness he isn't here! What a fool you would have made of yourself, running to him for protection! At best, he would have been bewildered and uncomfortable. At worst, he would have taken it as proof that you're just what he always said you are: a romantic fool who rebuffs gentlemen, throwing herself instead into the arms of dangerous brutes who've made their disinterest and disdain clear from the start.

When she reached the narrow staircase that led to the attic, her thoughts veered sharply away from lost fantasies, and back to a very real problem. Somehow, at some time in the last few days or weeks, a disturbed young boy had climbed these very steps, his movements furtive, his motive worrisome. And he could come back at any time, so she needed to discover how he had accomplished it, and how she could prevent it from ever happening again.

It must have been quite easy for him, she decided with a shudder. *People come and go here all the time, visiting Mrs. Blake and making deliveries. And she spends all her daylight hours in the back part of the house, cooking and doing laundry, out of sight of the front hall and stairs. As for the other boarders, if they're not in the kitchen, they're relaxing under the peach tree in the backyard, oblivious.*

Feeling slightly foolish, Maggie still allowed herself the precaution of sweeping her muslin curtain to the side with one finger and surveying every corner of her tiny room before stepping into it. Then she crossed to her bed and smoothed her hand along the blue-and-yellow fabric of the baby quilt, apologizing and absolving in one wistful motion. Her most precious possession, and even now, her most comforting. A reminder of the fact that she had been loved once—by a mother she would never meet. By a father who for all his flaws had done his best. By two brothers . . .

They each had loved her—would have given their lives for her. But they were gone, and she was all alone, despite her foolish belief that a man had come into her life.

Don't think about him! she reprimanded herself. *You can be quite certain he's not thinking about you! One hour—that's all he needed to wait, and he could have said goodbye to you. That's how little you mean to him, Maggie Gleason.*

To her dismay, tears began to sting the corners of her eyes, and she banished them angrily. He wasn't worthy of them! He didn't deserve her friendship, much less the amorous thoughts she'd wasted on him. And had she honestly been foolish enough to see him as her protector? Wielding his pistol like a sword—the warrior-poet of her childhood fantasies?

"It wasn't foolish, it was reasonable," she consoled herself finally. "You didn't imagine that sketch, did you? He drew it with his own hand. How do you explain that?"

It's for your future husband . . . so that you will always be surrounded by books.

No romance after all. An odd sort of friendship,

perhaps. And maybe one day, Maggie would learn to appreciate it, but for the moment, it meant less than nothing to her. All that mattered was that he was gone. She needed him, and he hadn't been able to wait one short hour before leaving for a month without a word.

A breeze had come up, causing a tree branch to brush against the window, and Maggie felt her insides begin to knot. She had forgotten all about that lovely maple, but was that the way the intruder had been able to spy the quilt? Half expecting to see a troll-like face peering back at her, she forced herself to go to the window and evaluate the situation. The tree was good-sized, and could easily support the weight of a person, even at this height. But one couldn't climb too close to the house without venturing onto slender branches. And from the safety of the trunk, wouldn't the leaves keep a climber from being able to see into the attic?

And did it matter? Whether he'd been watching from the tree, or sneaking right up the stairs, she had to put a stop to it. Otherwise, she wouldn't be able to sleep, or change her clothes, or even read in peace in this room, ever again.

Since the only man in your life right now is Denny, you'll have to trust that he'll handle this discreetly, for the child's sake. And effectively, for yours, she decided grimly. Then she located the first three love notes, tucked them into the pages of her lesson book along with the garish drawing, and headed back down the stairs and out onto the street, calling goodbye to Mrs. Blake without pausing to explain herself.

As she hurried toward the sheriff's office, she assured herself that no child was going to be beaten or branded because of this. There had to be a constructive way to stop this sort of behavior—to educate the boy without humiliating him. Denny had a temper, and a lawman's need to right a wrong, but he also had a big heart. He'd never treat a child the way the police and the neighbors had treated Ian.

"Afternoon, Miss O'Connor."

She tried to smile at Denny's part-time deputy, who was seated outside the office, his hat pulled forward to shield his eyes from the sun. "Hello, Frank. Is the sheriff inside?"

"Sure is. Hey, Denny! The teacher's here! She looks mighty upset."

"Oh, for goodness sakes." Maggie raised her voice and called out, "I'm perfectly fine," then quickly pushed open the door, announcing, "I need your help with something, but it's hardly an emergency and—oh!" She looked past the sheriff to the man standing at the desk and added lamely, "Mr. Coburn! I didn't realize anyone was here. I didn't even know you were still in town. I can come back—"

"Why in blazes would you do that?" Denny demanded. "What's wrong? You look like you've seen a ghost."

She forced herself to smile at the sheriff. "Do I? It's been a harrowing day, but fortunately, no ghosts were involved. Just one badly behaved little boy. Which is why I'm here. But as I said, it's hardly an emergency." Her gaze fell on the WANTED posters spread across the desk and she added in a tight, unfamiliar voice, "Please, finish your business with Mr. Coburn first."

Denny scowled. "It was only a matter of time before those Lawsons started giving you trouble. Which one was it? Junior? Maybe a night in a jail cell would teach him some manners."

"Jail?" Maggie stepped backward, aghast at the suggestion. "I can only pray you're joking."

The sheriff shrugged. "If someone had thrown Jed in a cell once or twice, years ago, he might have learned a lesson about watching his temper. The whole family could benefit from a night behind bars, if you ask me."

"That's a terrible thing to say, Denny Riordain."

"What did he do?"

"It wasn't one of the Lawsons. And I have no intention of telling you one more word about it. I came for civilized advice, not barbaric suggestions."

Denny shot Coburn a grin. "She's like a mama-cat protecting her young."

The bounty hunter nodded, his face expressionless. Then he asked, "What sort of misbehavior was it?"

Maggie's chin jutted forward in proud defiance. "Nothing I can't handle on my own, thank goodness. Forgive the intrusion, gentlemen. And Mr. Coburn? Have a safe journey."

"Thank you."

She spun away, fighting a new wave of hurt and embarrassment. Here he was, face-to-face with an opportunity to say goodbye, and he still couldn't quite muster the interest.

Too preoccupied with choosing whom he'll kill this time, she told herself in disgust. *To think you considered allowing him to touch you! Be grateful he showed his true nature so clearly before you made even more of a fool of yourself.*

"Don't run off this way, missy," Denny was protesting. "Tell me who the little hooligan is—"

"That's quite enough, Sheriff." She turned back to eye him sternly. "The children admire you, did you know that? I believe they trust you, too. You'd do well to trust them in return, rather than treat them as criminals."

"For you to come here, he must have done something serious."

"For me to come here, I must have been out of my

head," she retorted. "From now on, I'll handle the children by myself. You can concentrate on your WANTED posters and posses."

"Maggie!" Denny grabbed her by the arm to prevent her from storming out of the office. "I didn't mean to upset you."

"You didn't." She touched his hand in apology. "It's been a trying day, is all. I shouldn't have raised my voice. Forgive me?"

"Sure."

She wanted to turn to Coburn, to assure him that he didn't have anything to do with her mood either, but she wasn't sure she could be convincing. And the very fact that he hadn't said another word told her more than she needed to know. He could see her this way, upset and hurting, and couldn't be bothered enough to ask, or wonder, or even pretend to care.

"Give my love to June," she murmured, then she extricated herself from the sheriff's grasp, gave him a wistful smile, and took her leave of the men as gracefully as she was able.

She was tempted to go to June and seek advice concerning the letter writer, but was afraid her perceptive friend would know that something else was also bothering her. June's opinion of Coburn was so low, Maggie didn't dare let her discover that she had entertained amorous thoughts of the man, unrequited though they had been.

There was no one else she trusted, except perhaps Mr. Braddock and Father James, either of whom, she knew, would give her valuable advice. But they were too far away to offer her what she really needed—a sense of security in a town that had felt so much like home, from the time she'd stepped foot into it, until today.

You chose to be alone, she reminded herself. *Part of that decision is learning to protect yourself. Perhaps this experience will prove to be a valuable lesson. When all this is over, you'll ask Mr. Gentry to supply you with a pistol, and Denny can teach you to use it. Then you'll never need a man again. But for now . . .*

For now, she didn't trust herself with a loaded weapon. On the other hand, she had wielded a kitchen knife all her life—for culinary purposes, of course, but at least it felt comfortable in her hand, so she confirmed that her landlady was still in the parlor, then borrowed a razor-sharp paring knife, intending to sleep with it under her pillow.

She was safe now, she decided, although she couldn't imagine any set of circumstances under which she'd stab a child. "You won't need to actually hurt him," she assured herself as she hid the weapon in the top drawer of her dresser. "At worst, you'll just show him you're armed, and he'll be so frightened and disenchanted, he'll wonder how he could ever have loved you. And the truth is, even that won't be necessary. He'll never approach you in a threatening manner. But knowing you have this will help you get some sleep tonight."

It was true. She had been dreading the idea of sleeping in her room unprotected, knowing that her admirer might walk right up to the bed and stare at her. As it was, she couldn't manage to eat more than a bite of her dinner, and while she tried to participate in the parlor activities thereafter, her heart wasn't in it, and she was soon back in her room, where she hastily donned her nightgown, then dug out the knife and clutched it tightly as she crawled under her quilt.

She discovered quickly that she still didn't feel safe.

The boy didn't know about the knife, so he could still come to her room, and what good would any weapon do if she was sound asleep when the intruder came around?

In the meantime, every sound—the branches against the window, the creak of the steps as the boarders headed to their bedrooms, the howl of a dog in the distance—made her heart beat with rapid, uneven insistence. The more she tried to steady herself, the worse it seemed to be, until she finally realized there would be no sleep for her that night.

As soon as she was certain everyone else had gone to bed, she threw a robe over her nightgown, gathered up the knife and the admirer's four notes, and crept downstairs. Then she built a fire and curled up on the sofa, with the knife and the "love letters" on her lap.

"Who are you?" she asked the writer sadly. "Poor, odd little boy—if only I knew who you were, I could tell you, kindly but firmly, why this is not appropriate behavior. For anyone." She let the crude drawing float to the floor, concentrating instead on the first little poem. "This is so sweet," she assured the absent child, relaxing as she reread the words. "Poor, innocent dear—it's so clear from this that you could never hurt anyone. And I won't let anyone hurt *you,* either. We'll find a way to deal with this, you and I. I give you my word on that.

"If only someone had done that for you, Ian," she murmured as she drifted into sleep. "We'd all be together to this very day. You and me, and Papa and Brian. And Lettie, too, somehow. Just like in the story Brian used to tell. There should have been a way for that to happen. I was too little then, and I didn't really understand why they were all so afraid of you . . ."

She found herself engulfed in a dream, and to her delight, she was with her brothers again. Brian and

Ian, playing with tin soldiers on the floor of the kitchen, while Maggie cooked dinner. Her father stood by the fire, his eyes shining with pride as he surveyed his family. Then she heard a noise in the parlor, and announced cheerfully, *Uncle Eddie must be here. You boys should put the toys away now.* Brian complied immediately, but Ian jumped up and ran into the parlor to greet the guest. Maggie followed, wiping her hands on her apron as she walked, but when she got to the parlor, it was empty, and so she shouted, *Ian? Where are you?*

When he didn't answer, a sense of foreboding enveloped her. Slowly, she turned back to the kitchen, but her feet were like lead.

She wanted to warn Brian and her father to be careful, but her mouth was too dry. And her chest was beginning to ache from the force of her heart, pounding and pounding against her ribs. She was going to faint, and decided to welcome it, when a rough hand grabbed her by the shoulder and began to shake her.

"Maggie! Wake up!"

She shrieked, then pulled away, curling into a terrified ball, while staring at the intruder through a haze of confusion and disbelief. She could only pray she was still dreaming, but knew, even as he reached for her again, that she was not.

Twelve

"It can't be you!" Maggie's hand began to search frantically for the knife. "Why are you here?"

"Looking for this?" he drawled, holding the weapon in view for a moment before setting it down on the floor next to where he was kneeling.

"That's mine!" She wanted her words to sound angry, but instead, they were more of a confused gasp.

"Take a deep breath," he instructed, adding tersely, "Now."

She nodded, then took several gulps of air. The third steadied her enough to speak in a reasonable tone. "Why are you here? Mrs. Blake said you wouldn't be back for a month."

"I want to talk to you about these." He gathered up the poems and drawing and waved them under her nose. "Is this what you meant by 'misbehavior' at the sheriff's office?"

"Give me those!"

"I want to talk to you about them," he repeated. "Come with me."

"Pardon?"

He grinned in frustration. "I want you to come with me, to discuss these perverted love notes. In my room."

Maggie gathered her robe tightly about herself, then

eyed him in cool dismissal. "We can discuss them in the morning, sir. Here, or at the sheriff's office. But not in your—oh!" She shrieked again as he threw her over his shoulder and strode toward his room.

"Mr. Coburn!"

"I want to talk to you. In private. Undisturbed." He deposited her on the bed, kicked the door closed, and then pulled the desk chair up and sat in front of her. "Tell me who's been writing these notes to you."

She scanned his expression, and saw only clinical interest, so she scooted a safe distance away, then tried to relax. "One of the children—"

"These weren't written by a child," he interrupted her.

"Pardon?" She sighed, finally understanding his bizarre attitude. For some reason, he believed an adult male had dared send notes of this sort. And like any lawman, mercenary or otherwise, he had his limits when it came to insulting the opposite sex.

Nice to know even a coldhearted bully like yourself can be chivalrous on occasion, she congratulated him silently. Aloud, she was more reassuring. "I worried, too, when I first read this one." She tapped the long, graphic note. "But it's the same handwriting as the others. Look at this one. It was the very first to arrive. See how sweet and juvenile it is. No man wrote that."

"No child wrote this," he countered, tapping the third note as Maggie had done.

"We disagree, sir. May I ask you a question?"

He nodded.

"Why have you returned so abruptly? Did you forget something?"

Coburn shrugged. "I kept remembering your behavior at the sheriff's office. It was bizarre, even for you."

"If you're going to insult me, I'm leaving."

He grasped her by the arm, preventing her retreat. "You asked a question. I'm trying to answer it honestly."

"Fine." She settled back down. "Continue, please."

"At first, I thought you were just uncomfortable. Because you were upset that I left the boardinghouse without saying goodbye."

"I can't imagine why you think that would upset me."

Chuckling, he insisted, "I *knew* it would upset you. That's why I did it. To make a point."

"Pardon?"

He raked his fingers through his thick, dark hair. "It was clear to me that you were beginning to misunderstand our relationship. I thought the kindest thing to do, under the circumstances, was to be cruel. Or rather, dismissive. I didn't take any pleasure in it, Maggie. In fact, it was one of the hardest things I've ever had to do."

"But you did it for me? I'll be forever grateful, Mr. Coburn. And now, if you'll excuse me—"

Again he caught her by the arm. "I'm not finished."

His hand was strong, and she was curious about the rest of his explanation, so she shrugged her shoulders and instructed him to go on.

"I knew you'd be upset, so when you seemed nervous and combative at the sheriff's office, I attributed it to my behavior."

"When, in fact, it had nothing at all to do with you?"

He nodded, smiling ruefully. "Somewhere between here and Redding, I realized that. You're too tough to fall apart just because some worthless fellow broke your heart. And you're not a very good liar, yet that business about the misbehaving child had a ring of truth to it. And you were scared. You—the woman who has refused to be scared by any of *my* tactics, which are ordinarily very effective."

"Your tactics? You admit then that you've tried from the start to frighten me, for the same reason you frighten the children? To keep me away?"

He nodded. "In those days, I didn't know about your peculiar need to vanquish bullies with your flaming sword of justice and compassion."

"My what? Oh, dear. June told Denny about my childhood? And *he* told *you?* I'm honestly surprised." *And a bit disappointed in them,* she added to herself.

"I didn't need anyone to tell me about your need to rescue children," Coburn said quietly. "At our very first meeting, you defended the Lawson boys. And then you insisted on going out to their cabin alone. And you've called me a bully more than once, right to my face."

"That's true."

"Is there something else? Someone bullied you as a child?"

"Not exactly. I had a sickly brother who was taunted mercilessly."

"That must have been difficult." He cleared his throat. "I need a list of every man you've met since you came here. And any from your past who might have followed you here, from San Francisco or elsewhere."

"For goodness sakes! I keep trying to tell you, these weren't written by a man."

"I see." He handed her the third note. "Read this aloud."

"Don't be tiresome."

"Shall I read it to you then? You actually believe a child wrote about his need to—"

"Don't!" She covered her ears and glared. "Perhaps

you should just go back to your bounty hunting, and leave this alone."

"Bounty hunting?"

Maggie cursed herself silently, but tried to maintain an even expression. "The sheriff's desk was covered with WANTED posters today. Should I assume they were just a subject of idle conversation?"

Coburn hesitated, then repeated flatly, "I need that list."

"It's preposterous, and I won't be a party to it. The men here have treated me like a princess."

"An emerald-eyed Irish princess?" he asked, quoting Denny in a mocking tone.

"As a matter of fact, yes."

"Fine." He picked up the drawing of the naked woman on a quilt. "Let's talk about this instead. Beloved Maggie. You believe an innocent child sees you this way?"

Maggie averted her eyes. "Couldn't we discuss this in the morning?"

"It's an elaborate drawing. Is it accurate?"

"I beg your pardon!"

Coburn chuckled. "I was referring to certain details, such as these marks on your thigh."

"What are you talking about?" She flushed and took the drawing from him, and realized that indeed, there were several faint marks on the naked woman's right thigh. She had been so busy noticing the quilt, and the breasts, and the smile, she hadn't paid attention to lesser details.

Coburn exhaled with impatience. "If you don't cooperate with me, I won't be able to—" He broke off, apparently noticing that Maggie was staring in openmouthed amazement at the drawing. "What? Talk to me."

"How does he know this?" she whispered, more

confused than alarmed. "They're so faded, I don't notice them myself anymore."

"Faded? Are you talking about scars?"

She nodded, intrigued by the puzzling development. "A dog bit me, when I was eight years old. But it's been more than ten years, and they've faded almost to nothing."

"Let's have a look."

"Pardon?" She drew back in haughty disgust as his meaning hit her. "I assure you, sir, they're unremarkable."

"But visible, apparently."

"Visible to whom?"

"That's the question," he agreed. "I didn't notice them when you got out of the bathtub, so they can't be very prominent."

"The bath tub?" She winced at the memory. "You're suggesting this boy has seen me bathing?"

"I'm not suggesting anything until I have a look, so just—"

"No! You can't be serious."

"This is no time for false modesty," he said with a chuckle, then before she could protest further, he was on her, pushing her shoulders back into the mattress with one arm, while pulling her nightgown high on her right leg with his free hand.

"Alex Coburn!" she wailed, but he didn't seem to hear, and also didn't seem to be taking lustful advantage of the situation. In fact, he was studying her as though she were a bug under a magnifying glass. And he hadn't pulled her garment any higher than necessary.

And she couldn't have freed herself in any event, so she gritted her teeth, alert to any mischief. "Well?" she demanded finally.

"See for yourself. They're just where the culprit

drew them. He's seen your leg, Maggie. There's no other explanation." Releasing her, he laughed as he watched her straighten her nightclothes primly. "Who else has seen that leg?"

"I beg your pardon?"

"The man who kissed you on your father's front porch—what's his name? Have you kept in touch with him?"

"What on earth are you ranting about? What man?"

"He kissed you on your father's front porch, then asked you to marry him." Coburn's tone betrayed the return of impatience. "I do my best not to hear the gossip that runs rampant through this town, but you're a popular topic at the saloon, and when I play cards there, I hear more than I care to."

"You mean Robert?" Maggie narrowed her eyes in deliberate warning. "You're suggesting that I allowed him to peek under my skirts? Are you insane?"

Coburn grinned. "Can you think of anyone else?" When Maggie simply glared, he shook his head as though further amused. "You're saying that to your knowledge I'm the only man—"

"Be quiet!" She calmed herself before adding, "The doctor who treated the bite saw the original wounds, of course, but he died years ago. My father and brother saw them, but they're both dead, too. So yes, to my knowledge, you're the only man who has seen that part of my leg."

"This Robert—he's the chess master?"

Maggie nodded.

"And he lives in San Francisco?"

"No. Chicago."

"Chicago?" He arched an eyebrow. "When was the last time you and he communicated?"

"When I left for San Francisco, I severed all ties.

Everyone I loved was dead, and I was desperate to begin a new life, away from the painful memories."

"What sort of memories?"

"Death. My mother died when I was born. My brothers both died before they reached manhood. My father died last year. I'm the only one left." She stared into his eyes and pleaded with him, saying, "There aren't any men in my life, Coburn. I wish there were, but there aren't. No bad men, and no good ones."

His gaze softened. "That's not quite accurate. You have the sheriff, and you have me. And Kirk Waller, and countless others. We'll make that list—"

"It's a boy, Coburn. In my heart, I'm sure of it. He's troubled, and perhaps even a little dangerous— and if he's been watching me bathe . . ." She shuddered. "There's no other explanation, is there?"

"Apparently not. I'll have a look at your bedroom window in the morning."

"There's a tree, right outside the attic. And there's no door on my room, did you know that?"

He grimaced as he nodded.

She shuddered again. "It's too brazen to be believable. That he might stand outside the bathroom window, where anyone could catch him—"

"To catch a glimpse of 'beloved Maggie,' " Coburn muttered. "There are men who become so obsessed—" He stopped himself and smiled in apology. "There's not much else we can do tonight."

"That's true," she said, relieved.

"In the morning, I'll pay another visit to Lawson, just to be sure he's not behind any of this."

" 'Another' visit? When was the first?" Maggie noted that he had winced, and asked carefully, "Are you saying it was you who—well, who caused his injuries? You and Denny, I suppose?" She exhaled in frustration. "I appreciate the sentiment, but it was pre-

sumptuous, don't you think? And an abuse of the sheriff's authority."

"I went alone," Coburn assured her. "And I didn't
go there to fight with him. Just to warn him. But he
took such pleasure in showing disrespect for you, I
decided to render him harmless, just in case."

"He said it was a gang of lumberjacks."

"That's what I told him to say."

"And that's why you asked me so many questions
that evening—to make certain he did as you instructed?" She smiled in reluctant gratitude. "That's
why he had Junior escort me home safely?"

"He knew it would be his hide if anything happened
to you." Coburn's smile was rueful as he added, "I'm
glad he cooperated. I didn't want to have to go back.
My knuckles were raw as it was."

"From pounding his face? I should think so." She
studied him intently. "Why did you pretend not to care
about my welfare?"

"I didn't want you to misunderstand. To see a
knight in shining armor where there wasn't one." He
cleared his throat, then asked, "Who else has shown
interest in you since you came here?"

"There's been nothing unusual. And as you said,
there's not much more we can do about it tonight."

Coburn was examining the drawing again. "What's
this about? These letters—M, and R, and T, and Z.
Does that mean anything to you?"

"My mother made it. They're baby blocks, do you
see? M for Maggie. M through Z." An unexpected sob
caught in her throat, but she swallowed it back dutifully. "It's always been my favorite possession, but it's
tainted now. *Everything* is tainted. He's been looking
at me, through windows or worse. I felt so safe when
I first arrived here—"

"You're safe," he reassured her, slipping his arm

around her shoulders. "You trust me to protect you, don't you?"

"Yes," she admitted, cuddling against him. "You're a confusing man, but I suspect this is what you're good at."

"That's right. There's only one more thing we need to do tonight, Maggie. Then you can go to sleep. How does that sound?"

"Wonderful," she admitted.

"Good." He pushed her gently backward until she was lying under him. "I need to look at your leg again. Just for a minute. You trust me, don't you?"

Maggie hesitated, then gave him an uncertain smile. "Do what you must."

His hand slid under her nightdress, caressing her skin, and she allowed herself the secret luxury of enjoying the callused warmth of his fingers. To him, this was simply a criminal investigation, but to her, it was the culmination of an innocent fantasy—a moment she would cherish forever, although he'd never know it.

"That's good." With his hand still exploring her upper leg, he leaned his mouth close to her ear and whispered, "Your perverse admirer believes you belong to him. You can see that in the notes, can't you? He believes there's no man in your life to protect you. But he's wrong, isn't he?"

Maggie closed her eyes and sighed with relief. "Yes, he's wrong."

"I want him to *know* he's wrong. When he sees you tomorrow, I want him to realize that you're *my* woman, not his. I want him to smell me all over you."

"What?"

She tried to wriggle out from under him, but he pinned her and insisted, "This is important. You want him to stop, don't you?"

Maggie gulped, then nodded.

His gaze locked with hers. "You trust me, don't you?"

She nodded again, just before his mouth covered hers, and his hands began to ravage her with gentle thoroughness.

Her body began to throb with excitement, and she returned his kisses without hesitation. She had dreamed of this, knowing his touch would ignite her. And there was passion in his blazing eyes; in the deep, hungry thrusts of his tongue as he sought hers; in the demanding way he moved himself against her. Then his hand slipped between her legs and teased at her, and she knew she should stop him, but he was talking again. Talking nonsense, but in that voice of his . . .

"I want him to smell me on you. To know you're my woman. The men here are afraid of me, sweetheart, and with good reason. I won't let them touch you. No one but me can dare look at you, or touch you, or write love poems to you, or draw you. That's how you want it, isn't it?"

"Yes," she said, gasping for air. "That's how I want it."

"That's right, Maggie." As he freed himself from his trousers, he continued to kiss her with ravenous thoroughness. Then his hand was between her legs again, pushing her thighs apart, while stimulating her with intimate thoroughness, and before she could believe what was happening, he was thrusting himself into her, gently but without any hesitation. She wanted to scream for him to stop—to let her think, for just a minute—but her mouth was too busy kissing him to scream, and her pelvis was rising up to welcome him. To welcome the searing heat that gave way to glorious confusion as tight, focused waves of pleasure began to pulsate through her.

"You're so beautiful. So goddammed beautiful." He was crooning the words, his voice raspy with appreciation. "Don't worry about anything, sweetheart. Not ever again. I swear I'll take care of you."

"Love me," she dared to demand in return. "That's all I want."

She heard the laugh rumble through his chest, and for once, the sound was filled with joy rather than mockery or self-derision. Then his thrusts intensified, and he was groaning her name, and her own joy shifted into something so glorious, she had to cling to his neck, throw back her head, and call out his name in grateful delight.

He inhaled and exhaled, slowly and steadily, as though reorienting himself after the burst of hedonism. Then he gathered her against himself, brushing her damp hair away from her face so he could stare into her eyes. He seemed about to say something, then kissed her cheek instead. "Go to sleep, Maggie. Morning will be here before you know it."

"Tell me what you were going to say."

"I'm glad I came back."

"So am I." She snuggled against him.

"You're safe now. No matter what happens, you're safe."

"Because he can smell you all over me?"

Coburn grinned. "That's right. It may sound crude to you, but he'll know. And unless he's a complete imbecile, he'll stop bothering you."

"Good."

"And between myself and the sheriff, we'll track him down, and then he won't bother anyone, ever again."

"Don't hurt him, though," Maggie murmured. "He doesn't mean anything by it." When Coburn didn't respond, she repeated, "Don't hurt him. Not on my account. Is that clear?"

"Go to sleep," he suggested. "Leave the rest to us."

"But, Coburn . . ."

"Under the circumstances, shouldn't you consider calling me Alex?"

She felt her cheeks warm under his teasing gaze. "It's such a nice name." She stroked his jaw, then added softly, "Promise me you won't hurt him."

"Don't ask for promises I can't keep." He kissed her forehead, then gathered her into his arms, her cheek cradled against his chest. It was a loving motion, but also seemed calculated to foreclose further eye contact and, presumably, any more questions.

But his words rang in her ears—*Don't ask for promises I can't keep*—and she needed to know if he was referring only to the fate of the admirer, or to Maggie's future with Coburn as well. Not that she was sure she knew what promises she wanted him to make, even if he were willing.

Did she want him to marry her? Had things changed so much that she was now willing to start a family, and with a virtual stranger who made a living as a bounty hunter?

And what if he said just the opposite—that this night had served its purpose, which was to convince the admirer that the schoolteacher had a man in her life. Wasn't that the truth? Coburn had left town that very afternoon for the purpose of avoiding an entanglement with Maggie. The only thing that had changed since then was the necessity to protect her from unwanted attentions.

No, she told herself with quiet confidence. *That's not the only thing that changed tonight. It can't be. Not with him holding you this way—so tenderly, and with such ferocity of commitment.*

His breathing was strong and steady, just as his lovemaking had been, and Maggie wanted nothing more than to snuggle against him and fall asleep. But the unspoken question seemed to hang in the air, and she decided there'd be no real rest until she asked it. In some ways, she even suspected he was waiting for it.

"Alex?"

"Go to sleep."

There was an edge to his voice—barely perceptible, yet also undeniable—that silenced her more than the actual words. It might as well have been a wall between them, despite their physical closeness.

And she no longer wished to know what he was thinking. She didn't even want to know what the ensuing days, and nights, would bring for them.

The tension and regret in his voice already told her everything she needed to know: that somehow, in a haze of innocence and need, she had made a terrible, terrible mistake.

When Maggie awoke the next morning, she reached for him instinctively, then flushed and sat up quickly. He wasn't there, of course. Why should he be? What amazed her was how easily she had accustomed herself to sleeping with a man. Rather than lie awake all night fretting over her predicament, as she had been certain she would do, she had luxuriated in the feel of him, waking up occasionally, only to be lulled right back to sleep by his strong, even breathing.

The sun was filtering through a crack in the curtains, and she pulled the covers more tightly around herself, fearing that the peeping child might be out there, watching her. Then a more practical concern occurred to her—Mrs. Blake was probably in the kitchen, fixing breakfast for the boarders, and would realize that Maggie had spent the night in Coburn's room!

Lunging out of the bed, she pulled her robe over herself and belted it tightly, then crept to the door, which she inched open. Perhaps she could make a dash for the stairs when the landlady's back was turned.

"Well, look who's finally awake!" Mrs. Blake called cheerfully from the library. "Did you need something, dear?"

Maggie grimaced, then stepped into view, knowing that her cheeks were crimson, but knowing also that further delay would only make things worse.

Mrs. Blake hurried over to her and pulled her into a hearty embrace. "Poor dear. Mr. Coburn told me all about last night. It must have been so dreadful for you."

"I beg your pardon?" Maggie stared in dismay. "What exactly did he tell you?"

"That you've been receiving offensive love notes from some reprobate, and you were so frightened, you couldn't bear to spend one more night in a room without a door. Why didn't you tell me, dear? I would have given you my bedroom in a heartbeat!"

Maggie smiled a weak but appreciative smile. "I should have thought of that."

"I'm just so grateful to Mr. Coburn for returning so fortuitously, and for taking you under his wing the way he's done." She beamed as she pretended to scold. "To think you didn't believe he could be a gentleman."

Maggie eyed her with frustrated amusement. "I thought you'd be scandalized."

"If it were anyone else, I suppose I would be. But

the situation was desperate, was it not? Let people say what they will. I know he'd never take advantage of an innocent girl like you, and even if he would, you'd never allow it. And your safety comes first, so if he wants to sleep on the floor next to your bed for the rest of his life, I won't say a word about it."

"Thank you." Maggie bit her lip, then dared to ask, "Where is he?"

"Examining every window in the house. He seems to think this fellow has been prowling around, trying to spy on you. It sends a shiver down my spine. You should have told me," she repeated firmly.

"I didn't know what to think. And I wasn't really frightened, until last night. I think it's just one of my students—an innocent but misguided child."

"Mr. Coburn seems to think it's a man—a very bad man."

"We disagree on that. And," Maggie said with a sigh, "I hope you won't say anything to anyone about it yet, just in case it is a child. I don't want him to be humiliated in front of the whole community for one tiny error in judgment."

"Mr. Coburn seems to think it's more than that."

"As I said, Mr. Coburn and I disagree." She regretted the displeasure in her tone, and smiled to soften it. "I should hurry and dress for school."

"Mr. Coburn doesn't want you to change upstairs anymore. Bring your dress down here and change in his room."

Maggie arched an eyebrow. "I'll make certain no one is looking in my window before I undress." *After all,* she added in tart silence, *Mr. Coburn himself could be in that tree at this very moment.*

Then she laughed at herself, remembering that he had seen all there was to see of her the night before, and had no need to climb a tree for such a purpose.

At that moment the back door slammed, causing Maggie to whirl toward the sound just in time to see the bounty hunter stride into view. He nodded toward her, his eyes twinkling. "Good morning, Miss O'Connor. I hope you slept well."

Maggie squared her shoulders. "Good morning, sir. Mrs. Blake tells me you've been inspecting the windows."

His mood sobered visibly. "I don't want you changing your clothes in that room of yours anymore. My bedroom is the most secure in the entire house."

When she started to protest, Mrs. Blake scolded her, saying, "This is no time for modesty, young lady."

The twinkle returned to Coburn's blue eyes. "Exactly what I said last night. Isn't that so, Miss O'Connor?"

"I'm afraid last night didn't make as much of an impression on me as it did on you," she retorted. "Excuse me, please. I don't want to be late for school."

"You'll have breakfast before you go, won't you?" Mrs. Blake patted her arm and added in a soothing tone, "We know you're upset, dear, but you have to eat. You need your strength now more than ever. Isn't that so, Mr. Coburn?"

Maggie sent him a warning glare, then turned back to her landlady. "I'd love some coffee and toast. And you're sweet to worry about me, but please don't. I'm not in any danger, and I never was."

"Then why did Mr. Coburn find you sleeping in his room with a kitchen knife in hand?" Before Maggie could answer, Mrs. Blake did so for her. "Of course you're frightened. Any woman would be after the night you had. And I imagine you're exhausted, too—"

"Mrs. Blake?"

"Yes, dear?"

Maggie kissed the older woman's cheek. "Let's just pretend last night never happened, shall we?"

The landlady smiled. "If that makes you feel better."

"It does. Infinitely better." Without giving Coburn the satisfaction of another look, Maggie headed up to her room, where she plopped facedown onto the bed.

Was he her lover now? She simply didn't know. The sparkle in his eye could just as easily have been amusement at her expense as a shared secret. And he had protected her reputation, but hadn't that protected *him,* too, from the consequences of his behavior?

What would the landlady say if she knew he had capitalized on Maggie's fear by appointing himself her bodyguard and proceeding to confuse her with frightening tales of perverse men, and to seduce her by pretending to examine scars on her leg while actually caressing her?

She'd think he was a scoundrel. And if she knew how much Maggie had enjoyed Coburn's attention, Maggie too would plummet in her estimation. Even now, the confused schoolteacher could remember how masterful his lovemaking had been, and how thrilled she had been to receive it. The mere thought of it was beginning to make her tingle again!

That's enough of that, she scolded herself as she scooted off the bed and cinched her robe more tightly before heading for the washroom to dress and prepare for her day.

With any luck, Denny and Coburn would solve the mystery of the secret admirer before the day was out. Then Coburn would leave on his bounty hunting, which would tell her all she needed to know. Or he would stay, and try to make love to her again, which would confuse matters further. But only if she allowed it, and as she readied herself to rejoin him in the kitchen, she decided coolly that whatever else happened, she wouldn't allow herself to make that mistake again.

Thirteen

Mrs. Blake stood on the front porch, her eyes filled with concern as she waved goodbye to Maggie and Coburn. "Take good care of her."

"Don't worry." The bounty hunter flashed the woman a reassuring grin, then slipped his arm around Maggie's waist.

"Stop that!" Maggie batted his hand away in disgust, then gave her landlady an apologetic shrug.

"Don't be stubborn, dear. This is Mr. Coburn's strategy."

"Pardon?"

Coburn nudged her. "Don't you remember, Miss O'Connor? We discussed this last night. I want the men in this town to stay away from you until we've solved the mystery of these notes."

"Do you see?" Mrs. Blake smiled with delight. "They'll believe Mr. Coburn is courting you. And they're so frightened of him, they won't dare come near his girl, much less send her love letters. Isn't that clever?"

"Brilliant," Maggie drawled, wondering if her new lover had told their landlady about the rest of his strategy: ensuring that his "smell" was all over her!

"Let's go." His arm encircled Maggie once again. "Have a good morning, Mrs. Blake."

"Are you enjoying yourself?" Maggie demanded as he escorted her down the street. "What will people think? Oh, fine. There's Gladys. Now, stop it!" She brushed his arm away again, then smiled toward her nosy neighbor. "Good morning, Gladys."

The woman stared back, clearly unable to think of anything to say.

"Mrs. Blake will explain all this to you," Maggie assured her. "It isn't what it seems."

"I should hope not," Gladys said with a sniff, then she bustled past them, almost bursting with clear intent to interrogate the landlady without mercy.

"Why did you say that to her?" Coburn muttered under his breath.

"She's such a gossip. The whole town will hear about it."

"That's exactly what we want."

"They won't let me teach anymore if they think I'm some sort of loose woman."

"For walking with a man?"

"For allowing myself to be compromised in public by a gunfighter," she retorted.

Coburn chuckled, then anchored his hand securely on her hip. "Just pretend you're madly in love with me, and I'll take care of the rest."

She shook her head, but didn't pull away. Instead, she allowed him to guide her across the street toward the path that led to the schoolhouse. At least he had used the word "pretend," which meant he knew she wasn't *actually* in love with him, despite her midnight indiscretion.

And she did feel safe with him, she realized sheepishly, remembering other mornings, after she'd received the third note, when she had scrutinized every face, every expression, for some sign of guilt. If Coburn hadn't come home and offered to help her,

she would have slept on the sofa with a knife, having
nightmares about Ian, and would have been exhausted
and wary by morning.

"That's better," he murmured as she relaxed against
him. "You're not angry with me, are you, Maggie?"

"I don't know," she admitted. "I'm confused, and
worried about what you and Denny will do today."

"That again?" Impatience had invaded his tone. "I
promise we won't string him up. At least, not without
a trial."

"Alex!" She pulled free and began to stride up the
path away from him.

"Hey!" He caught her again, then forced her to
gaze directly into her eyes, repeating his earlier in-
struction—"Pretend you're in love with me"—in a
low, gravelly voice. Before she could react, he began
to lower his mouth to hers.

She was trembling with anticipation, but forced herself to protest that the children would see them.

"Aren't you the person who insists the letters were
written by a child?" he countered seductively. "Aren't
they the very ones who need to witness this, and to
understand that you're spoken for?"

It made sense somehow, and so without further protest she curled her arms around his neck.

"You're so beautiful," he whispered, then his mouth
crushed against hers, while his fingers kneaded the
small of her back, urging her to press closer to him.

She felt the rest of the world recede, leaving them
alone on that hillside, drenched in one another's ardor.
Every detail of their lovemaking returned to tease her,
and she could tell beyond a doubt that he, too, was
becoming aroused.

"Alex," she warned in groggy delight. "The children."

"I want everyone in this whole damned town to

know," he answered, his voice as thick with passion as it had been during their lovemaking in his bed.

"I'm sure they do." She pulled free, but only slightly, leaving her hands resting on his shoulders. Then she stared up into those midnight blue eyes and told him simply, "You need to leave now. I have students to teach."

Coburn smiled. "You should see how pretty you look. The morning air has coaxed a beautiful flush from your cheeks."

"That's embarrassment."

"It's arousal," he corrected. "I was just trying to be a gentleman."

"Save that nonsense for Mrs. Blake," Maggie suggested, stepping back and trying for a more sensible mood. But he was so amazingly handsome, and his attention was so intently focused on her, she almost found herself stepping back into his embrace.

Then she happened to glance toward the schoolyard, and was catapulted back to reality by the expression of confused dismay on her students' faces. "Oh, dear."

"Do any of the boys seem jealous?"

"I believe they're horrified."

He laughed and took her arm, leading her up toward the gate. "I knew the men would notice, but I suppose your younger admirers were bound to see the difference, too."

"The difference? Oh . . ." Maggie grimaced as she realized what he was implying: that every man in town would see that she was no longer a virgin. Was that possible? Turning to him, she blurted out unhappily, "I don't want to look different. I don't want to *be* different. I want to be what I was—Maggie O'Connor. I was happy that way, for the first time in years."

"Happy? You were being victimized by a stranger."

"And now I'm being victimized by you. Is that an improvement?"

It was Coburn's turn to wince. "Is that how you feel?"

"No." She flushed and looked down at the ground. "I shouldn't have said that. I know you needed—or at least, thought you needed—to do what you did. What you're still doing. But it's destroying my reputation. Can't you see that?"

He touched her cheek. "Once we've apprehended the culprit, Mrs. Blake will make certain everyone knows the truth."

"But the truth is a lie," Maggie reminded him. "And you said yourself, the men can see the difference just by looking at me."

When his eyes flashed with amusement, she glared in disgust. "It isn't funny, Alex. Couldn't you at least pretend to care about me?"

"I can do more than pretend." He caught her by the waist and kissed her quickly, then released her before she could catch her breath. "Your students are still watching us."

"Oh!" She had forgotten all about them again, and now turned to wave in apology, calling out, "Go on inside. I'll be right there." Then she instructed Coburn, "Don't bother to come back. I'm perfectly capable of walking home without a bodyguard."

"I'm not going anywhere."

"What?" She shook her head, almost frantic at the thought. "You can't possibly stay! Please? I thought you were going to meet with the sheriff."

"I sent word to him to meet me here."

"No." Summoning her most confident tone, she took his hands in her own and squeezed them. "I'll be safe as long as the other children are around. And if anything goes awry, there's a bell." She inclined her head toward the apparatus in question. "I promised Denny I'd ring it at the first hint of danger, and now I'm promising you, too. Please, Alex? I won't be able to teach if I know you're out here."

Coburn eyed her sternly. "If any male over the age of fourteen, other than myself or the sheriff—"

"Absolutely! Even if it's the reverend."

To her surprise, Coburn didn't smile at the joke, but simply asked, "Do I have your word?"

"You honestly think it could be Reverend Fletcher?"

"I don't know him," Coburn said with a shrug. "And neither do you. Go on inside now. I'll be back before you're finished for the day."

She nodded and thanked him, then dashed up the walk. Once on the porch, she turned and was charmed despite herself at the sight of him, lounging against the fence post, watching her with dark blue eyes that shone with vigilance and determination. She wanted to thank him again, but there was an unexpected lump in her throat, and so she settled for a wave instead before hurrying into the classroom.

She hadn't seen the children this way—so uncomfortable, or so curious—since the first day of school. And she had never seen them so confused. She even suspected that the older boys were looking at her through knowing eyes, and Coburn's goal reverberated in her imagination. Was it possible? Were they actually smelling him all over her?

Three of the children—Josh Deighton and the two older Lawson boys, seemed particularly shaken, but it was little Joey Lawson who finally dared raise his hand.

"Yes, Joey?"

"Are you gonna marry that Coburn fella?"

She flushed, wondering what she was supposed to say to that. That she was "his woman"—whatever *that* meant?

Mary Ellen took advantage of Maggie's hesitation to explain, "He means, do you love Mr. Coburn?"

Maggie licked her lips, then explained simply, "He's the most important man in my life."

She surprised herself with those words, but knew that they were true. And they had a nice ring to them, so she decided to capitalize on that fact by announcing, "That's all you need to know. I don't want to discuss anything else about Mr. Coburn today."

"Can we talk about him tomorrow?"

It brought a reluctant smile to Maggie's face. "We'll see."

Then, to her amazement, Joey Lawson exploded. "He's bad! Everyone knows it! You said you weren't gonna marry anyone, then you start kissing *him!*"

Maggie bit her lip. Of all the boys on the list—the students, and the other children from the camp—Joey had seemed the least likely suspect. So why was he the most concerned?

Coburn had you so convinced it was an adult, not a boy. But what if it's someone as darling as Joey? Denny and Coburn won't be understanding. They'll mortify the poor child! Remember Ian's face, when Captain McLaughlin told Papa he should be locked up, far away from decent women? He was so hurt. So confused. So pure, no matter what they thought!

She flashed Joey a reassuring smile. "Mr. Coburn is a complicated man, but a good one. Now, the subject is closed."

For the rest of the day, they looked at her as though she were a stranger, and in a sense, she was. But who? Not Maggie Gleason anymore—she had left that girl behind in Chicago, hadn't she? Who would have known she'd miss her so much at times like these? Only Maggie O'Connor was here, and that particular Maggie had proven to be somewhat undependable, succumbing to the charms of a dangerous man, just as Coburn had predicted she would from the start. There was no going back, but there was also no future, or at least, not that she could see.

She finally decided to dismiss the children an hour early, if only so she could walk home alone, and perhaps decide what to do next. "Give my best to your parents," she called after the students as they made their traditional rush toward the door. "I'll see you tomorrow morning."

To her surprise, a logjam formed inside the doorway, as though none of the children wanted to be the first one out into the yard. For a moment, she didn't understand, then she winced just as Mary Ellen announced in a loud whisper, "He's out there. Waiting for you. I think he wants to kiss you again."

Maggie felt her cheeks warm. "There's no need to be frightened of Mr. Coburn. Run along now. If he asks, tell him I'll be out as soon as I put these books away."

They exchanged wary glances, then Mary Ellen shrugged. "He knows she won't kiss him anymore if he's mean to us, so . . ." Squaring her little shoulders, she marched out into the yard.

Maggie laughed in spite of herself, impressed by the girl's logic. The other children seemed similarly reassured, and began to file out of the room, with Maggie herself bringing up the rear. As she watched, the students moved, quickly and nervously, past the tall, dark-haired gunman who had resumed his position against the fence post.

He had pulled the brim of his black hat down to

shade his eyes, and had folded his arms across his chest. Seemingly relaxed, yet anyone with any sense would know instinctively that he was alert. *And* he was dangerous. And so incredibly attractive. Maggie's heart ached as she looked at him, wondering what it would be like to run to him and throw herself into his arms. It would startle him, she knew, despite the fact that he wanted her to pretend to be in love.

He was halfway to Redding yesterday, anxious to put as much distance between himself and your hopeless romantic fantasies as he could, she reminded herself. *He only came back to protect you, nothing more. Don't see romance where there isn't any, Maggie-Margaret.*

Securing the door behind herself, she walked down the path toward him, and was pleased when he straightened respectfully, tilting his hat back so that they could look into one another's eyes. "Good afternoon, Miss O'Connor."

"Mr. Coburn."

He started to reach for her, but she restrained his hand. "I've decided this charade is completely unnecessary."

"I see." He seemed completely amused. "On what theory?"

Her cheeks warmed. "I'm certain the whole town has already heard about our scandalous conduct, so there's no need to repeat it. And—" she paused for a breath—"I've had time to think about the culprit's identity, and I'm absolutely sure it's a harmless child. I can handle the situation myself, although I appreciate your offer of assistance more than you'll ever know."

"You have two choices. I can put my arm around you, or I can carry you."

Maggie jutted her chin forward in a show of defiance. But she also took another backward step, just in case. "You wouldn't dare."

"The drama alone would make the story spread like wildfire. But as I said, it's your choice."

There was a twinkle in his eyes that told her he'd be more than happy to follow through on his threat, so she joined him quickly, tucking her hand into the crook of his elbow. "You'll have to settle for this, sir."

Coburn pushed open the gate with a flourish, then smiled down at her as they began the walk down the hillside. "So? Did the children ask you questions?"

"A few. And I imagine Denny had a few of his own?"

"I had to stop him from ripping the drawing into shreds, he was so furious. I may not be able to restrain him when he gets his hands on your admirer." Dropping the light tone, he added, "He knows the men around here better than anyone, and can't name one who'd do something like this."

"Well, that's reassuring, isn't it?"

Coburn shrugged. "We also managed to rule out another possibility—that it might be one of the outlaws I've been hounding lately. I was concerned one of them might have decided to turn the tables on *me* by bothering *you*."

"That seems unlikely, doesn't it?"

"Yes. But just to be thorough, we did some checking. Each of them has been spotted a safe distance from here at some point in the last two weeks. One scoundrel in particular—" He stopped himself abruptly. "As I said, it wasn't one of them."

"Which rather proves my point, does it not? It isn't one of the townsmen, or some criminal. It's one of my students. Which means it has to be handled delicately. It doesn't sound as though Denny's the man for that job. And . . ." She eyed him sternly. "I doubt whether you're suited to it either."

"It needs a woman's touch?"

"Precisely."

"If those letters are any indication," Coburn told her with a chuckle, "your touch is exactly what he craves."

"That's quite enough."

"The sheriff wants to question you. At his house, over dinner tonight."

"Oh, dear. I don't want June involved. I mean, I adore her, but she's—well, she's protective of those she cares about."

"She also knows the people in this town. Denny's hoping she'll think of something he's missed. So, we're going."

"We?" Maggie bit her lip to keep from smiling. "Are you sure *you're* welcome? According to June, you left halfway through the meal with no explanation the last time you ate with them."

His laughter was rueful. "The sheriff tells me I'll be taking my life in my hands."

"It should be quite an experience," Maggie agreed, imagining how much fun it would be to see June put this arrogant man in his place. The dinner invitation was sounding better and better all the time. "If we're to be guests in the Riordain home, I'd like to bathe first, unless you have an objection."

"Why would I object?"

Maggie looked around quickly, to confirm that no one else could hear. "Last night you said you wanted him to smell you on me. So I thought you might not want me to bathe."

Coburn burst into laughter. "That was just a figure of speech."

"Oh." She grimaced and nodded. "I see."

"Even after you've bathed, he'll know you were in my bed."

"That's enough." She tried not to be charmed by the mischief in his eyes. "Give me your word you won't bother me while I bathe. Or later, when I'm resting in my room."

"You'll bathe and nap in *my* rooms," he told her. "But I'll give you complete privacy. Once I've ensured that the place is secure and the curtains tightly drawn, I'll stay in the library until it's time for us to go."

Maggie gave him an appreciative smile.

"That's better," he murmured, pulling her into his arms. "If your secret admirer is watching us at this moment, he'll think you're a woman in love with a very dangerous gunman. That should discourage him."

"Coburn," she protested, without pulling away.

"Alex," he reminded her seconds before his lips came down to taste hers.

Instinctively, her arms wrapped themselves around his neck, and she melted against him, allowing her body to flood with warmth and anticipation. But when his tongue began to explore her mouth, she pulled away quickly, for fear he would know that it was much more than pretense on her part, and how easily she could be seduced again.

Coburn placed his hands on her shoulders and studied her intently. "You trusted me last night. Has something changed?"

"Everything has changed." She took a deep breath. "Last night, you had me convinced I was in some dreadful, perverse danger that only you could rescue me from. That's why I trusted you. I was mistaken."

"About the danger? Or about trusting me?"

"The danger," she assured him softly. "I know you

mean well, Alex, but can't you see? I'm not at all frightened or alarmed by these silly notes."

"You were sleeping with a knife in your lap."

She took another deep breath. "That's true. It seemed wise to take precautions."

"That's all *I'm* doing."

You took more than precautions last night, she grumbled inwardly.

"Do you still trust me?"

"Yes," she admitted, adding sharply, "But not like last night."

Coburn laughed. "I see. You'll allow me to protect you, though?"

"Within reason." Backing away from him, she flashed a rueful smile. "I'll just run ahead and ask Mrs. Blake to draw that bath for me. In *your* bathroom. And you'll remember your promise, will you not? To stay in the library?"

"Have I ever lied to you?"

The twinkle in his eyes made her blush, and she knew her voice might betray even more if she spoke, so she turned away quickly and sprinted the rest of the way to the boardinghouse.

Maggie bathed hastily, certain that at any moment, Coburn would find an excuse to barge into the room. Perhaps to see her scars again? She half wanted him to do so, despite the fact that it would lead to another mistake.

But by the time she had toweled off, bundled herself up in a robe, and crawled into his bed, she knew he was going to keep his word. And she had to admit she was disappointed, but it was for the best, so she decided to use the opportunity to analyze what had happened over the last twenty-four hours, and what she should do from that point forward.

Unfortunately, she was distracted by the fact that his bed was warm and masculine and reminiscent in a thousand ways of their lovemaking. She couldn't help but wonder if that one night had been enough for him— enough to satisfy his curiosity, and to put his mark on her, so that other men would leave her alone.

Or were they destined to have an affair? Right under Mrs. Blake's nose? It seemed improbable, but the alternative seemed unbearable. Could they live under the same roof without remembering, and being tempted to repeat the mistake? Even if Coburn could manage it, she was fairly certain she could not.

And what if Coburn *couldn't* manage it, and decided to find somewhere else to live? Not because Maggie was irresistible, but because their night together had forever undermined the detached relationship he wished to have. He would stay until he was sure Maggie was safe, but what then? Would he go off on one of his hunts, send for his books, and never return to Shasta Falls?

You need to resist him these next few days, if only to prove to him that you and he can reestablish a friendship, and put the lovemaking behind you. Prove that he can stay here, reading night after night, without a lovesick female stealing glances at him from across the room, hungry for attention or romance. If he ever left Shasta Falls on your account, it would be so difficult for Mrs. Blake. And impossible for you.

Given Coburn's determination, coupled with his experience in hunting down criminals, she had no doubt that he and Denny would identify the letter writer in the next few days. And whether the culprit was a boy or man, they'd deal with him decisively, and the situation would be resolved. Now if only she could resolve her confused feelings for her protector as easily.

"Maggie!" June literally bounded down the walkway of the Riordain house, then pulled Maggie into a fiercely protective embrace. "I've been worried sick! Come inside this instant."

"I'm fine, June."

"Fine? According to Denny, someone's been writing awful notes to you."

"It's been disconcerting, I'll admit, but I'm convinced there's no danger in it."

"No danger? Denny says the notes were obscene and disgusting. Speaking of which . . ." She turned to fix Coburn with a haughty glare. "Look who's come back for the rest of his meal."

Maggie struggled not to laugh out loud. "Alex has been investigating the matter out of concern for my welfare."

"Alex?" June sniffed, clearly offended. "Since when is he concerned for anyone's welfare but his own?"

"Junie!" Denny stepped between his wife and Coburn, then offered his hand to his dinner guest. "I warned you she'd be mean."

Coburn shook the sheriff's hand, his face expressionless. "It's fine." To June he added simply, "I apologize for leaving so abruptly the last time I was here. It was unforgivable."

"Well, at least we agree on something," June drawled. "Come on, Maggie. Dinner's on the table, and I can't wait another minute to hear this from your own lips."

"Wait a minute." Denny touched Maggie's shoulder. "Look at me, missy." When she'd raised her eyes to

his, he murmured, "I know now that you came to my
office yesterday for advice and protection. I'm sorry
I scared you away. When I heard you were frightened
enough to sleep with a knife in your hand—"

"That's enough," Maggie interrupted, touched by
the shame in his eyes. Then she kissed his cheek and
insisted, "At first, I was frightened. But the truth is,
the situation is not dangerous. The reason I left your
office yesterday was that I was afraid you'd be too
hard on the poor child. If you can promise me you
won't do anything rash, then I'll welcome your assistance. Otherwise . . ." She arched an eyebrow in
warning, leaving the rest of the threat dangling in the
air.

"Coburn here told me you thought it was a child.
I disagree. The poems were one thing, but that long
letter. And that drawing." Denny's expression dark-
ened, as though the slightest memory of those insults
were enough to edge him into a rage.

June stroked her husband's arm reassuringly. "It's
time I had a look at the notes and the drawing. I'm
sure I can tell if they're the work of a man or a child."

"You're not to see them," Denny growled.

June turned to Coburn. "Did you bring them, sir?"

"Yes."

She held out her hand.

The bounty hunter cleared his throat. "Would you
settle for seeing just the two poems, Mrs. Riordain? I
have a feeling you'll agree that even they aren't the
work of a child. Then it won't be necessary for you
to see the other two documents, which are much more
offensive."

"But first, we'll go inside and have a bite," Denny
insisted, taking his wife by the hand and pulling her
toward the house. "I don't want you seeing any of

that rubbish on an empty stomach. Come along, you two."

"The poems are actually quite sweet," Maggie called after them; then she tucked her hand into the crook of Coburn's arm and allowed him to escort her onto the porch, and then into the dining room, where June had everything waiting.

Fourteen

"This looks wonderful, June." Maggie served herself some fluffy mashed potatoes, then passed the bowl to Coburn.

"If it looks familiar to you, Mr. Coburn," June interjected, "it's because it's the same meal I served last time you visited. I hope you don't mind."

"Not at all. As I recall, it was delicious."

"Really?" June drawled. "You have an odd reaction to delicious food, sir."

"She'll never let it go," Denny assured his friend with a grin.

"It was unpardonably rude of me," Coburn replied, adding toward June, "You have every right to be annoyed."

"If I'm annoyed, it's because you're forcing your attentions on my friend. And don't tell me it's all for her protection, because I've never heard such a ridiculous thing in my life. Where I come from, one doesn't protect a girl by ruining her reputation."

Coburn frowned. "I take it you've heard from Gladys Chesterton?"

"Half the town witnessed that display of yours. I was worried sick until Denny explained it to me. After that, as I mentioned, I was no longer worried. Just annoyed."

Maggie sighed. "Denny and Alex are convinced a grown man is bothering me, and they believe he'll think twice if he perceives me as being involved with a gunfighter."

"We should wait until after dinner to talk about all this," Denny protested.

"We have no time to lose," June reminded her husband. "At any moment, Mr. Coburn could run from the room, taking Maggie with him."

"That's enough." The sheriff eyed her sternly. "We'll discuss the notes now, if you insist, Mrs. Riordain. But you won't insult our guest again."

She grimaced but nodded, while Maggie struggled not to smile. Stealing a glance at Coburn, she was surprised to see that he was neither amused nor bothered. Instead, he seemed intent on appearing solemn and respectful.

"Since I'm the person most familiar with the situation, I should be the one to explain it," Maggie announced. When they had acquiesced, she began. "You remember how I told you, June, that one of the boys had sent me a poem? That first poem was very sweet. Alex? Do you have it?"

She waited until he had handed the paper to June. "Do you see? It's clearly written by a boy."

June nodded. "It's the penmanship of a child. And there's a quaint sort of innocence to it. *Just be mine, all the time.*" She pursed her lips, then announced, "It could be a child. Let me see the second one." Accepting the paper from Coburn, she read softly: *"When I don't see you, I'm not me. When I see you, I'm me."*

June's hazel eyes clouded as she raised her gaze from the paper and fixed it on Maggie. "So, he really has been watching you to an unusual extent. Odd, isn't it?"

"In what way?" Maggie asked. Then she realized

that June was thinking about Ian peeping through windows, so she added quickly, "I'm quite certain it isn't as odd as one might think. I'm sure hundreds of little boys have these sorts of thoughts, but with time and patience, they outgrow them, or learn to direct them in a more positive direction."

"Hundreds?" Denny snorted. "There'd better not be more than one in this town. And that one had better watch himself, or he'll have me to answer to."

"Denny, don't be harsh." June arched an eyebrow in warning. "If it's a child who's writing these notes or looking through a few windows, we'll deal with him gently, for Maggie's sake. Can't you see you're upsetting her with all this bluster?"

"Bluster? You didn't read the third note, or see the drawing, or you'd be wanting to string him up, same as me."

"Denny!" June jumped to her feet and began to pace, while the men watched in clear confusion. Finally, she announced, "You were right after all. We shouldn't talk about this at the dinner table."

"Come and sit with us, June," Maggie urged. "We won't discuss it anymore. There's actually nothing left to say, is there? You agree that it's a child, which means there's no need for official reprisals. I'm the schoolteacher in this town, and the children are my concern. If the three of you are willing to help me identify the child, I'll be grateful. But I'll also insist on handling the matter without any interference."

"It isn't a child," Coburn muttered. "No child is capable of this sort of perversity."

June ceased her pacing and stepped over to the bounty hunter, surprising everyone by resting her hand on his shoulder and saying in a soft, almost pleading voice, "You mustn't say such things, sir."

Alarmed by her friend's behavior, Maggie shook her

head in oblique warning. "June? Please just sit and eat with us. We'll talk about something else. I for one can't stomach any more discussion of this unfortunate situation."

"Because they're breaking your heart with every word they say," June agreed, returning to her chair, then reaching for Maggie's hand and squeezing it. "Surely you realize they're trying to help you. They have no way of knowing why you're so vulnerable on this topic. You have to tell them about Ian, Maggie. They'll surely understand."

"June!" She pulled her hand free and stared at her hostess in dismay. "Not another word. You promised. And—" She tried to smile toward the men. "It's nothing. Nothing at all. I simply have a tender heart where little boys are concerned, because I lost my own brother when he was a child."

Coburn's gaze was fixed on June. "Is that it, Mrs. Riordain?"

"You'd best call me June," she murmured.

He hesitated, then turned to Maggie. "It's something else, then? You have to tell us, Maggie, even if it's painful. Despite your naivete, I can assure you that the person who sent these notes to you is not a child. He's a perverse and dangerous creature intent on molesting you, and if your past holds some clue to his identity, you're going to tell me. The sheriff and I can't help you if you don't."

"I assure you, sir, there are no perverse creatures in my past," Maggie told him through gritted teeth.

"Fine," he growled. "If you won't tell me here and now, you can tell me tonight, when we're alone. One way or the other, I'll hear it."

She could see from the glint in his eyes that it was true: he would find a way to make her tell him everything. He might even enjoy it, and if it were any subject other than Ian's transgressions and demise, she might enjoy the interrogation herself. But as it was, she couldn't bear the thought of it, and silently berated June for creating so volatile a situation.

Denny interrupted her thoughts by insisting, "Coburn's right, missy. It almost surely has to be someone from your old life, or someone you met while traveling here. There's no one in Shasta Falls—boy or man—capable of this sort of filthy, disgusting—"

"Dennis Riordain!" June pounded the table with her fist. "Not one more word. You're torturing Maggie with that kind of talk." Grabbing Maggie's hand again, she pleaded, "Tell them, or allow me to do it. I can't bear to see them hurt you so unthinkingly."

This time, when Maggie pulled herself free, she did it roughly, then folded her arms across her chest and announced, "The only person hurting me is you, June Riordain. I told you about my brother in confidence. And for you to bring it up in this horrid context is unforgivable. However . . ." She fixed her friend with a cold stare. "It's obvious you won't rest until you've told them everything, so be quick about it. And then Mr. Coburn will take me home. All I ask is that you not blame him this time for the abrupt end to the meal, since it's your meddling that is chasing us away."

"Well now," Denny interjected nervously, "it can't be as bad as all that. And I'm sure this little secret, whatever it is, can wait for later—"

"Let's get it over with." Maggie arched an eyebrow toward her hostess. "You were anxious to tell them, so please do so."

June's hazel eyes were glistening with tears, but she nodded and squared her shoulders, then began in a soft, gentle voice. "Every little girl and boy should have a mother to love and cherish them, but Maggie's mother died in childbirth, and there was no one to watch over her, or her two brothers, when they needed it most. Little Ian in particular was completely helpless and innocent—the sort of child who needs special care. But instead, the adults in his life vilified him for simple transgressions, and turned their backs on him when he needed them most. And it was left to our poor Maggie—just a baby herself—to try to make everything right.

"And then—" A sob caught in June's throat, but she proceeded doggedly, while Maggie and the men stared in mesmerized silence. "Then they did the unthinkable, and wrenched Ian away from the one person in the world who loved him. The pain from that separation twisted the poor boy's heart into knots, and by the time he found his way back to Maggie years later, it was too late. He lashed out at the other brother—a wonderful boy named Brian—and in that one horrible moment, both boys were lost to her forever."

Covering her hands with her face, June wailed, "Do you see why you must choose your words with care? Ian Gleason's sins were nothing more than childish mistakes—and yes, he peeked in a window or two, and made the neighbors shake their heads. But a firm, gentle hand could have guided him to another, better path. Instead, the authorities and his own father treated him like a common criminal—an outcast!—and where did it lead? To tragedy for the whole family, and lifelong misery for Maggie."

Slipping out of her chair, Maggie knelt before June, then hugged her gently. "That was so beautiful. I never dreamed you saw it that way. It's as if you knew him—"

"Through you," June reminded her, sniffing back her tears as she spoke. "I know them both—Ian and

Brian—through you. Forgive me, Maggie, but they had to hear it."

"I agree." Maggie wiped her own tears from her cheeks, then stood and gave Denny a wistful smile. "I think your wife's heart is made purely of gold."

"That it is," he agreed, and to Maggie's delight, his eyes too were damp.

And Coburn? She was suddenly curious, and turned to him, certain that even a hardened gunfighter would have been moved to tears by June's tender soliloquy.

Instead he appeared almost stunned as he demanded, "This all happened in Chicago? Five or six years ago?"

And then to her dismay, he spoke the words she had prayed she'd never have to hear again.

"My God, Maggie. You're the little Gleason girl!"

By the time they left the Riordain home, Maggie was completely drained, and didn't resist Coburn when he slipped his arm around her waist and led her silently through town and up the boardinghouse steps. Even when he ushered her into his bedroom and closed the door firmly, she simply sighed and moved to sit on the foot of the bed, then gave him a wistful smile.

"You must be exhausted," he murmured. "Get undressed and into bed, while I take a quick look around the house. Lock the door behind me," he added as he disappeared into the library.

Shrugging to her feet, she closed the door, but didn't lock it, for fear she'd be fast asleep by the time he returned. Then she stripped down to her petticoat and chemise in the dark, climbed back onto the bed, and snuggled contentedly under the covers.

Thanks to June, it had been easy to talk to the men

about Ian. Denny in particular had been touched, and had apologized profusely for having made rash statements about little boys and their transgressions. In his own way, Coburn had been equally apologetic, although he had stubbornly insisted that the parallel, while eerie, was inaccurate, because "these notes were *not* written by a child."

Then the four of them had gone over it, again and again. Every man Maggie had ever met. And everyone who might possibly know about your unfortunate association with the stories that had dominated the Chicago newspapers five years earlier.

Maggie had cooperated as fully as possible, although she kept Russell Braddock's confidence by insisting that all the arrangements for the teaching position had been made by Father James. Fortunately, Denny had confirmed that this was just the sort of thing "the good father" did constantly, and wasn't at all surprised that the priest hadn't asked Maggie anything about her past. The letters of recommendation from Headmaster Robert Grimes, coupled with Maggie's gentle demeanor, would have been all the information he had needed to determine that she would make a wonderful teacher.

To Maggie's chagrin, she had learned that Denny and Coburn had made inquiries about Robert to authorities in Chicago. With frustrated affection, she had assured them that they had wasted their time, and that when the response came, it would prove conclusively that the headmaster was a saint.

Now alone in Coburn's bed, she tried again to think of anyone else who might have followed her, but there was no one. The neighbors had all been sympathetic—too sympathetic, in fact—but none had shown an inordinate amount of interest in Maggie or her father those last few years. And the voyage to San Francisco had been relatively uneventful.

She heard Coburn reenter the room, and half expected a scolding. Instead, there were the unmistakable sounds of a man undressing, and she burrowed her face more deeply in her pillow, hoping he'd think she was asleep. Not that his arms wouldn't feel wonderful at that moment, but she had no idea where such cuddling would lead, and no energy to either fight or welcome further complications.

Then he was under the covers with her, and he didn't hesitate to pull her into a hearty embrace before murmuring into her hair, "Didn't I tell you to lock the door?"

"I knew I was safe."

He chuckled. "No paring knife tonight?"

She smiled as she snuggled against him, relieved that so amiable a tone had been established so easily.

"Maggie?"

"Hmm?"

"I know you're too tired to talk. But do you have the strength to listen for a while?"

She wriggled free and peered into his eyes, trying to fathom why his tone suddenly sounded so bleak. His mood at the Riordains had been confident and energetic, but now, he seemed almost wistful. And his blue eyes were uncharacteristically lackluster. "Don't look so discouraged." She stroked his face with her fingertip. "I promise I'll be more careful in the future. From now on, I'll lock the door whenever I'm in here alone."

"It's not that. It's something else. Something personal."

"Oh, no." A wave of exhaustion swept over her. "Couldn't it wait for morning? I really am tired of it all. You were so sweet and understanding about Ian, and I'll gladly answer any questions, but—"

"It's about *my* past, not yours."

"Oh!" She hesitated, then touched his face again. "Why tonight?"

"I asked you so many personal questions. And tomorrow, there will be dozens more. It seems only fair. And"—he took a deep breath—"it's time you knew."

She could tell, from his expression and his tone, that he wasn't going to talk about bounty hunting or books. This was something else—something fraught with pain. Somehow, the anguish of talking about Ian and Brian must have touched him, deep inside. And now he needed to confide in her in return—to be fair, and because it was time, whatever that meant.

She started to scoot into a seated position, but he gently restrained her, pressing her back into the pillow and then hovering over her, his eyes dark with memories.

"I'm listening," she murmured. "Tell me anything you want. But remember, there's no need."

He smiled at the remark. "It's so like you to say that. You're remarkable, Maggie. Do you know that?" Before she could respond, he cleared his throat and added in a self-mocking tone, "Can you see I don't know exactly where to begin?"

"Why don't you begin with the day you met her?"

"Is it that obvious?"

"Yes."

"Well, then . . ." He cleared his throat a second time. "I met her in Chicago, five years ago. She was a young widow, expecting her first child. I was practicing law, with plans to head west eventually. To seek fame and fortune," he added dryly.

"And you fell in love with her? And married her?"

"Yes."

"What was her name?"

"It was Christine." He sat up and stared into the darkness. "As soon as the baby was born, we packed up everything we owned and moved to Virginia City, where a friend of my father's had already made a fortune with an extensive mining operation. I was ambitious—specifically, I intended to make a name for myself as a prosecutor, and to thereafter secure an appointment to the judiciary, with the ultimate goal of becoming a justice on the Supreme Court of California before I turned thirty-five. My father was a judge—a very well respected one. It was his dream, as well as mine, that I was pursuing."

"It was a noble goal."

"Perhaps." His eyes clouded. "In the meantime, Christine was a perfect wife—devoted to me and our son, with no thought to any need of her own. We hadn't been in town six months when she told me we were expecting another child, and I was very pleased. Life was perfect. The only thing that was missing was a prosecution that would attract the attention of powerful men in San Francisco and Sacramento."

"Why didn't you just practice law in one of those two cities?"

"It was a calculated maneuver—to have a reputation firmly in place before I went there. I needed one celebrated victory. And on the very day my second son—a beautiful boy named Jason—was born, it happened."

Maggie wanted to silence him with a loving embrace. To tell him he didn't need to say another word. She already knew that somehow, through some horrid mishap, the wife and sons had perished, and she couldn't bear to watch the memories overwhelm him.

She remembered how it had been for her, trying to find the words to tell June about Ian. And she was certain that this was the very first time Coburn had ever told of his loss. The pain would be unbearable, and yet, if Maggie could listen well, and respond with love, as June had done, perhaps he'd be able to sleep soundly tonight, despite the torture she could see behind his eyes.

So she murmured, "A particularly infamous criminal came to trial in Virginia City? With you as prosecutor?"

He nodded. "Two criminals: John Evans and Daniel Wiley. Vicious men, who had robbed a stage, butchering the driver and six passengers in the process. Evans had a reputation as a brute, but Daniel Wiley was relatively unknown in the area, although we learned that he and his brother had committed a series of petty crimes in Oregon before they had a parting of the ways.

"Wiley hired a talented defense attorney—a man known for his histrionics. The courtroom was packed, and it seemed for a while that Wiley at least might have established an alibi. I wasn't about to lose the case, though, so I conducted an investigation and managed to discredit the alibi witness. The newspapers carried glowing accounts of my performance. Of course, such fame is fleeting. More importantly, though, I was contacted by the governor of California, who congratulated me and said he'd like to discuss my future with me."

"And you had such high hopes." Maggie shook her head, remembering all too well how it could feel. So many nights, she had sat by the fire in her father's house, knitting or doing needlepoint, while Brian had entertained her with her favorite story: how he'd buy a big, fancy house, with servants and stained glass windows, and Ian would come to live with them.

"Yes. Evans and Wiley were hanged for their

crimes, and I left immediately for a meeting with the governor. Christine and the children stayed behind, of course. The baby seemed much too young to make the trip."

"Oh, Alex."

His face hardened, as though he had to banish all emotion if he hoped to make it through the story without breaking down. "Wiley's brother Sean came to Virginia City. He'd heard about the trial, but didn't arrive until after the execution. He went wild with vengeful grief, and would have torn me to pieces had I been present. But of course, I was safe in California, so he visited my family instead."

Coburn shuddered visibly. "I learned a lot about cruelty during the trial, but nothing could have prepared me for what that animal did to my children. Nothing . . ."

When a sob caught in his throat, Maggie couldn't bear a second more, and lunged into his lap, wrapping her arms around his neck and insisting, "Don't say any more. Please don't make yourself say another word. Just let me hold you, Alex. Please?"

"He didn't kill Christine."

"What?" She recoiled slightly, not from the words, but from the icy tone. Then she looked into his eyes, and saw self-loathing so acute, she simply didn't know how to react. Moistening her lips, she managed to murmur, "Go on."

"Wiley was skillful and meticulous, causing her as much pain as possible, while keeping her alive, so that she could recount every detail to me. Every detail of the butchering of my sons. And the repeated raping and disfigurement of my bride."

"Oh, no. Oh, Alex, it wasn't your fault."

"Do you think that matters?" he asked, but his tone was gentle again. "Nothing mattered, Maggie. Nothing in the world. I tried to pretend it did, for Christine's sake, but she had nothing to live for, either. The doctor had to keep her sedated twenty-four hours a day, just to keep her from shrieking like a banshee. And she didn't want to tell me about the boys—she didn't want to give Wiley the satisfaction. But I had to hear it. I had to hear every word. It was . . . horrendous."

"I can't begin to imagine."

"I think you can. How old were you when you watched your brother bleed to death? When you imagined Ian cringing in a prison cell, tormented and alone?" He pulled her close and whispered, "I wanted you to know this, so you'd see that I understand."

"Is Christine still alive?"

"She asked me to do something for her."

Maggie winced. "What was that?"

"To find Sean Wiley and kill him. And then, to spit on his grave."

"Yes. You needed to do that."

He nodded. "She urged me to leave right away. By all reports, he'd gone back to Oregon, and she was afraid he'd disappear completely. I didn't want to leave her alone in her condition. She had numerous wounds, and was haunted by nightmares. But she said she'd never get a decent night's rest until Wiley was dead, so I finally agreed."

He paused, clearly lost in thought for a moment, then winced apologetically. "Sometimes, I can't believe it really happened."

"I know *that* feeling all too well," Maggie told him. Then she stroked his cheek and urged, "What happened next?"

"I knew how to use a pistol, but the truth was, I hadn't ever shot at a man, much less killed one. I'd had some fairly lively brawls in my youth, but nothing lethal. On the other hand, I despised Wiley from the bottom of my soul, and I was confident that if I could find him, I could kill him. He had—or rather, has—a reputation for being quick with a gun, and of course, merciless. And while I didn't care about my own life, I wanted to stay alive, for Christine. It was a confusing time. Gut-wrenching, yet also deadening."

He coughed to clear the raspiness from his voice. "So I set out after him. Christine made me promise not to come back until he was dead, but something nagged at me. A feeling. I couldn't explain it, but somehow, I knew I should go back to her. The conflict grew stronger, and finally, after two sleepless nights, I turned back." Then he interrupted himself to explain, "Do you remember the other night, when I came back unexpectedly, and you asked me why? I had that same feeling then, along the trail, and couldn't ignore it."

"So you went back to Christine? Was she angry?"

"She was at peace. Believing that I wouldn't rest until I avenged her babies, she took her own life the day after I left town."

"Oh, Alex. Oh, no. I can't bear it." Maggie twined her arms around his neck and pulled him close. "I'm so dreadfully sorry, darling."

His arms wrapped around her just as tightly, and they clung to one another in tearful silence, until he gently urged her away. "There's not much more to tell. I went after Wiley, but he had disappeared completely. I interrogated his neighbors and former associates, as well as every lawman who'd ever had the misfortune of tangling with him. One thing became clear: he was a monster, with an uncanny ability to inflict injury on others while keeping himself safe. He supported himself through robbery, but for pleasure, he murdered. An ungodly spree, every five or six months, and then he'd vanish for a while.

"I learned everything there was to know about him.

And in the meantime, I learned to use a pistol. Not just for target practice, either. I needed practice shooting at human beings, so I started going after bounty. I'm not ashamed of it, either," he declared quietly. "I always give my quarry a chance to surrender. Most do, and I turn them over to the authorities right away. But every once in a while, I'm luckier, and the fool puts up a fight." He smiled apologetically. "Are you shocked?"

"By your behavior? No. I can't see how life left you any choice."

Coburn nodded. "I didn't care about my life anymore. All my ambition was converted into my need for revenge. Even after months had passed, I avoided situations in which I might make a friend, or meet a nice woman. I knew enough about Wiley to know he'd take a perverse sort of pleasure in killing someone I loved again."

"Oh, dear."

"I was careful for so long. The closest I came to making friends was with Denny. And, of course, Eleanor. But I made sure no one would mistake either of those relationships for anything but practical, impersonal arrangements."

"But they're more than that?"

He licked his lips before admitting, "In some ways, they probably kept me alive, until you could get here."

"Oh, Alex." She snuggled gratefully against him. "Isn't it strange, how much we have in common? The books, the tortured past, the determination never to allow ourselves to love again."

He stroked her hair for a few moments, then pushed her away and cupped her face in his hand. "Wiley is still out there, Maggie. When I saw that drawing, I almost lost my mind, thinking that he was playing some depraved game with you. But there's a confirmed report that he was seen in Monterey two weeks ago, which makes it impossible for him to have sent the second or third note."

Maggie shuddered. "What a dreadful thought. No wonder you were so—well, so insistent that I spend the night with you."

He chuckled. "Actually, I had more than one motive in that regard."

She felt her cheeks redden. "Did you?"

"You're a beautiful girl."

"Was Christine beautiful?"

He hesitated, then nodded. "In a different way, but yes. She was lovely, although she didn't seem to know it. She was raised by an uncle who treated her like a servant, and then he had the nerve to arrange a marriage for her, to an elderly gentleman who made unreasonable demands on her. It took me months to convince her that she was something more than a servant to me." He shook his head. "Barbaric, in these times, to think of marriages between strangers, isn't it?"

"I suppose it depends on who does the matchmaking," Maggie replied carefully.

Her reply brought a scowl to his face. "You sound like Christine. Would you like to hear how I met her?"

"Yes. Very much."

His tone softened. "Her husband died in a penniless state while she was carrying little Paul. She didn't want to return to her uncle's house, for fear he'd find her another, even less acceptable husband. But her prospects were few, and she made the absurd decision to consult a professional matchmaker."

Maggie gasped. "In Chicago?"

"Unbelievable, is it not?" Coburn grumbled. "I had heard about this fellow—a man named Braddock—and I had made my opinion of him clear. In fact, I felt such activity should be outlawed. For the protection of the brides, who are invariably victimized in such barbaric arrangements."

Maggie had to struggle to keep her face expressionless, despite her amazement over hearing that she and Coburn had even more in common than they had guessed. They both knew Russell Braddock, although their reactions to his business had been quite different.

Coburn smiled. "I can see you're horrified, as was I. And this Braddock was making a fortune plying his unsavory trade. A sort of legend had grown up around him—by his own design, I'm certain. He styled himself as a true romantic, making love matches between strangers. I despised the hypocrisy of it all, and one evening, when I found myself face-to-face with him in a card game, I told him so."

"Oh dear."

"He pretended not to take offense. I learned quickly that he could be charming—a necessary skill in a business such as his, where one trades on the confidence of others. He gave me countless examples of the supposed love matches he had arranged, and when I remained skeptical, he suggested I speak with one of the happy couples, or better still, one of the prospective brides. He said he was sure I'd walk away from such a meeting with a new view on arranged marriages."

"Oh!" Maggie clapped her hands in unexpected delight. *"That's"* how you met Christine? It's so—I mean, it's so interesting."

"So romantic?" he drawled. "You sound like Braddock. When Christine and I married, he had the nerve to send a gift, with a card that took full credit for the 'match'—as though he had planned from the first for us to fall in love and marry."

"But it wasn't that way at all?" Maggie asked, stifling a smile.

"It was fully the opposite. I agreed to meet with one of the brides for the precise purpose of convincing her that she shouldn't go through with Braddock's scheme. Christine and I dined together, and I convinced her to withdraw her name from Braddock's list of prospective brides. I arranged decent employment for her in the home of an acquaintance, and visited her weekly, to see that her health and spirits were good. Over time, we developed a rapport, and—" he smiled wistfully—"I was aware of the progress of the baby. Growing, kicking, thriving. And over time, I began to regard the child as mine. And Christine as my closest confidant."

"I see. She must have been so happy."

"Yes, she was. Instead of a loveless match by a mercenary broker, she found herself in a loving relationship that developed slowly, and from mutual regard. *That's* romantic."

"Utterly."

He smiled apologetically. "You don't mind?"

"I only wish you hadn't lost her."

"I know. Thank you."

She snuggled against his chest, half hoping he'd begin making love to her. "Are you as tired as I?"

"Yes," he admitted.

She waited a moment, but it seemed he was falling asleep, and so she pulled free and nestled into her own pillow, scolding herself for wanting more. He'd just relived his courtship of another woman, after all! And before that, the nightmare of losing her and his sons in a hideous manner. Did she honestly expect him to be amorous so soon after all that?

Or ever? Because as much as she loved being in his arms, she knew he had told her the story of Sean

Wiley for more than one reason. Yes, it allowed them to share their grief, but it also warned Maggie that Coburn wasn't ready for involvement yet—not with her or anyone else. He had to keep his promise to Christine—to spit on Wiley's grave. And he couldn't take a chance that Wiley might discover their romantic relationship and practice his evil ways on Maggie.

But perhaps one day, after Wiley was dead . . . ?

Even then, two obstacles remained: Maggie and Coburn themselves. Would they be able to love again, knowing the pain that would result if they ever lost one another?

Don't think about it, she pleaded with herself. *Go to sleep! It will be time to get up and dressed for school before you know it. And the hunt for your secret admirer will start again. It's all so relentless, and not at all romantic.*

She smiled despite herself, charmed again by the fact that Coburn had met his wife through Russell Braddock. It was such an amazing coincidence. She wondered if she'd ever dare tell him she herself had used the services of the matchmaker, although not for finding a husband.

Alex would be shocked and disapproving, she told herself gleefully. But he'd have to admit that Mr. Braddock did a wonderful job of it.

And if Mr. Braddock hadn't sent you here, you and Alex never would have met, so—oh!

She literally jumped as the truth hit her, and Coburn responded immediately, grappling her against his chest. "Did you have a nightmare, sweetheart?"

She groaned in confusion. "Just an odd thought."

"I shouldn't have told you so gruesome a story right before bedtime," he muttered. "Try not to think about it."

"I'll try." Pulling free of him quickly, she moved

as far away as possible, still stymied by the realization that Russell Braddock had sent her to Shasta Falls for something more than just a teaching position.

Because she was now almost certain that the wily matchmaker had known full well that Alex Coburn lived in the same boardinghouse. Coburn, who had scoffed at Braddock's talent, even after he'd found him his first wife.

And so to prove a point, Braddock had done it again.

And Coburn was going to be outraged.

Not that their relationship was going to end in marriage, of course, but still, Braddock had instinctively known Coburn and Maggie would be attracted to one another, and had probably known they would eventually act upon that attraction in some way.

And it would fall to Maggie to tell Coburn about Braddock's benevolent interference. But not until this business of the note writer had been resolved. And even then, she knew she'd have to prepare herself for an angry reaction. The thought of it made her shudder involuntarily.

"Maggie?" Coburn's arm slipped under her, turning her toward him and pulling her against himself in one strong motion. "Try not to think about it."

"I'm fine." She twined her arms around his neck and kissed him lightly. "Go to sleep."

"Not until I'm sure you're not thinking about Christine and the boys." His hand cupped her left breast. "I'm determined to find a way to distract you."

Maggie sighed with confused delight as his fingers teased at her nipple. "It's not necessary."

"It's my pleasure," he assured her, then his mouth crushed down to hers, and she easily returned the kiss. Then his hands began to roam, igniting everything they touched, and she had no choice but to grind against him, alive with need. But this time, he was in no hurry, and as she trembled with arousal, he proceeded to make love to her from head to toe with his mouth and his hands until she cried out in decadent surrender. Only then did he satisfy himself inside her, with her blissful cooperation, until he groaned and collapsed onto her, then rolled slightly to the side and flashed an appreciative smile. "Very nice, Maggie-Margaret."

"You were supposed to be distracting me, not yourself," she reminded him playfully.

"I thought I did that. Was it my imagination? Shall we ask the other boarders if they heard you cry out my name?"

She felt her cheeks flush scarlet. "It wasn't that loud, was it?"

His smile softened. "I alone had the pleasure of hearing it." His lips brushed hers. "Can you sleep now, sweetheart?"

"Mmm." She cuddled gratefully against him, and was quickly lulled by the strong, steady sound of his breathing as he, too, drifted off to sleep.

Fifteen

To Maggie's amazement, Coburn was already nibbling on her neck before she had rubbed the sleep from her eyes the next morning, and they made love with abandon despite the fact that Mrs. Blake was only two rooms away, making breakfast. But if the landlady suspected anything, she didn't show it when she greeted them. Instead, she served them coffee and eggs, chattering breezily about her oldest daughter's latest letter.

This time, when Coburn walked Maggie to the schoolhouse, he didn't urge her to act like a woman in love. He didn't even walk with his arm around her waist. Instead, they strolled side by side, their hands barely touching, yet Maggie imagined that all eyes were on them, and that everyone in Shasta Falls must be sensing the incendiary nature of their affair.

Not that she knew what to make of it herself. They had barely spoken a dozen words to one another that morning. Yet she had never seen him so relaxed and lighthearted, and she knew that it was due not only to their lovemaking, but to the fact that he had shared his tragic story with her, confident that she was a kindred spirit because of her own experience of violent loss.

The fact that he no longer seemed overly concerned

with the secret admirer also pleased her. Perhaps she had finally convinced him that it was a child, and that that child posed no threat to her well-being. In any case, he was smiling when he kissed her cheek at the schoolyard gate, and there was no undercurrent at all to his voice when he admonished her to "be alert, and ring the damned bell if you feel the least bit uneasy."

Trying not to beam, she forced herself to pay attention to the children, although she was acutely aware of each passing hour, knowing that soon she would see Coburn again, and he would escort her back to his bedroom and close the door, and they would make love until common sense demanded they make a brief appearance for supper.

By the time she dismissed the children and gathered up her books, she was tingling with anticipation, but wisely waited inside until she was certain most of the students had left the yard. The last thing she wanted to do was misbehave in front of them, but if Coburn decided to greet her with a kiss, she wasn't sure she could control the intensity of her response.

At least it will teach them not to be afraid of him, she teased herself as she finally made her way onto the porch. *And if your little admirer is still here, he'll see once and for all that your heart belongs to another. That's the kindest way to end this, so kiss Alex with all your might.*

She expected him to be standing at the gate, and was disconcerted to find him at the bottom of the steps, staring up at her. Despite his quick smile, she sensed something was wrong. And when he didn't even try to kiss her, but instead just patted her arm and asked how her day had been, she felt a tremor of foreboding.

And so she prompted him in a calm but determined voice. "Tell me what's wrong."

"I'll tell you when we're home."

She liked the fact that he called the boardinghouse their home, but didn't like the strain she could now clearly see behind his eyes. "Tell me now."

"No." He slipped his arm around her waist. "I won't discuss it with you in public, so don't ask again. How were the children today? Any problems? Any lighthearted moments?"

"If there had been problems, I would have rung the bell," she reminded him. "Just tell me if anyone's hurt. Please?"

"No one you care about is hurt."

She pulled free and stared at him. "Someone *you* care about? Oh! Is it Sean Wiley?"

Coburn scowled. "I should never have told you about him. No, Wiley's not hurt. If he were, I'd be celebrating."

Maggie had to smile. "I've missed that frown of yours, Mr. Coburn. It's been ages since you lost your temper with me."

His eyes finally regained some of their luster. "You're in a good mood. You must have slept particularly well."

She felt her cheeks warm. "Yes, I did." Reaching up, she stroked his rigid jaw. "Can I assume you and Denny have determined the identity of my admirer?"

He scowled again and took her by the arm. "No more questions until we get home."

As she hurried to keep pace with him on the walk to the boardinghouse, she ran down the list of suspects in her mind one last time. From Coburn's grim expression, she suspected it wasn't a child after all. A man, or perhaps one of the older boys from the logging camp. Given the fact that Coburn hadn't befriended anyone other than Denny, he couldn't be worried for the suspect's sake. But perhaps it was a

friend of Denny's. Someone who was so beyond reproach that they hadn't considered him the night before.

Someone beyond reproach . . .

She remembered how Coburn had refused to dismiss Reverend Flectcher as a suspect. Could it be
him? Or worse, Father James? Her brain recoiled from
the notion, then an even more upsetting thought occurred to her. Had Coburn found out about her connection to Russell Braddock? Did he despise her now,
for keeping that secret from him?

Stop it, she instructed herself finally. *You'll know
soon enough, and from the look on Alex's face, you'll
wish he'd never told you.*

By the time they reached the boardinghouse, her
nerves were so raw, she was barely able to exchange
a few pleasantries with Mrs. Blake before dumping
her books on a library table and hurrying into
Coburn's bedroom. He was already in there, pacing,
and so she closed the door, then moved to sit on the
edge of the bed, where she waited in silent apprehension.

The bounty hunter cleared his throat, then flashed
an uneasy smile. "Denny offered to do this, and I
realize now his instincts were correct."

"Are you angry with me?"

"Angry?" He strode over to her and pulled her into
an embrace, kissing her hair as he cradled her. "Never,
sweetheart. I'm just so sorry that you have to hear
this. If I could protect you from it, I would."

"You said no one was hurt!" She wriggled free and
stared up at him in dismay. "You're frightening me,
Alex. Please just tell me. I can't bear one more minute
of suspense."

He nodded. "I'm going to tell you quickly. Not because that's easy for you, but because it's easiest for me. After that, we'll go over it again and again, until—"

"Alex!"

He winced and nodded again. "First, I have to ask you a question."

"Oh, for goodness sakes!" She caught her temper and waved her hand for him to proceed quickly.

"It's about Lettie Price."

"Lettie? Oh, dear." Maggie sighed. "You needn't worry, Alex. I always felt sorry for her, and a small measure of reproach, but we weren't at all close. Is she dead? Is that the response you received from your inquiry to the Chicago authorities?"

He scowled slightly. "My question is, did you tell Lettie Price you were taking a teaching position here in Shasta Falls?"

"Yes. I wrote to her from San Francisco. Not that I really thought she might care, but she had no one, and we shared an odd history, and—" Maggie's hand flew to her mouth. "You can't possibly think Lettie is a threat to me! Oh, Alex—no. You couldn't be more wrong." Recovering her equilibrium, she gave him a reassuring smile. "I can almost see why you thought it—"

"You wrote to her, and you specifically told her the name of this town?"

"Yes, Your Honor," she said, her tone now weary. "Is the interrogation over yet? Because if it is . . ." She dared to arch an eyebrow. "I've spent the day dreaming of being alone with you. And here we are. Can't you think of a better use for our time than talking about poor Lettie?"

She hoped he might relax, but instead, his jaw visibly tensed. Then he said simply, "Lettie Price was murdered three months ago."

"Murdered? By whom? The only person who really hated her was my father, and he's been dead for nearly six months."

Coburn took a step backward, then looked Maggie directly in the eyes. "She was murdered by her son."

"Her son?"

"Ian Price."

"Ian Price?" Maggie shook her head, dazed. "What on earth are you saying? There were two Ians?"

"No, sweetheart. There was one Ian." He sat on the bed, then pulled her into his lap. "He didn't die in prison, Maggie. That was a story your father and the warden made up, so that you'd stop trying to contact him."

Maggie wriggled to her feet and turned to face him, completely confused. "He didn't die in prison?"

"You wrote every week, and cried every time the letters came back unopened. Your father believed you would spend the rest of your life in a hopeless quest, so he convinced the warden to pretend Ian was dead. Then, when you—"

"Wait!" She licked her lips, not daring to believe it was true. "Are you telling me my brother's still alive?"

"I'm telling you Ian Price is alive," Coburn growled. "He escaped from the prison, went to Chicago, and savagely murdered his mother, then ran off before he could be apprehended."

"Ian killed Lettie?"

"Pay attention, Maggie." He stood and grabbed her by the shoulders. "My God, I knew this would be difficult, but you have to listen to what I'm telling you. If Lettie told Ian where you were before she died, or if he found that letter—"

"Wait!" She batted his hands away and strode across the room, then sank onto the desk chair and forced herself to take a deep breath. "He's alive? And he killed Lettie? After all these years?"

"After all these years, he's going to complete the killing spree that started with Brian. He would have killed you and your father that night—"

"No, Alex. Papa believed that, too, but it wasn't true. I mean," she corrected herself quickly, "he would have shot my father, but not me. Never me. Ian loves me, Alex. And I—I love him. And he's alive." A tremor of joy possessed her, and she repeated softly, "He's alive. Oh, Alex! It's a miracle!"

"Maggie . . ." He crossed to stand before her. "How can I make you see—?"

"Isn't it wonderful?" She flung herself into his arms. "Hold me! Hold me, and make love to me, and let me talk to you." Pulling his face down, she covered it with kisses. "My little brother. I can't believe you're actually going to meet him. And June! Does June know? She's had a soft spot in her heart for him from the moment she first heard his name, and now he'll know it. It was always so cruel to think he died, not knowing—but he's alive!"

"My God, Maggie." Coburn held her with a fierceness that made no sense to her. Then he insisted, "You're hysterical. I should have realized—"

"I'm deliriously happy!" she confirmed, wrapping her arms around his neck. "Forget about Lettie, darling. He shouldn't have killed her, but surely you can see why he did. He spent five horrible years alone in prison, with no one to love him, all because of what she did to us when we were tiny babies."

"He's had five long years to plot his revenge," Coburn said, his tone gentle but firm. "I agree with everything you're saying, sweetheart. In his twisted mind, he had to kill her, just as he had to kill Brian and your father—*everyone* involved in that terrible mess. He somehow believes that if everyone's dead, then it's over."

"Exactly! And everyone *is* dead, and so he can begin to heal, with our help." She felt a second burst of joy, and clapped her hands in glee. "Who better than a bounty hunter to help me find him? You must know just how we can track him."

"Yes. I know how we'll do it."

"We'll leave at daybreak tomorrow. Don't ask me to wait a second longer! The town will have to understand. Angie Deighton can teach in my place for a few weeks, and after that, if we haven't found Ian, Father James will have to arrange for a new schoolteacher. An ugly man," she added playfully.

"Maggie?"

"Yes?"

"Will you let me talk now?"

She suppressed a giggle. "I'll try. But really, Alex, you can't imagine how I feel." Cocking her head to the side, she teased, "You should be glad, at least, that we're leaving town. You won't have to protect me from my secret admirer anymore."

"That's enough. Sit down, now. And listen to me."

"There's more? Oh, no . . ." She shook her head, refusing to accept bad news. "Please, Alex. Don't tell me something's happened to him. I couldn't bear it. You said he ran off before they could apprehend him. You said—"

"I said he was intent on killing everyone from his past. Including you. I said he knows you're here in Shasta Falls. He's had three months to come after you. We don't have to track him down, Maggie. He's already done the reverse." A glint of anger shone in Coburn's blue eyes. "He's here. He's been watching you. He won't rest until you're dead, too. You have to pay attention to every word I'm saying. And you have to do everything I tell you to do, without question."

Maggie exhaled sharply, then shook her head. No wonder Coburn had been behaving so strangely. He actually believed Ian would hurt her! It was a ludicrous concept, but she could understand why he and Denny—the prosecutor and the sheriff—had leapt to that conclusion.

Taking him by the hand, she led him back to the bed, then sat down and patted the cover for him to join her. He scowled but did so, and then she said soothingly, "I'm sorry you've been so worried about this, darling. From your vantage point, I'm sure Ian looks like some sort of dangerous criminal, but believe me, he isn't. He's as gentle as a lamb."

"Humor me," Alex drawled. "Pretend he killed your brother, tried to kill your father, and killed his own goddamned mother."

She pulled back sharply. "There's no reason to be sarcastic. I'm simply reassuring you that Ian would never hurt *me*. In his mind, I'm the only person who ever loved him. He'd die before he'd hurt me."

"He refused to see you after Brian's murder. He returned your letters unopened."

"Because he was hurt and confused."

"Or, because he believed you had turned your back on him. You accepted Brian into your heart. You and Brian were celebrating a birthday together—the birthday you once celebrated with Ian. You even let Brian sit in Ian's chair. You betrayed him."

"Is that how you see it?" Maggie frowned. "I suppose I don't blame you. But when you meet him—"

"I'm not going to 'meet' him. I'm going to arrest him, and return him to Chicago for trial."

"Alex!" She shook her head frantically. "Don't say that, please? Not until you've at least met him—"

"I'm not going to meet him!" He caught her quickly, as though guessing she was about to run away from him, and insisted, "I'm sorry, sweetheart. Forgive me for raising my voice. I'm just concerned that you won't take the proper precautions."

"Is there a price on his head? Is *that* why you're being so horrid?"

"If there isn't, there should be," Coburn retorted. "He murdered Lettie Price—his own mother!—in cold blood. You have an idealized vision of him, which frankly baffles me, considering the fact that you saw him shoot your twin brother."

Maggie grimaced. "I apologize for what I said about a price on his head. I know you're just worried about my safety. But I can hardly have you threatening my brother—"

"He's not—" Coburn caught himself and smiled grimly. "He's not actually your brother, is he, Maggie?"

"He most certainly is," she said with an haughty sniff. "You're beginning to sound like my father in the worst possible way." A new wave of anger crashed over her. "I can't believe *he* dared to lie to me about Ian. And Warden Hayes lied to me, too? What gave him the right to do such a thing?"

"They were wrong to do that, but their motives were pure. They believed you'd never have a life of your own, because you'd be obsessed with Ian's predicament. And I'm beginning to think they were right."

"I would have continued to write to him," she admitted. "And, of course, I never would have come to Shasta Falls."

"You would have moved closer to the prison?"

She winced. "Perhaps."

"And spent the rest of your life trying to visit a man who refused to acknowledge your efforts?"

"I don't know. I suppose in time I would have . . ." She stopped herself, admitting silently that she never would have abandoned Ian. But she wouldn't have been obsessed. Simply close by, in case he decided to allow her to visit.

"You say he's your brother. But it's apparent that he no longer sees you as a sister."

Maggie squared her shoulders. "What proof could you possibly have of that?"

Coburn stood up, crossed to his armoire, and located a stack of papers, which he brought back to Maggie. "Is this enough proof for you?"

She stared at the papers—the poems, and the drawing—without comprehending for a moment, and then she gasped. "You're suggesting Ian drew that picture? How dare you, Alex Coburn! He's a sweet, innocent boy—"

"And therein lies the irony." Alex fixed her with a steady stare. "You've always claimed a child wrote these, and I've always maintained it is the work of a man. And the truth is, we were both correct."

When Maggie didn't respond, he added more gently, "According to the warden's telegram, Ian never really did grow up, sweetheart. The same slowness that hampered him as a child persisted, and in some ways, he is still childlike. But he has the urges of a man. The urge to kill the persons who ruined his life. The urge to make love to a beautiful woman—"

"Alex, please," she whispered uneasily, knowing somehow that he was right, but not yet ready to accept it. "It's enough for now that he's alive. I don't want to talk about the rest."

"That's fine. We'll talk again later. You should rest for a while."

"You think he drew this?" She touched the scars on the drawing. "He must have remembered the day the dog bit me. The wounds were horrible, and very deep. He knew I had scars, but of course, he didn't realize they faded these last ten years."

It was too much, and she felt tears welling in her eyes. Was it possible that Ian was nearby? Hiding somewhere, watching Maggie? Afraid, perhaps, to approach her, or more realistically, afraid the authorities knew about his escape?

She picked up the first poem and smiled sadly. It made a certain odd sort of sense, that he could write this innocent, trusting verse. He was still a child. A "slow" child, to use Coburn's terminology. But he was also a man, and so he had drawn a naked woman. Beloved Maggie.

"He must be so confused. And frightened. And lonely."

"What about you?" Coburn asked. "Doesn't this confuse you, too? And frighten you, at least a bit?"

"I could never be frightened of Ian," she assured him with a sad smile. "But yes, I'm confused."

"The sheriff and I are going to help you. You trust us, don't you?"

Maggie bit her lip. "That depends on whether you meant what you said about sending him back to Chicago for trial. I can't be a party to that, Alex. And I can't be friends with anyone who'd do that to a child."

He exhaled sharply, and she knew that he was doing his best not to shout: *He's not a child!*

"To me, he's a child. And the warden says he never grew up, so doesn't that mean he's a child in the eyes of the law?" When Coburn didn't answer, she asked softly, "What is it you and Denny intend to do?"

"Find him. Our primary concern at this point is to make sure he doesn't pose a threat to you. After that, we can discuss what to do next." He gave her a wary smile. "Do you have a photograph of him?"

"You don't need a photograph," she retorted. "He and I are twins. If you see a boy who looks like me, arrest him immediately."

Coburn shook his head, chuckling. "Are we back to this? Beloved Maggie, protecting Ian from bullies—in this case, myself and the sheriff?"

She shrugged, then her bravado faded and she took his hand in her own. "Promise me you won't let anything happen to him."

"Don't ask me to promise that."

"Oh, I'd almost forgotten. You can't make any promises to me at all, can you?"

"What?"

"Never mind." She turned away, frustrated and concerned for Ian's future. If she didn't find a way to change Coburn's mind, he and Denny were going to hunt Ian down and send him back to Chicago, where he would be tried for murder and hanged! What cruel twist of fate had given her a bounty hunter for a lover, and a sheriff for a close friend?

"I want to talk to June. She's the only one who can possibly understand."

"I agree. They invited us to dine with them again, and I accepted."

Maggie nodded stiffly.

"In the meantime, you and I could rest for a while—"

"No, thank you." She jutted her chin forward defensively. "I'd like to be alone, if you don't mind."

A shadow of something—hurt, annoyance, anger?—passed over his face, but he nodded. "Whatever you want. I'll go and read—"

"In the library? Couldn't I—?" She flushed and asked more sweetly, "I'd like to read in the library. It's been ages, or at least, it feels as though it has."

"I miss those evenings, too," he told her. "Although I wouldn't trade them for the last two nights in here."

Maggie flushed. "You don't mind reading in here, then? Or I could go up to my room—"

"I'll be here if you need me. And you'll stay in the library. But if you get lonely, and want to talk or be held—"

"I won't." She stood up and moved to the door.

"Maggie?"

"Yes?"

He seemed about to say something kind, then his face hardened. "I'm determined to keep you safe. There's no price too high, including your affection."

"Or my trust?"

"Yes. I hope it won't come to that, but in any case, I'm going to keep you safe."

She wanted to glare at him, but had a feeling he was talking to Christine as much as to her, and so she allowed him one wistful smile, then left the room, closing the door behind herself. By the time she'd reached the sofa, the door had opened again, and she sighed in confused disgust. Yes, he was determined to keep her safe. If only she could convince him that it was Ian, not she, who needed his protection and concern.

She stared at the cover of Tobias Blake's *Ivanhoe* without even bothering to open it. How could she concentrate, knowing Ian was in Shasta Falls? She had to find him, and hug him, and tell him she had never once stopped loving him—not even in that awful moment when Brian had fallen into a heap.

And she had to warn him about Coburn. To tell him that the authorities now suspected he was in Shasta Falls.

It occurred to her that perhaps she could leave a message for him the same way he had left the poems and drawing for her—in the pages of her lesson book. Unfortunately, it was Friday, which meant she'd be teaching at the logging camp rather than the schoolhouse for the next two days.

But you could leave your lesson book at the schoolhouse, in plain view on the desk. And inside, place a note, telling him how dear he is to you, and telling him to go to Sacramento and wait for you. You can arrange to meet at the Catholic Church there—surely there must be one. And surely the priest will be willing to help you.

She thought of Father James again, but his connection to Denny was a danger. And Mr. Braddock? She still wasn't certain what to make of him, for having used her to prove a point with Coburn.

You mustn't trust anyone, she decided finally. *If it means you need to leave Shasta Falls—and Alex and the Riordains—behind, then you'll do it, until you're sure Ian is safe.*

She thought of June, and sighed. Surely her friend would approve of this plan. She might even assist her. But she might not, and Maggie couldn't take that chance. Still, it made her heart ache, and she vowed to make the best of the remaining days of their friendship.

You'll see her and Denny tonight, and you'll try to keep the mood light. And thank them for all they've done for you. In fact, you should make them a pie! You're certainly not going to get any reading done.

Pleased to have something other than Ian to occupy her thoughts, she roamed through the kitchen and parlor in search of her landlady, but without success. *Surely she won't mind if you use the oven,* she told herself, *especially if you make a second pie for the boarders, as you did last time. But not berry this time. The peaches in the yard are just too scrumptious to resist, so . . .*

Scooping up a basket from the pantry, she headed out onto the porch, and was soon gathering huge, soft peaches. It reminded her of her childhood, when Ian would plead with her to bake pie every night. He was the reason she had mastered the skill so completely, and now, ironically, he was the reason she would put those skills to good use.

Her chest tightened, with apprehension and with excitement. Ian was alive! It was a miracle. And if her plan for contacting him proved successful, she'd actually be hugging him soon.

The soft sound of footsteps on the matted grasses of the yard told her someone was walking up behind her, and she shook her head, already annoyed at the thought that Coburn might scold her for leaving the house. It was so ludicrous that he saw Ian as a threat! Of course, if the bounty hunter apologized, and promised to help her protect Ian from the authorities, her resentment would fade quickly, so she summoned a hopeful smile before she turned to face him.

Sixteen

Before her stood a slender young man, dressed in simple brown pants and a threadbare beige shirt. His dark hair was shaggy, his thin face sunburned but not otherwise weathered. And he was, quite simply, the most heartbreakingly welcome sight Maggie had ever seen.

"Ian!" She threw her arms around his neck, and was surprised when he didn't hug her in return. His body was stiff, and his arms hung at his side, as though he didn't know quite what to do with them.

Pulling him quickly behind the tree, so that they couldn't be viewed from the house, she demanded, "Aren't you happy to see me?"

"Yeah." He flashed her a lopsided grin that made her heart ache. "I wasn't sure you'd want to see me, though."

"Look at you! All grown up! I'm not sure I would have recognized you in a crowd."

"You're big, too," he said, blushing deeply. "When I saw you, I was surprised."

"I can imagine." She pulled him into another embrace, then explained with a sob, "They told me you were dead. I never, ever would have stopped writing, or trying to see you, if I'd known you were alive."

"Yeah. Miz Price told me about that. She told me *he* made you go away."

"He? Oh, you mean Papa? It was wrong of him, but he did it out of love for me."

"And hate for *me*," Ian replied in a matter-of-fact voice. "Miz Price told me he died."

"Yes, Ian. He died earlier this year."

"Did you cry?"

"Yes, I did." She stepped back and studied his face. "I cried at the prison, too, when they showed me a grave and told me you were buried in it."

"Good. I thought you were cross with me, because I shot the new boy."

Maggie sighed. "That was a sad day, too."

"I had lots of sad days, while you played with him. Sometimes, I came and watched you."

"Oh?" She touched his cheek. "We'll talk about that later, shall we? For now, you need to go. There's a man who lives here—"

"Yeah. The one that kisses you."

"Yes. He could come out here at any moment, and I'm not sure exactly what he'd do."

"I almost killed him yesterday, but I was afraid it'd make you cross with me."

A chill ran through Maggie, and she repeated nervously, "You almost killed Alex? Why?"

"I don't like the way he kisses you."

"You mustn't kill anyone else, Ian. Promise me you won't."

His face contorted with indecision, then he shrugged. "I won't, unless they try to hurt me or you."

Maggie nodded. "There's no school tomorrow. I usually go to the logging camp—"

"Yeah, I know."

Maggie smiled at the impish bragging. "Tomorrow, I'll find some excuse not to go to the camp. I'll come up to the school instead. Meet me there, and we'll leave town together."

Ian's face lit up. "Then we'll get married, and have babies?"

"Married?" Maggie shook her head, then asked wryly, "It's true, then? You don't think of me as a sister anymore?"

"You're *his* sister."

"And yours. Always yours. Always."

Ian grimaced. "It's better that you're not my sister. It means we can have babies."

Maggie shook her head again. "I can't ever feel that way about you, Ian. I love you more than life itself, but as a brother. In my heart, that's what you'll always be."

He shrugged. "Then I'll get another girl for babies."

"We'll see."

To her surprise, it made Ian burst into laughter. Then he sobered quickly and explained, "You always said that to me. When I wanted to have pie, or to go look at the horses, or get a puppy. We'll see. We'll see. We'll see."

"Well, we will," she said with a smile. Then she sandwiched his face between her hands and kissed his forehead. "I'm so happy, Ian. So happy I can finally tell you how much I love you. How much I missed you, for all those years you were with Lettie. Every night . . ." Her voice choked on her tears.

And Ian was sobbing, too, and they clung to one another, until Maggie remembered Coburn and pulled away, wiping her face frantically. "You have to go right away."

"Or he'll shoot me?"

"No. I don't think so. But," she admitted sadly, "I don't know for certain what he'd do if he found you here. So please go?"

"I've got a place where I'm safe. I'll stay there to-night. And then, tomorrow . . . ?"

"Yes, tomorrow morning. At the school. If you're not there, I'll just assume something detained you, and I'll try again at noon. And every four hours after that, until we're successful. Don't take any chances, Ian. They know about you now, and they'll be looking for you."

"I'll be careful." Ian studied her closely. "Will he let you come to the school alone? Seems like he's always with you. Kissing you."

"He's very fond of me," Maggie agreed. "But there's something he doesn't know about me. Something that will make him leave me alone for a while."

"What is it?"

She smiled sadly. "It's a long story. I'll tell you while we're traveling together. I have so many things to tell you, Ian, but only one thing really matters." She stroked his face. "I adore you. I have since we were babies, and that love never wavered. And it never will."

His blue eyes filled with tears. "Sometimes I knew that, and sometimes, I figured you hated me. For killing the new boy, and scaring you with the gun."

She embraced him fiercely. "All the killing is behind us now, Ian. We're going to find someplace where no one can hurt you, and you can't hurt anyone, either. I'll take care of you—"

"No, *I'll* take care of *you*. I'm the man. I'll make all the decisions, and all the rules, like Papa did."

Maggie smiled through her tears. "We'll see."

When Ian laughed at the joke, she felt as though her heart might burst with joy. Then she remembered their situation, and sobered quickly. "Go back to your hiding place. Be very, very careful."

"I will."

When he turned away, she grabbed his arm, acutely aware of how quickly things could change. Never again would she let him out of her sight without first telling him how precious he was to her. "I love you, Ian Gleason. Nothing can ever, ever change that."

"I love you, too," he assured her, then after a quick glance about the yard, he dashed away.

With a contented sigh, Maggie picked up the basket of peaches and headed for the house. After ten long years, she had finally been reunited with her brother. And in every way that counted, he was as sweet and loving as he'd been right up to that awful day when the policemen had taken him away from her. And he finally knew the truth: her love for Brian, and her sorrow over the loss of him, had never come between them.

So much for the past, she told herself ruefully. *Now, what do you intend to do about the future? Ian is a fugitive. You can take him to Mexico, I suppose, but Alex will come after you.*

She winced sadly at the thought of trying to outsmart Coburn. He was a born strategist, and had spent the last two years learning to track and apprehend fugitives.

Stepping into the kitchen, she placed the basket on the table, then selected the ripest, most fragrant peach to bring to her lover. If he were any other man, she would try to convince him to help her hide Ian. But Alex was a former prosecutor, a bounty hunter, and a man whose past drove him to protect his woman with fanatical devotion. He might agree to help Ian with representation, and to avoid execution, but would insist that the boy needed to be locked up—for everyone's good, including Ian's. And Maggie understood that sentiment, and might have agreed with it, had she not been convinced she could keep her brother from hurting anyone else. And she could heal him with love, and keep him safe. And so she would.

Which meant she had to turn her back on the other man in her life: Alex Coburn. It would be so very difficult, but she would remind herself that their future looked bleak in any event. He couldn't give his heart to her until Sean Wiley was in his grave. He needed to concentrate on hunting criminals, yet he would be worried about ever leaving Maggie alone.

In a sense, you'll be setting him free from that hopeless dilemma, she told herself as she approached the doorway to his room. *But before you set him free, you'll shower him with love—all the love you have to give. He deserves that, after all he's given you.*

With a wistful sigh, she stepped through the doorway, then approached the bed, conscious of his gaze on her. He was propped against a pillow, with his journal opened in one hand, but his attention was on Maggie's expression. She gave him a reassuring smile, then handed him the peach.

"Thank you." He scanned her face. "Does this mean you aren't angry with me?"

"I could never be angry with you," she told him simply. "I love you dearly, and I always will."

He seemed stunned by the statement. Moistening his lips, he murmured, "I've been thinking about Ian—"

"I don't want to talk about Ian," she said, scooting up onto the bed next to him as she spoke. "And I don't want to visit the Riordains again tonight. I want to make love with you until we're both exhausted, and then I want to sleep in your arms."

Coburn's blue eyes warmed. "I like the sound of that. But in the morning, we'll need to talk about Ian."

"In the morning," she corrected, unbuttoning her

dress slowly, "we'll go and find Ian at the logging camp."

"What makes you think he's there?"

"I go there every Saturday. If he's been watching, he knows that. We'll find him there. And you and he will get acquainted, and once you've seen what a nice boy he is, and how unfairly life has treated him, you'll agree with me that sending him to Chicago isn't a good plan."

"Maggie—"

"Let me finish." She slipped her shoulders free of her clothing, then wriggled until the dress was down to her waist, enjoying the flicker of arousal in Coburn's eyes. He was trying so hard to concentrate on business, but clearly wanted nothing more than to devour her. "After you've met Ian, and talked with him, if you still believe he's dangerous, then I'll do whatever you recommend, as long as we take steps to protect him."

"What steps?"

She sighed. "He didn't have a trial last time, so he didn't have an attorney. You must know which lawyers in Chicago are the best. With the proper representation, isn't there a chance Ian can be placed in a hospital rather than a prison this time? It will be easier for me to visit him that way. At least once a year."

"I'm amazed to hear you talking this way," Coburn admitted, brushing his knuckles lightly over her breasts. "I was going to say almost the same things to you, if you were willing to listen. I'm determined to see that he gets a good defense. I believe we can protect him from execution, and as you said, try to have him incarcerated someplace more humane than last time. I can't guarantee any of that, of course—"

"Can you guarantee that you'll do your best?"

"Of course."

"Starting now?"

"Now? Oh, I see." A grin spread slowly over his face. "Be careful what you ask for, Maggie-Margaret."

"I'm not afraid of you, Mr. Coburn." With a mischievous smile, she twined her arms around his neck, then gasped with delight as he began to make good on his warning.

For twelve straight hours they engaged in a giddy cycle of lovemaking and slumber, and while it was primarily joy that engulfed them, there were moments when Maggie was unable to keep herself from sobbing gently against his chest or into his pillow. She was afraid he'd know that she was already mourning the upcoming loss of him—of the lovemaking, and of the companionship and hope he had brought to her life. Fortunately, he assumed that she was crying for Ian, not herself, and his reassurances and promises only served to make her fall more and more deeply in love with him.

Still, when morning arrived, she knew what she had to do. She had to break his heart, and she'd hate herself forever for doing it, but he would survive. Perhaps he would even love again one day. And Ian would be safe. That was all that could matter for the moment.

So she dressed for the ride to the logging camp, although she knew she'd be making a very different journey. Then she waited until Coburn had strapped on his gun belt, then patted the bed, inviting him to join her for one last talk.

"Don't worry about the pistol," he said. "It's just a precaution. I have no intention of using it on Ian."

"I know that," she assured him. "There's something else I need to tell you. I should have said something last night, or the night before, but—" She smiled sadly. "You kept distracting me with your kisses."

Coburn grimaced. "This sounds serious."

"It's actually rather amusing. But at first, you'll be angry."

"With you? Never."

She tried not to notice the love blazing in his eyes. "Just promise me you'll listen to everything I have to say before you react."

"I promise." He patted her hand. "You underestimate my feelings for you, sweetheart. Nothing you say will change those."

But Maggie knew otherwise, and it was all she could do to continue. "You remember my mentioning Father James?"

He nodded. "Denny's friend. He arranged for your coming here. I should thank him one day soon."

"Shh." Maggie ordered herself not to dare cry, then continued. "Father James acted as go-between, but there was someone else involved. Someone to whom I wrote, after my father died. I wanted to start a new life, away from Chicago, and this particular man had a reputation for helping girls find new lives. He had conducted business in Chicago for years, but had moved to San Francisco. I hesitated to contact him, because he didn't usually arrange teaching positions, but he agreed to help me, so I made the long voyage to San Francisco."

She could see that the truth was dawning on Coburn, but he didn't interrupt. Instead, he nodded for her to continue.

"He usually arranges marriages, but I assured him I had no intention of ever being a bride. All I wanted was to teach, and to live alone in peace. I thought he would understand and respect that, but it became clear, when I finally met him, that he was too much a matchmaker—and a romantic—to ever accept my plan of spinsterhood."

"Braddock?"

He had spoken the word softly, but still Maggie recoiled. "Please don't be angry. He was so kind to me. And so well intentioned. He insisted that the right husband could chase away all the old, painful memories. And he said—" She took a deep breath, then used the phrase she had rehearsed silently more than once during the night. "He said he knew just the right man to do it. A man who loved books as much as I, and who was as determined as I—"

"Stop it!" Coburn was on his feet, staring in dismay. "I don't believe you."

"It's not as diabolical as it sounds, Alex," she insisted, struggling against a rush of self-loathing. "I assured Mr. Braddock that I had no interest in meeting a man, not even one who loved books. I agreed to come to Shasta Falls for the teaching position, but I had no intention of ever becoming involved with you. And when I first met you, I thought Mr. Braddock was insane for even suggesting it, but over time, as we sat together, and you teased me . . ."

She could see clearly what was happening, as the truth sank into his heart, and then into his brain, and hurt and anger began to well up visibly in his face. "You never said a word."

"I promised Mr. Braddock I wouldn't."

"I see. You promised Braddock. That, of course, justifies everything." His eyes narrowed with disgust. "Did you enjoy making a fool of me?"

"I didn't see it that way. I only saw that Mr. Braddock was a genius. A miracle worker. And I was glad he warned me, Alex. If he hadn't, your moods would have made me run away. But I trusted his instincts—"

"That's enough!" He turned away, as though afraid he might say something even harsher.

"Alex?" She slid to her feet, then touched his shoulder. "It all worked out for the best, didn't it?"

"Did it?" His voice was raspy and unfamiliar as he turned back to her. "You let me tell you that story, about Christine and about my sons, when all along you knew——"

"No!" She hadn't anticipated that, and couldn't bear the thought that he believed she could be so cruel. Deceptive and manipulative, yes—that would be the price she'd pay for keeping him at a distance until she and Ian could get away. But not this! "He didn't tell me about them, Alex. I swear it."

"Then he used us both," he growled. "And you were his willing pawn. So irresistible. So innocent. But you're not so innocent after all. And there's a heartless side to you I never would have believed possible, Maggie."

"You'll feel differently once you've had time to think about it. Alone."

"I don't want to think about it," he told her, his voice now eerily quiet. "Let's just go and find your brother."

"If you promise not to hurt him, I'll—I'll let you go after him alone."

Coburn's eyes narrowed. "What?"

"You need to be alone. And I want to prove to you how much I trust you. How much I love you. Go to the camp, and bring Ian back safely. And then we'll talk this through again and again until you understand that Mr. Braddock and I only deceived you out of love."

When he just stared, she added quickly, "This is my way of showing you how much you mean to me. And the truth is, I can't bear the thought of watching you arrest Ian. I'll stay at the sheriff's office, safe and sound, until you and Ian return. You can even lock him up in a cell, as long as you let me stay there to visit with him, and reassure him."

"You give me your word? You'll stay with the sheriff until I'm back?"

"Where would I go?" she asked with a rueful smile. "You and Ian are my whole life. I'll wait patiently for as long as it takes. Just promise me you won't shoot him."

"I won't shoot him, unless it's necessary to save a life. Including mine."

Maggie nodded. "Let's go, then."

They walked together in silence, and for the first time in days, the connection between them, both physical and spiritual, seemed broken. He was clearly lost in thought, and she knew from his expression that she had hurt him more deeply than she had intended. She had known he'd be furious over the deception, and Braddock's interference, but she hadn't counted on his believing she'd known about Christine. And his poor murdered babies. He would spend the rest of his life believing Maggie had played games with his heart, despite knowing how cruelly life had tortured it.

Isn't this what you wanted? she taunted herself. *Look at his face! He can't bear the sight of you. He'll ride off for the camp without a backward glance, and he'll wait there for hours, glad of the opportunity to be away from you. This is just what you and Ian need, so accept it. Alex can go back to hunting Wiley, and you can take care of your brother. That's the way it has to be.*

When they reached the livery stable, she touched

his arm. "Alex? Why don't you just watch me from here?"

"Huh?"

"Your horse is here. Just watch me until I safely reach Denny's office. The sooner you leave for the camp, the sooner I'll hold Ian in my arms again."

Coburn shook his head. "We don't even know Denny's there."

"Someone is always there by this time of day. But if it makes you feel better, I'll send him out to wave to you, so you'll know I'm safe."

He nodded. "If that's how you want it."

"It is." She wanted to kiss him farewell, and to tell him she loved him, but was afraid she'd burst into tears, so she patted his arm instead. "Be careful, and take good care of my brother."

"I will."

She started to walk away, and was surprised when he spoke her name softly. Turning back, she winced at the pain in his eyes, then murmured, "Once you've thought it through, you'll understand."

"I'll never understand why you lied to me," he corrected her. "And I'm not sure I'll ever trust you completely again. But I do love you. I just—I just wanted to be sure you didn't doubt that."

She bit her lip, desperate not to run to him, and forced herself to think about Ian, waiting at the schoolhouse. "I love you too, Alex. Take care." She turned and rushed toward the sheriff's office, and was relieved when he made no further effort to stop her.

But she knew his eyes were on her, and she allowed herself to take comfort in that, one last time. Then she stepped up to Denny's door and peeked inside at the sheriff.

"Missy!"

"Come out here and wave to Alex."

"What?" He hurried to the door. "Where is he?"

"Over there? See?" She waved brightly toward her lover. "Now that he knows I'm safe with you, he's going to have a quick look around town. Then he and I are going to ride out to the logging camp, to see if we can find Ian."

Denny draped one arm across Maggie's shoulders, then waved to the bounty hunter with his free hand. Coburn tipped his hat, then disappeared into the stable, and Maggie sighed. Her last glimpse of him. Much like the first. If only she'd known that day that the dusty gunman was the only true love she would ever be allowed to know.

"How are you, missy?"

"I'm fine."

"Come inside for a while."

"For just a minute," she agreed. "Then Alex wants me to hire a horse and join him on the outskirts of town, so we can head for the camp. He's sure that's where Ian will be, since I usually go out there every Saturday."

"He's probably right." Denny cupped her face in his hand. "I'm sorry about your brother, missy. June cried her eyes out all night over it."

"It's tragic, but with your help, and Alex's, it will work out. I'm sure of it."

He studied her intently. "June insists Ian would never hurt you. But I'm not so sure about it."

Maggie smiled. "June's such a dear. And it's true, Denny. Ian loves me."

"He loved you once—"

"I'm not going to quarrel with you, Sheriff Riordain." She patted his arm to soften the scolding. "You've been a wonderful friend. I'll never be able to thank you for all your kindnesses."

He flushed. "You make it sound as if you're going somewhere."

Maggie berated herself silently, then rallied. "If you and Alex insist on returning Ian to Chicago to stand trial, I'll be going with him."

The sheriff sighed. "I never thought of that. But I suppose, if it was my brother, I'd do the same thing."

"Of course you would." She glanced toward the doorway, anxious to find Ian and leave as quickly as possible. They'd take a southern route, with no danger of encountering Coburn, whose path was now leading west.

"Walk with me to the stable, Denny. I don't want to keep Alex waiting."

The sheriff's eyes narrowed. "Waiting where? If he wanted you to go to the camp, why did he leave without you in the first place?"

"I told you, he wanted to scout around town and its outskirts first, to be sure Ian wasn't lying in wait somewhere. He wanted to know I was safe with our big, strong sheriff for a few minutes. Then you're to send me to him. He'll be waiting for me by the school."

"Why there?"

Maggie shrugged. "He didn't explain the details to me. I suppose he thinks it's the safest spot in town, aside from this office. And so do I." She took a deep breath and added in a more casual tone, "You're to watch me ride up toward the school, but not come with me. Alex says you're needed here. He didn't explain that either but as long as you watch me until I'm safely to the school, where's the harm? I'll wave to you when I catch sight of Alex."

"That doesn't make any sense."

Maggie glared. "It's not *my* plan, so don't ask me to defend it. If you want to defy Alex Coburn, fine, but my experience is that he knows exactly what he's doing. I learned that playing chess with him. He's a master strategist."

Denny shrugged. "He's had more experience tracking men than anyone I know, so I bow to his judgment on that score. But not on other matters."

"Oh?"

His expression hardened. "This business between you and him. You sleeping in his bedroom and all. That has to stop."

"I agree."

The sheriff exhaled in relief. "You do?"

"He's been a perfect gentleman," she assured him. "But I agree, it's harmful to my reputation. And a schoolteacher's reputation is priceless." She gave him a brisk hug. "Please don't worry about me, Denny. I'm happier than I've been in years."

"You don't look happy."

Maggie sighed. By all rights, she should be all aglow, given the fact that she was about to be reunited with Ian. But the circumstances were so bizarre and fraught with complications. And in exchange for time with Ian, she was turning her back on a love affair, and a lover, that had turned her simple life into an exciting and passionate adventure.

"I'm happy," she insisted stubbornly. "And it's time for me to meet Alex, so give me a hug, and then watch me until I wave to you."

"None of that," he growled. "I'll come with you."

"Denny—" She stopped herself and strained to hear the unfamiliar sound that was suddenly filling the air. "What on earth is that?"

Denny strode to the doorway and stepped onto the sidewalk. "It's the schoolbell, although I'll be hanged if I know who could be ringing it."

"The bell?" Maggie pushed past the sheriff, and as

she reached the outdoors, there was no mistaking the sound. A bell—not beautiful, like a church bell, but like something from a firehouse, signaling trouble.

"Ian!" Maggie sprang forward, only to be grabbed and hauled back by the sheriff.

"We don't know what this is about, missy. Stay here—"

"It's Ian! It's my brother, and something is terribly wrong, so let me go." She batted his hands away and blurted out, "He was waiting for me there, Denny. And now he's ringing the bell. *Please* let me go."

"Wait." The sheriff dragged her back into his office and grabbed a shotgun. *"Now* we can go."

She wanted to scream at him that he couldn't bring a firearm, but what if Ian needed protection?

From Coburn? Was *that* it? Her mind reeled, and she was grateful that she had the sheriff's hand to steady her as they raced up the path that led to the schoolhouse.

The bell was no longer ringing, but it had done its work. Throngs of people, in twos and threes, were headed up the hill, curious but not overly concerned. Maggie and Denny pushed past them, then stopped short when the school came into view.

"Oh, no . . ." Maggie felt a stab of terror at the sight of Coburn, standing guard at the gate, his rifle at his side, his blazing eyes fixed in the direction of the sheriff's office.

She looked around wildly, hoping to see Ian gesture to her from some hiding place, but there was no sign of him. And the schoolhouse door was open wide. From the knotting of her stomach, she knew that was a very bad omen.

Tearing free of Denny, she sprinted for the gate, determined to push past Coburn and find her brother, but the bounty hunter caught her by the arm; then, to her shock and dismay, he grappled her to his chest and murmured, "I'm so sorry, sweetheart."

"No!" She tried to wriggle away, screaming, "What have you done? How could you? *Where is he?*"

Her gaze darted toward the open schoolhouse door again, and again she tried to push past Coburn, but he restrained her, growling to Denny, "Go and see. But prepare yourself first."

"Prepare?" Still struggling, Maggie looked from one man to the other. "What does *that* mean?"

It was Denny who understood first. "Wiley?"

Coburn nodded. "He left a note. Not that there would have been any question. It's still in there with— with the body."

Denny nodded, then squared his shoulders. Turning to the crowd that had formed outside the fence, he shouted, "Go home! We have enough trouble here without worrying about you folks. Go home, and you'll hear about it soon enough." Then he strode up the walkway, onto the porch, and disappeared into the building.

Coburn held Maggie by the shoulders and said quietly, "Sean Wiley killed your brother, sweetheart. He killed him as a means of taunting me. I'd give anything if I could change that, or trade places with Ian."

"No . . ." She stared into his eyes, transfixed by the pain, then she collapsed against his chest and began to wail. "No, no, no! He was so sweet. So pure. I know you don't believe that—"

"I believe it, Maggie." Tightening his hold, Coburn told her in a shaky voice, "I never saw my sons' bodies. Did I mention that? They were buried before I returned to Virginia City. Christine told me, and I read the coroner's report, but I never saw what that monster was capable of. Until now."

"Oh, Alex!" She wrapped her arms around his neck. "What will become of us?"

"I don't know," he admitted.

"I have to see Ian. I have to hold him, one last time—"

"You will. But let the undertaker work on him first. I won't allow you to see him like this, and neither will the sheriff. It's—it's not something Ian would want you to see. And I swear, Maggie, it looks like Wiley killed him quickly, and then did—did the rest afterwards. I know that's small comfort—"

"Oh, Alex."

Stroking her hair, he confessed, "This happened because of your association with me. Can you ever forgive me?"

"Alex . . ."

"I know you think I'm heartless, but I never would have hurt your brother. I was determined to take him safely, and then to find a way to help him. I couldn't make promises to you, but I made that vow to myself, and I swear I would have kept it."

"I believe you," she sobbed. Then she raised her eyes to his and stammered, "I s-swear, I never knew you existed until Mrs. Blake told me about you, the day I arrived in town. I swear it. Mr. Braddock didn't tell me about you—"

"It's fine, Maggie. It doesn't matter."

"It matters to me! What happened between us was so sweet, and so slow, and so very unexpected. So exquisitely honest and heartfelt. Oh God," she groaned. "What will we do now?"

Denny's voice interrupted softly from behind her. "Take Maggie home, Alex. I'll deal with all this."

"You read the note?" Coburn asked.

Maggie turned to see Denny's response, and then flinched to see that his eyes were red-rimmed from crying. "Oh, no . . . My poor Ian. Please, let me go to him."

"I'd kill myself first," Denny growled, blocking her path. Not that it was necessary. Coburn's hold on her was like iron, and deep inside she knew they were correct. There was nothing she could do for Ian now. And while her imagination was reeling with images of what Wiley had done, she had a feeling the reality was a thousand times worse.

"I saw him last night," she murmured, wiping at the tears that continued to pour down her cheeks. "I told him how much I loved him. And he was happy. He was his sweet self, so trusting and so gentle."

"That's something, isn't it?" Coburn said. "He'll rest in peace, knowing he was loved, and needed, and cherished." With a quick movement, he bent down, scooped Maggie up into his arms, and carried her back down the hill to the boardinghouse.

Coburn tucked her into his bed, then sat, holding her hand, while a tearful Mrs. Blake fussed over her. Between sobs, Maggie told them about her brief meeting with Ian under the peach tree. "I'd almost forgotten how beautiful his smile was," she admitted. "Five years in that awful prison, and yet he was still as innocent and vulnerable as he was when he was a little boy."

With a rueful smile, she added, "I know I should be in mourning, but I've mourned him for the past two years. In so many ways, this gave me something precious, despite the horror of it all."

"It must have meant the world to Ian, too," the landlady said. "He came all this way, just to see you again. And I agree—as tragic as this is, it would have been so much more unbearable if you two hadn't had some time together before that awful man did what he did."

"Speaking of that monster," Coburn murmured. "I can't stay too long, Maggie. Not if I hope to catch up with him."

"I know." She sandwiched his face between her hands. "After you spit on his grave for Christine, do it again for Ian."

"I will." Turning to Mrs. Blake, he asked, "Eleanor? Could I have a moment alone with Maggie?"

The landlady wiped her eyes, then bustled toward the doorway. "I'll be in the kitchen if you need me."

When she'd gone, Coburn reminded Maggie, "He's already hours ahead of me."

"Go," she urged him. "I'll be here waiting. Forever, if necessary."

"That's not acceptable, sweetheart." He took her hands in his own and tried to smile. "I intend to find him quickly, and then, one of two things will happen. Either I'll kill him, or he'll kill me."

Maggie nodded, her lower lip quavering.

"I want you to stay with Denny and June while I'm gone. They won't let you out of their sight, I'm sure. If I'm not back in a week, and you haven't heard from me—"

She yanked her hands free to cover her ears. "Don't!"

"Maggie, listen. I won't be able to concentrate on protecting myself if I'm worried about you. I have to be absolutely sure you're safe, so you have to promise to follow my instructions to the letter."

She sighed and nodded for him to continue.

"If you don't hear from me in a week, Denny will take you to San Francisco. To Braddock."

Speechless, Maggie simply nodded again.

"Don't let anyone but the Riordains know where you'll be."

"I won't." She forced herself to smile. "Mr. Braddock will take good care of me. And he'll be pleased that we turned to him for help. Don't worry."

Coburn moistened his lips. "Will you promise me one more thing?"

"Anything."

"If something happens to me, let Braddock find a husband for you."

Maggie stroked his face. "That's nonsense, but it's lovely nonsense."

"Take the sketch with you," he continued stubbornly. I want your husband to see how much you need to be surrounded by books."

"Oh, Alex . . ."

"And tell Braddock he has my undying gratitude and admiration," the bounty hunter added, his expression solemn. "He truly is a genius. He found Christine for me, and then, by some miracle, he found you. The great love of my life."

Stunned, Maggie choked back a sob and threw herself into his arms.

"Learn from me," he pleaded. "I didn't trust Braddock. And I didn't believe I could ever be happy again after I lost my family. But these last few weeks with you—my God, they've been paradise."

"Take me with you," Maggie pleaded.

"No. You'd slow me down." Grasping her face between his hands, he insisted, "You can fall in love again, with Braddock's help. And the next time might even be more incredible. Promise me you won't waste time mourning me. I want your word on this."

She wrenched free and said, scolding, "Alex, don't."

"I don't want to be haunted by unfinished business

between us," he countered stubbornly. "I've had that sensation for too long. I need to concentrate on outsmarting that bastard Wiley."

She knew that much was true, at least, so she nodded dutifully. "You have my word on it. If I don't hear from you after—after a while, I'll visit Mr. Braddock, and—"

"One week, Maggie. If you haven't heard from me by then, it means I'm dead and Wiley is still alive. He'll come after you, if only for sport. You won't be safe in Shasta Falls. You need to go to San Francisco." Grasping her by the shoulders, he insisted, "Promise me."

"I promise." She wrapped her arms around his chest. "I love you so much."

"And I love you." He returned the hug briskly. "Now get some rest. Let Mrs. Blake and the Riordains take care of you. I have to go."

She watched in dismay as he gathered up his holster and hat from the foot of the bed. Then he turned back to her, and for a moment she thought he was going to say something else, or at least, to come and kiss her one last time. But all he did was nod stiffly, his face expressionless; then he turned and strode out of the room.

Epilogue

For so many years, Maggie had cringed at the thought of Ian's prison funeral, imagining it to have been an abbreviated, impersonal, and perhaps even disrespectful affair. If only she could have been there, she had told herself. If only Ian had died knowing he was loved.

And so, as she stood in the Shasta Falls churchyard, listening in rapt appreciation as Reverend Fletcher talked about the poor departed soul—as though he'd been an honored member of their community, rather than a troubled stranger—she reminded herself that for all the horror of Ian's death, there had been some small blessings. And while her heart ached for a few more minutes, or weeks, or years, she reminded herself that she had been given something priceless in that brief meeting under the peach tree. And she hoped that Ian, too, had gained a measure of happiness and peace from it.

The cemetery was overflowing with mourners, each of whom offered comfort to the bereaved sister. Her students in particular were visibly distraught, and she knew they were remembering her playful mentions of her brothers. She imagined how odd it must be for them, yet they seemed determined to be strong and loving for her, and as she met each pair of sympathetic eyes, she tried to smile in grateful acknowledgement of their devotion.

Denny and June had barely left her alone since the tragedy, and even now, stood on either side of her, offering love and support so selfless and complete, she wondered how she could ever hope to repay it. And while Coburn wasn't there, she felt his love as well. She hadn't heard from him, but she told herself he was certainly alive. Doing what he needed to do— for himself, and for Christine and Ian and the little babies. At any minute, he could appear in the distance, and she would run to him. But even in his absence, she drew strength from him.

Reverend Fletcher finished his last prayer, and as the congregation murmured, "Amen," Maggie stepped up to the coffin and took one last look at Ian's sweet face. Thanks to the efforts of the undertaker, the boy appeared peaceful and serene, despite the brutal nature of his last few moments of life.

Forgive us, Ian, Maggie told him as she brushed her lips across his forehead. *You deserved a full and sheltered life. But know at least that I will never forget you, never stop loving you. And you'll be here, in this beautiful cemetery of this beautiful town, where there is so much love. I can visit you here.*

"Maggie, look over there. Near the fence," June murmured, touching her shoulder from behind.

Maggie raised her eyes and scanned the crowd, certain that Coburn had come back to her. Then she saw Jed Lawson, standing with his sons, his eyes filled with sympathy as he nodded in her direction.

So many second chances, she told herself as she returned the simple greeting. *So many reprieves, especially for you, Maggie-Margaret.*

All that was left now was to ensure that Ian would be warm, so she unfolded her baby quilt and draped it over him, tucking it securely into place. A feeling of peace washed over her as she bent to kiss his cheek one final time. Then she nodded to the pallbearers to place the wooden lid on the coffin, and they lowered Ian into his final resting place.

For the rest of the day, mourners came by the boardinghouse to offer love and sympathy; it was almost eight o'clock before Mrs. Blake and June finally put the last of the food away. Then they settled down in the backyard with Denny for a little quiet conversation, while Maggie wandered into the library and, for the first time in days, curled up on the sofa with a book in her hand.

In some ways, she felt closer to Coburn here than in his bed, and she sighed as she thought of their nights by the fire. If only he would send word that he was still alive. If only she hadn't allowed him to go after Wiley. If only she had insisted on going with him.

She had tried not to think about his last-minute instructions. How could she consider going to San Francisco, when Ian was here in Shasta Falls? She feared Wiley, but not enough to allow him to come between her and her brother again. And if Wiley hurt Coburn—

She cringed at the thought, then remembered Coburn's other orders. Would she follow those, allowing Russell Braddock to find someone else for her to love?

She shook her head, knowing she could never do that. But this time, her refusal to entertain thoughts of marriage would not be based on fear of love, or of the heartache that love could bring. She had learned over these past months that true love could heal as surely as it could hurt, and she would never forget that lesson.

"Maggie?"

Startled, she looked up to see him standing there, a rueful smile on his handsome face. "Stay there for a minute," he instructed. "You look so beautiful. So perfect. I kept this image with me, day and night—"

She jumped to her feet and ran into his arms. "Thank God! Oh, Alex, thank God." They clung to one another in wordless relief, then she raised her gaze to his and asked simply, "Is it over?"

Coburn nodded.

"You spit on his grave?"

"I did worse than that," he admitted. "Then I left him for the buzzards."

"Good. That's one bounty we don't need."

Coburn cupped her chin in his hand. "That's all behind us now, you know."

"And what's ahead of us?" She smiled gently. "Justice Alex Coburn has a nice ring to it."

"As does Mrs. Alex Coburn."

She smiled shyly. "Yes, it does." Then she slipped her arms around his neck. "It's almost a miracle, that we can start over, together. The family neither of us ever expected to have again."

"And the kind of love I thought only existed in books, until I met you. It's fitting that we found it here, in a library."

Maggie's eyes filled with tears, and she pulled his head down toward her, then kissed him gently.

"Of course," he murmured, scooping her up into his arms as he spoke, "the bedroom is romantic, too."

"And the bath," she agreed with a hopeful smile. "You're awfully dusty, Mr. Coburn."

"And you're overdressed, Miss Gleason-O'Connor."

With a roguish grin, he began to nuzzle her neck until she suggested he do more. Then he carried her off to the bedroom to begin their new life together.

If you liked NIGHT AFTER NIGHT, be sure to look for Kate Donovan's next release in the *Happily Ever After Co.* series, FOOL ME TWICE, available in November wherever books are sold.

Trinity Standish wants to honor the terms of her grandfather's will by restoring his ranch to its former glory, thereby keeping it out of the clutches of his lifelong nemesis. Unfortunately, a condition in the will requires Trinity to be married before her interest vests. So she turns to Russell Braddock, who remembers hearing amazing stories about a man named Jack Ryerson, who can save any business. Jack is irritated to hear from the marriage broker—after all, it was one of Braddock's ridiculous matches that caused Jack's former fiancée to run off with a sea captain! But he can't turn down a good business deal, and soon he finds himself trusting his heart to feisty Trinity . . .

Other books in the series:

GAME OF HEARTS
CARRIED AWAY
MEANT TO BE

Readers may contact Kate at katedonovan@hotmail.com.

COMING IN MAY 2002 FROM
ZEBRA BALLAD ROMANCES

__JUST NORTH OF BLISS: Meet Me at the Fair

by Alice Duncan   0-8217-7277-5 $5.99US/$7.99CAN

Belle Monroe is considering letting a handsome stranger at the World's Columbian Exposition take her portrait to publicize the fair. Although she's terrified of posing, the persistent photographer's tender advances soon make Belle wonder if this brash Northerner and a proper Southern girl like her could actually be meant for each other.

__A PRINCESS BORN: Of Royal Birth

by Sandra Madden   0-8217-7250-3 $5.99US/$7.99CAN

When Edmund Wydville returned to his country estate, Kate Beadle was fully grown—and uncommonly beautiful. She had loved Edmund since childhood, but understood that nobility had no business wooing women of uncertain origin. Edmund would find that love was far less concerned with noble blood than with the way Kate made him feel.

__FLIGHT OF FANCY: American Heiress

by Tracy Cozzens   0-8217-7350-X $5.99US/$7.99CAN

Hannah Carrington had been whisked off to Paris by her mother. She was glad to explore the City of Lights, but husband-hunting was another matter, for Hannah dreamed of studying science. Marriage would put an end to all that—unless it was to a man as inclined to scholarly study as she was, namely Lord Benjamin Ramsey.

__SUNLIGHT ON JOSEPHINE STREET: The Cuvier Widows

by Sylvia McDaniel   0-8217-7321-6 $5.99US/$7.99CAN

After her husband's untimely death, Marian Cuvier felt determined to find a new place in the world. That led her to Louis Fournet, Jean's former business partner. When the darkly handsome man awakened feelings Marian found unfamiliar, she discovered that convincing herself not to fall in love again would be the most difficult task of all.

Call toll free **1-888-345-BOOK** to order by phone or use this coupon to order by mail. *ALL BOOKS AVAILABLE MAY 01, 2002.*

Name _____

Address _____

City _____ State _____ Zip _____

Please send me the books that I have checked above.

I am enclosing $_____

Plus postage and handling* $_____

Sales tax (in NY and TN) $_____

Total amount enclosed $_____

*Add $2.50 for the first book and $.50 for each additional book. Send check or money order (no cash or CODs) to: **Kensington Publishing Corp., Dept. C.O., 850 Third Avenue, New York, NY 10022.**

Prices and numbers subject to change without notice. Valid only in the U.S. All orders subject to availability. **NO ADVANCE ORDERS.**

Visit our website at **www.kensingtonbooks.com.**

DO YOU HAVE THE
HOHL COLLECTION?

The Queen of Romance

Cassie Edwards

Enjoy *Savage Destiny*
A Romantic Series from
Rosanne Bittner

__#1: **Sweet Prairie Passion**   **$5.99**US/**$6.99**CAN
  0-8217-5342-8

__#2: **Ride the Free Wind Passion** **$5.99**US/**$6.99**CAN
  0-8217-5343-6

__#3: **River of Love**   **$5.99**US/**$6.99**CAN
  0-8217-5344-4
